THE
RUSSIAN
PINK

THE RUSSIAN PINK

A Novel

MATTHEW HART

PEGASUS CRIME

NEW YORK LONDON

THE RUSSIAN PINK

Pegasus Crime is an imprint of
Pegasus Books, Ltd.
148 W. 37th Street, 13th Floor
New York, NY 10018

First Pegasus Books cloth edition November 2020

Interior design by Maria Fernandez

Library of Congress Cataloging-in-Publication Data is available.

ISBN: 978-1-64313-550-2

10 9 8 7 6 5 4 3 2

Printed in the United States of America
Distributed by Simon & Schuster
www.pegasusbooks.com

for Heather

yet from those flames

No light, but rather darkness visible

—*Paradise Lost*, Book I

PROLOGUE

All diamonds are blood diamonds. It's just a question of whose blood.

On a black August night Piet Louw and Denny Vorster vacuumed a 1,512-carat diamond out of the Chicapa River, Lunda Norte Province, northeastern Angola, not far from the Congo border. The scent of jungle orchids drenched the air. The screams of animals tore strips out of the velvet night.

Piet was taking a leak from the side of the barge. It was Denny's turn in the water. Breathing through an air hose, he was down below on the riverbed, harvesting the gravels with a suction tube. The river was quiet. The only sounds were the shrieks from the bush, the rhythmic whirring of the pump, and the rattle of stones on the sizing screen. Then came a loud clang as something heavy hit the steel mesh. It rolled off and landed on the wooden deck with a thump.

Piet turned around from where he was standing and stared. The stone lay in the dim circle of illumination outside the harsh light around the diamond screen. He zipped up his fly, stepped over, and squatted down to have a look.

The stone on the deck was caked in hard material, and yet it glowed. Light found its way into it through cracks, and the crystal fed on the light, magnifying it and driving it back out. In this way the power of the diamond pierced the covering. It pierced Piet's brain.

Through narrow fissures in the surface encrustation, the jewel's light throbbed like the pulse of a ferocious god.

Piet found a length of mooring chain and coiled it at the side of the barge. Then he dragged over the concrete blocks they sometimes used as anchors. He threaded the chain through the blocks. He took out his bush knife, knelt on the deck, and placed his hand on the cold, wet hose that pumped air to Denny. With a swipe, he slashed it.

Fifteen seconds later Denny burst to the surface gasping and choking. Piet leaned over and dealt him a crushing blow to the skull with a forty-inch pipe wrench. He pulled Denny alongside, wrapped the anchor chain and blocks around his torso, and let the body go. It vanished in the murky water.

Now Piet owned the whole diamond.

He wrapped it in a piece of sacking, climbed into the aluminum skiff, and headed downriver to his camp. He cut the outboard fifty yards from the dock and drifted in, guiding the boat with the oars so as not to wake the cook.

Quietly, his heart pounding, he carried the stone to the little diamond lab behind the machine shed. He went in and locked the door. He put the stone in a sink under a stream of water and picked and pried at the hard-caked mud. A sudden fear clutched at him. He snatched up a diamond tester, turned it on, and pressed the tip through a crack until it touched the stone.

Diamond.

The stone filled his hand like a grapefruit. He had a diamond scale in the lab, but the jewel was too big to fit on it. A staggering, incomprehensibly massive diamond.

But the color! It seethed. It clamored for release. A savage, unconquerable pink. Was that the true color, or was the diamond taking something from the rocky crust that he couldn't pick off? If it was a pink it would be worth tens of millions. No, *hundreds* of millions.

He packed it carefully in bubble wrap, swathed it in oily burlap, and stuffed it in a canvas bag. His mind was whirling. How could he get the diamond out of Angola?

He couldn't take it through the capital, Luanda, where all diamond exports were supposed to go. The Angolans would never let such a stone escape, no matter what bribe he paid. He would have to take it straight out of the country from Saurimo, the nearest city.

He hid the bag carefully behind a row of oil drums, turned out the light, and locked the door behind him.

No lock can keep out fear.

The jewel had established its power inside his head. The power swelled and spread outward into the night, flowing into the forest like a silent animal. As soon as he stepped away from the shack the animal was there already, writhing through the dark leaves that crowded the edge of the camp. Piet found himself gulping for breath. He stumbled back in a sudden panic, tearing and scrabbling at the lock when his key jammed. He rushed inside and hurled a drum aside and grabbed the canvas bag. He ripped off the careful packaging until the stone appeared and a lurid glow spilled out and lapped at Piet's crooked face. He stood still then, listening. No sound came from the cook's house. Lucky for the cook.

He carefully rewrapped the diamond, shouldered the bag, and took a path that led downriver to a neighboring camp where some Russians had a diamond mill that processed shoreside gravel. They had a beat-up

MI-6 Soviet military helicopter that they used to transport fuel and machinery from Saurimo.

He hated walking in the forest—the viscous, black, Angolan night clinging to his face, the fetid breath of the jungle, the sudden slithering of animals. Two days ago the cook had killed a dwarf python that got into the chicken run. Only in Africa could a six-foot snake be called a dwarf.

The weight of the bag dragged at his shoulder.

The Serb who ran the Russian camp sat on a canvas stool, a steaming bowl of curry in his lap, and listened to Piet's story. He didn't believe a word.

"Too bad for Denny, eh, Piet? Problem with air hose." He shook his head. "Tough shit for Denny." He forked a huge piece of butterfish into his mouth and wiped a yellow dribble from his chin with the back of his hand. "What's in the bag?"

"Stuff," said Piet.

The Serb jabbed his fork into the curry and speared another chunk of grayish flesh.

"Sure, Piet. Your stuff." He put the bowl of curry on the ground, grabbed a bottle of Russian brandy, and took a slug. He stared at Piet with bloodshot eyes.

"We going in the morning, Piet. Same time as usual. Six o'clock. We fit you in. Maybe even have room for your stuff." He gave Piet a big smile. As much of a smile as you can make with nine teeth.

When Piet got back to camp he called Johannesburg on the satellite phone and chartered a Learjet to meet him at Saurimo. He told the pilot to file a plan for an onward flight to Luanda. That was in case the Angolans were listening in. He did not sleep, but lay awake all night with the canvas bag clasped to his chest. Twice he opened it and unwrapped the stone, gazing at it as the jewel slid its fingers into the remaining spaces of his brain. In the morning he walked back to the Russian camp. Besides his bush knife, and the snub-nosed .38 in the ankle holster, Piet had a Czech-made Škorpion machine pistol concealed under his jacket. Serbs, you never knew. But they took him to Saurimo without incident.

The Learjet arrived. Piet flew straight back to Johannesburg. He took the diamond to Barry Stern.

Barry was as hard as steel, but he couldn't keep the look of blank astonishment from his face when Piet unwrapped the stone under the bright light on Barry's desk.

Barry drew a deep breath and closed his eyes for a moment, then reached for his loupe.

"We don't even know what this is, Piet," he said, knowing exactly what it was. His head churned with calculations. "So first things first. We clean it."

The normal way to clean the carapace of dirt from rough diamonds is to boil them in acid for twelve hours in a sort of pressure cooker. The acid takes off the surface encrustation and even gets at some of the inclusions—tiny specks of impurities that most diamonds contain. But who builds an acid washer big enough for a fifteen-hundred-carat diamond?

Barry rigged up something eventually. It took time. Very carefully, with repeated immersions, he coaxed the immense jewel into shrugging off its rocky shell. Bit by bit the crust dissolved in the boiling acid. Barry had never seen anything like the diamond that emerged. No one on Earth, living or dead, had seen such a jewel. Peering into it with his loupe each time he took it out, Barry saw a galaxy, a universe of pink. He put the stone back into the acid and blinked back tears. Naturally, he used the extra time to trash-talk the stone.

"The color, Piet—who knows? I'm not putting it down," he said, searching for the words to put it down, "but who has seen such a color? It seeks to hide. It comes and goes. And the structure, Piet, the fracture planes."

He shook his head slowly.

"Who can trust this stone? It's not clean, Piet. It's a danger stone. The man who tries to master this," he gazed sadly at the diamond, "will never know peace."

Piet was not the smartest man in Africa. He took $12 million for the diamond. Barry had a buyer already lined up. A Russian. The buyer knew the stone was problematic, but, on the other hand, it was stupefying. It almost defied belief. It weighed more than fifteen-hundred carats. Men had brought empires to their knees for lesser jewels. Forty million dollars appeared in Barry's account in Singapore. The Russian took the diamond to Antwerp.

THE
RUSSIAN
PINK

1

Slav Lily believed in God the Father almighty, maker of heaven and Earth, and in Jesus Christ, his only begotten son, but she also believed in a Glock 42 slimline subcompact. Sixteen ounces with the six-round clip fully loaded. She wore it strapped against her T-shirt, concealed by her short red leather jacket. You couldn't leave everything to God. She would have liked a nine-round clip, but fewer shots was a trade-off she accepted for a gun you could practically hide in your bra. If you couldn't put somebody down with six rounds of .380 Fiocchi Extrema, a really dependable hollow-point bullet Lily liked, you deserved what you got.

She sat in the eighth pew from the front and bent her head in prayer to her patron saint. There is no saint named Lily, but she had a special devotion for Saint Kateri Tekakwitha, Lily of the Mohawks. Extremely chic in a beaded deerskin way, as Lily saw it, plus she was a princess, plus knew how to float through the forest like a phantom. That last part about the forest Lily had made up. She felt that her own piety, as demonstrated by the $1,000 in twenties that she gave the priest for every diamond drop, gave her the right to add a few qualities that the saint must have had anyway but had escaped the notice of the seventeenth-century French Jesuits who'd written the history of that part of North America in between having their fingernails pulled out.

The ability to reconcile religious devotion with a utilitarian attitude to homicide is not uniquely Russian. But Lily had other attributes—a maniacal devotion to the Bolshoi Ballet, madly slanted eyes, a fondness for an expensive Siberian vodka called Beluga Noble Gold—that, taken all together, accounted for her nickname in certain twilit parts of the diamond world.

With her body turned at a slight angle, Slav Lily could see the whole interior of the Church of the Guardian Angel.

So could I. We had cameras in the church. I was running surveillance for a Treasury operation. There was a high-end money laundry rinsing dirty cash into the United States in diamonds. I had been planning to spring the trap, but not until I knew more about how it worked. Then I got an order in the middle of the night: The operation had been moved up. So here I was.

At 7:00 A.M. Mass, the sound of early traffic on Ocean Parkway was a light hiss of tires in the rain.

"Who was conceived by the Holy Spirit," the priest continued with his recitation of the Apostles' Creed.

The traffic noise got louder when the main door opened for a moment, then subsided when it closed. Lily heard the light pad of sneakers on the terrazzo floor. That was another thing she liked about Guardian Angel. With terrazzo, you could hear a fly.

"He descended into Hell," she intoned in time to the priest and the seven regulars. Always the same seven. That was good. No surprises. Today there was an eighth, a guy in his thirties in a denim jacket. Younger than the regulars. But Lily had watched him closely when he came in and had apparently decided he was OK. He'd dipped his hand

2

in the holy water and made the sign of the cross. Knew when to stand and when to kneel.

The only other people in the church were the paymaster Lavrov and his wife. They sat ten rows behind Lily with their mouths open, a matched pair of trolls with lantern jaws and squished-on noses like lumps of putty. Square yellow teeth showed in their open mouths. Lavrov had problems with his circulation, and his blue nose and large blue ears were the color of his cheap suit. A plastic penholder crammed with ballpoints protruded from his breast pocket. His wife wore a floral print dress. She had enormous breasts that strained the buttons at the front, but the dress would have been tight anyway because of the Kevlar vest. With both hands she gripped a canvas purse the size of a knapsack. The money was in the purse.

Everybody in the church was older than Lily, who was twenty-nine. She stood out because of her youth, her red jacket, and her striking appearance—the spiky black hair cut short, black eyebrows, and white skin so pale that the down on her lip showed as a faint shadow. She had stormy dark gray eyes and pointy, elvish ears. Strands of dark hair writhed around these delicate, strange shells like eels after prey.

"On the third day He rose again from the dead; He ascended into heaven, and sits at the right hand of God the Father almighty."

The man came up the side aisle: medium height, big chest, wrinkled khaki pants. and a light blue button-down shirt with a logo on the pocket. His shirt wasn't tucked in, so he was probably carrying. People in the diamond trade like to tell you it's a handshake business. Sure, except sometimes the hand has a gun in it.

"Give me a better shot of him," I said, and the screen in front of me flicked to a different angle.

We were parked a mile away in an equipment bay at Coney Island. An NYPD command vehicle is basically a windowless bus with a TV control room inside. A capsule sealed off from the outside world, filled with dim green light and whatever smells the occupants brought in with them.

A young cop beside me did the switching and controlled the audio. A captain in a starched white shirt surveyed the operation from a high-backed leather chair bolted to a dais in the corner. The chair creaked when he moved. He wore a sour expression in case I'd missed the fact that he hated civilians.

Slav Lily stiffened as the man approached. She didn't like the loose shirt either. He kept his hands in sight, holding them slightly away from his body.

He had thick, curly gray hair and sallow skin. I recognized him. A Brazilian diamond trader. Not too careful about where he got his goods.

He walked up the aisle with a limp, pit-PAT, pit-PAT on the terrazzo floor.

He slid into the pew two rows behind Lily. That was one of her rules: two rows. Close enough, not too close.

When he was in his seat he looked around the church. Finally he knelt and bowed his head, clasping his hands as if in prayer and extending his arms into the empty pew between him and Lily. A three-inch-long rectangular white shape slid into view between his thumbs. She plucked the folded-paper packet from his hands and took a long, slow look around the church.

She flicked the packet open with the fingers of the hand that held it, a display of deftness that revealed practice with the way diamond people fold their paper packets.

"I believe in the Holy Ghost."

A mist of pink light fizzed out of the paper and lapped at Lily's face.

She gazed at the contents of the package, her face softened by the rosy luminescence.

"Tighten up on that angle," I told the young cop.

The packet held a single pink diamond. It was shaped like a dagger, long and thin and pointed at one end. It glowed against the paper with a fiery intensity.

Suddenly the crackle of a radio pierced the quiet of the church.

Lily twitched the packet shut with a flurry of her fingers. She leaned back against the pew and looked across the church. The priest recited the last few lines of the prayer. Tight on Lily's face, I could see a bead of perspiration above her lip. It glistened in the soft dawn. She was looking straight at the guy in the denim jacket, who was fiddling frantically with his ear.

"Is that your guy?" I snapped at the captain.

"Not one of ours," the young cop muttered while the captain gaped at the screen, plainly uncertain what was going on.

The Brazilian reached forward and tried to snatch the parcel back, but Lily held it away from him.

"Please tell me you didn't add a backup," she said in her husky voice. It came rasping over the speaker.

He joined his hands together again and watched her, his black eyes steady.

"Darling," Lily growled reproachfully, "have you gone Brazilian on me?" She spoke English with a mid-Atlantic accent, too polished to be American and too slick with Russian vowels to be British.

"That backup whose radio betrayed him," she continued in an angry whisper. "That's very bad. We had no agreement. What are you doing?" She slipped the packet into an inside pocket. "Who else have you got here?"

"What's going on?" said the captain. His chair gave a loud squeak as he stepped off his perch and stood behind the young cop.

"It's going sour," I told him. "She thinks the courier is pulling a double-cross. He was supposed to come with a single backup." I glanced at a monitor. "That's him there, waiting outside the main door. I don't see anybody else, but this is not going well. Where are the arrest teams?"

"Here and here," the young cop tapped a screen that showed the grid of streets around the church. "There's a third over here. That's the on-ramp to the Belt Parkway."

We had two cars of our own but he didn't know where they were. That was another thing that pissed off the captain: NYPD teams would take out the Russians, and Treasury agents would swoop in for the collar.

"Where are the Russians' cars?"

"Black Escalade out front. That's it."

I didn't think that was all they had, but I let it go because things were starting to go off the rails inside the church.

The Brazilian shook his head. He held his right hand out toward Slav Lily. His left hand was no longer in sight.

"I take it back," he growled.

The pretense of a meeting under cover had evaporated. Neither took pains to keep a low voice. At the altar, the old priest soldiered on through the Mass. His flock, alarmed by the angry voices, stayed with him.

"Body of Christ," he said, and the congregation bowed their heads.

I hadn't seen Lavrov move until the young cop said, "the old guy." Lavrov was already out of his seat and halfway to the Brazilian's pew, hauling out an old Red Army Makarov semi-automatic as he went. It looked small in his enormous paw.

"I'm going to be very serious," Lily said to the Brazilian. "I need you to not do anything too completely stupid."

Lavrov's pistol pointed at his ear.

With a flourish the priest removed a cover from the chalice and turned in a swirl of vestments to come around the altar to distribute communion. The old people at the front got to their feet and began to shuffle from the pews into the main aisle. Distracted by the movement, Lavrov's attention flickered for the briefest moment. The Brazilian spun like a cat, leaning his head away from the gun and swiping his arm upward in a blur of speed. A bright red stripe opened from Lavrov's chin to his forehead across the center of his left eye. The Makarov boomed and behind the altar a flight of angels exploded in a shower of stained glass.

"Tackle One," the captain said into a microphone. "Disable suspect vehicle." His voice was calm.

Lavrov slapped at his face. A piece of his eye slid out onto his cheek. He lost his balance and toppled backward. He fired the Makarov again and a statue of the Blessed Virgin beneath the wrecked window burst into a cloud of white powder.

Outside, a matte-black NYPD Crown Vic with no insignia, unless you counted the ramming grid on the front, shot out of a side street and accelerated toward the church. On the wide-angle view we had from a building two blocks away it didn't look dramatic, but I wouldn't want to have been sitting in that Escalade when the Crown Vic torpedoed its ass.

"Fucking Russians," said the captain. "It's always an Escalade."

Lily was on her feet with her hand inside her jacket when the Brazilian's hand flashed again. It swiped across her forearm. She got herself out of the way of the next slash, and by then she had the Glock in her good hand. The Brazilian tried to duck, but a round of Fiocchi Extrema comes out at a muzzle velocity of 975 feet per second. You'd have to be pretty fast. A dime-sized hole appeared in the Brazilian's forehead and the back of his head blew off.

The priest stood rooted to the sanctuary steps, the chalice in one hand and the pale disk of a communion wafer in the other. He was still staring back over his shoulder at the blown-out window and the haze of plaster dust.

Holding her injured arm Lily staggered into the aisle and ran to a side entrance.

"She's screwed," the captain said. "That door is permanently locked. I checked it myself," he added. Unwisely. She disappeared through the door.

Lavrov's wife climbed to her feet and hobbled to her husband's side. She had swollen ankles and wore elastic compression stockings. She stooped and picked up the Makarov and handed it to him, giving him a little pat on the arm as she did. He struggled to his feet and they made their way up the aisle to the main door. Lavrov had one hand over his eye and blood streaming onto his neck, but other than that they looked like any elderly couple coming out of a church to find cops hauling Russians out of an SUV and spreading them face down on the road. I could see the Portuguese backup disappearing around a corner. Lavrov waved the Makarov in the direction of the street and fired. A cop with his knee on a captive's back rolled away in a spasm of agony. Lavrov's wife opened her big purse and pulled out a Stechkin machine pistol. Those big Stechkins have twenty rounds in the magazine and can fire them all in 1.6 seconds flat. You have to pull the trigger, though, and before she could, she caught a high-impact round from a sniper on a roof across the street. It's true that she wore a Kevlar vest, but, fatally, not a Kevlar hat.

Slav Lily came out the side of the church and disappeared behind the white rectory next door.

"Tackle Two," the captain said beside me, "target exited church south side. Apprehend target rear of house."

"Copy that," the speaker crackled, and the second Crown Vic appeared, gunning out of Ocean View Avenue and bouncing up onto the rectory lawn. It slewed badly on the rain-slicked grass. The driver twisted the wheel and tried to accelerate out of the spin, but the front end smacked sideways into a thick maple and erupted in a cloud of steam.

"Tackle Two—what the fuck?" the captain screamed.

The doors sprang open and four guys in full tac tumbled out and sprinted for the house.

"Have we got a camera behind that house?" I asked the young cop.

"Negative," he said, stunned by the disaster snowballing out of control on the screens.

"There's no way out back there," the captain said, but I think we both knew how much faith to put in that.

"Close the net," I told him as I tossed my headset on the console and hurried outside.

My driver's black Yukon was backed up to the trailer with the passenger door already open. The Yukon was the model with the 6.2-liter V8 engine. The driver was a former wheelman for a smash-and-grab gang. We were going eighty-five down Surf Avenue by the time I got my seatbelt fastened.

"Tackle Three," I heard on the speaker, "Tackle Three, come in," followed by an unintelligible burst of noise.

"Where is she?" I said.

A terse crackle came from the police-band monitor mounted on the dash.

"There's a motorcycle on the beach. They think it's her."

Over the radio came a staccato of laconic monosyllables as units moved to take up positions that transformed Brighton Beach into a trap. Picture Brooklyn sticking a sandy tongue into the Atlantic Ocean: that's Brighton Beach. Two bridges and a neck of land is all that joins it to the mainland, and we had those choked tight. Speeding further out toward the tip of the tongue, Lily was moving ever deeper into the trap.

The Yukon had strobes in the grill and one of those fire-truck horns that are supposed to clear even New Yorkers out of the way. But Brighton Beach is to the Russian mob what Little Italy was to the Mafia. Flashing

lights and a blaring horn made no impression on the stolid drivers plug-
ging the road.

The driver cranked the Yukon into a sharp turn, banged across the
sidewalk, and barreled up a flight of concrete steps. We blew across
the boardwalk and onto the beach. Offshore, a sudden breeze was
prying apart the overcast and piling it into stacks of cloud against
the bright blue sky. A hard, silvery light enameled the surface of the
ocean.

The truck wallowed and rocked through the sand. The driver's face
wore a beatific expression. His bejeweled hands gripped the steering
wheel. Far ahead along the shore, two NYPD squad cars shot out of a
street and onto the beach and churned off eastward, fishtailing through
the sand. Ahead of them the red dot that was Slav Lily sped along the
dark waterline and into a patch of light. The water shelving on the sand
gleamed like polished glass.

I studied the map on the dashboard screen. There was no way out, the
beach ended. After that there were some streets of houses, and then
the channel out of Sheepshead Bay into the Atlantic.

"She might be able to dodge around in there for a while," I said, "but
she can't get out. There aren't any bridges across Sheepshead Bay. There's
a line across the water, but I don't know what it is."

"Line?" the driver said.

He stabbed the brakes and slewed the Yukon around in a hard turn
that ended with the front wheels parked on the boardwalk.

"That line—it's a footbridge." A look of wonder transformed his
sagging face. "Jeez, I forgot about that." He pursed his lips and nodded.
"Smart girl. She's going to tie the pursuit into knots out there at the end
of the beach, and then cut back to the bridge. It's only a footbridge, but
it could take a motorcycle." He looked at me. "If she gets across that
bridge, she's out."

We thumped down off the boardwalk and went racing back along the beach. Five minutes later we had rounded the bottom of Sheepshead Bay and come up the other side, just in time to see a red motorcycle fly into view on the far side of the water. She almost made it past a car that was coming toward her on the wet street, but at the crucial moment it went through a puddle, and the sheet of spray smacked Lily off the bike. She hit the pavement and slid along the surface. The motorcycle plunged over the seawall. Lily picked herself up and stumbled to the footbridge. She held her injured arm straight down by her side, and in that hand she had the Glock. Her other hand was clasped tight to her forearm where the Brazilian had cut her. I got out of the Yukon and headed for the bridge.

Just then a police car with its siren wailing skidded to a halt. Two cops jumped out with their weapons drawn. Lily had reached the middle of the wooden bridge. She stopped, put her back to the railing, and hooked a heel on the lowest rung. She looked like someone posing for an ad.

The rain was heavier now. Her hair was plastered to her head. Black tendrils curled around her elvish ears. Her lips were gray. She locked her eyes on mine and smiled wanly before she arched her back across the railing and toppled over, splashing into the water a few yards from a rigid inflatable with twin 150-horsepower Mercury outboards that slid out from under the bridge. I could see how weak she was when they dragged her in, but she had enough strength to fire three quick rounds. A wooden post disintegrated, spraying my face with splinters. Lily disappeared up the channel and into the thickening rain.

2

"Well that was the trifecta," Tommy Cleary shouted as we came down the West Side Highway. "Russian gun moll disappears with the diamond, you get spattered in the face with wood chips, and the NYPD wants your head on a platter, which, knowing your boss, they will probably get."

The canvas convertible top snapped and rippled in the wind, but Tommy didn't really have to yell. He was just in a bad mood.

"I'm telling you, amigo," he said, stabbing a finger the size of a bratwurst at me, "I hope you're not counting on moving to a bigger office any time soon. My advice: Check the fine print on your employment contract."

What was really making Tommy mad was that I hadn't said a word about the $10,000 paint job on his 1957 Cadillac Eldorado. It had taken him months to locate a body shop that could recreate the original Dakota Red. They'd done the upholstery too and enameled the dash. A company in San Diego had cast a reproduction eighteen-inch Brougham steering wheel—add four grand just for that.

"And before I forget," he added, "your trashed face? That is not a hero look. It's a loser look."

Tommy was a former federal prosecutor now attached to our unit. He specialized in supplying the dense legal reasoning that gave our bosses in Washington cover when we did something embarrassing. So he was mad about that too. I wasn't the only one who was going to have a busy day.

I saw Tommy check his appearance in the rearview. He had recently traded in his dreadlocks for a close-to-the-head redesign, dyed blonde. Surprisingly, it made him look fiercer, even with the lilac bowling shirt that billowed against his black skin.

"I thought this operation was supposed to be planned to the nth degree," he said.

"I'm not the one who suddenly moved it up."

Tommy snorted.

"Be sure to mention that. We'll see where it gets you. Veteran field agent with full control on the ground and big-time resources messed up because the operation was advanced." He raised a hand and let it fall heavily on the steering wheel. "I'll try to think of something nice to say at the funeral."

It was going to be a long morning.

We hit a dip in the road. The Caddy sank and then rose again like a fairground ride. It was sprung too soft for a car that weighed more than two tons. I knew better than to open my mouth about it. One word and Tommy would start telling me about the Hydra-Matic transmission and the 364-cubic-inch engine.

Powerful gusts buffeted the car and lashed the Hudson River into whitecaps. Across the river a hydrofoil pulled away from the ferry terminal and dashed downriver for the Battery, slamming and shuddering through the waves. People save on their income tax by living in New Jersey. This morning they were going to pay for it.

"And another thing," Tommy said as we shot through the amber light at Fifty-Seventh Street. "The pink that showed up last night? I can feel the headache coming on already."

So could I.

The target of our operation was a hood named Sergei Lime. That's who Lily worked for. Lime had deep roots in Russian organized crime. With an American father, he had dual citizenship, and at the moment was living in New York. What caused my bosses worry were Lime's ties to an American billionaire named Harry Nash.

Nash and Lime were both connected to a hedge fund from which Nash had recently bought a diamond. A fantastically rare and previously unknown jewel, and—here's where the problem was coming from—also a pink.

Normally, no problem. The investigation of one target leads to another. You look for the links between them. Lime was a known criminal. He and Nash had business ties. A pink diamond shows up in an operation against Lime. Nash has a pink diamond too. Maybe more than a coincidence. So we open a file on Nash, tap his phone, and rummage through his bank accounts. However, we didn't. The reason we didn't was that Nash was running for office.

The Oval Office.

We got off the highway at Forty-Fourth Street. Tommy shoehorned the Caddy into a no-parking zone between two NYPD patrol cars. He slapped a piece of cardboard onto the dash and we climbed out. The sign said UNITED STATES TREASURY—OFFICIAL BUSINESS. But that wouldn't stop a New York cop from writing a ticket. What stopped them was that back in his twenties, before his left knee blew out and he went to law school, Tommy had been a New York Jet, and at a flyweight 205 pounds, the fastest and meanest linebacker in the NFL. In New York City, where people rank you by the damage you can do,

Tommy had more fans than Joe Namath. Every cop in the city knew what kind of car he drove. Tommy could park in Times Square, catch a show, and go for a late dinner; the Caddy would be waiting there when he got back.

The diner was full of cops, as usual. Tommy waded through the tables, slapping hands, until we reached the corner banquette.

"Let's put Nash aside for now," he said, sliding onto the seat and opening his briefcase. "Let's talk about your friend Lily." He found the file and was slipping on his half-moon reading glasses when the waitress arrived with coffee.

We gave her our orders, and when she left, Tommy resumed.

"Liliana Petrovna Ostrokhova, aka Slav Lily. At age seventeen, goes to work at Russgem, Russian state diamond conglomerate. Trains as a diamond sorter in Mirny, Siberia, grading rough diamonds from the Siberian mines. After some personal adventures we won't get into here, transfers to St. Petersburg for advanced training in polishing. Moves to Antwerp office, which is where she gets busted." Tommy glanced at me over his glasses. "By you."

He returned to the file.

"A year later she arrives in the United States and sets up as an independent diamond trader."

He closed the folder as a week's supply of protein and carbohydrates arrived in the form of scrambled eggs, breakfast steak, hash browns, pancakes, toast. Bagel on the side. Four little plastic tubs of peanut butter beside the bagel. Even the cops at the next table were impressed.

The waitress came back with my yogurt and banged it down in front of me with an expression of disgust. I didn't like it any better than she did, but I'd promised my daughter to clean up my diet. Unfortunately, she'd translated what I'd hoped was a general, goal-based agreement into specific menu items.

Tommy put his glasses aside, picked up his knife and fork, and began to whittle his way through the food.

"Everybody who reads your report is going to know you're running that girl. What they'll also be asking themselves is who else she's working for. Lime thinks she's working for him. You think she's working for you. Anybody else belong on that list?"

He speared a sausage and slathered on hot English mustard.

"Put simply," he waved the sausage, "was the girl in the middle of a gunfight, stabbing, and general mayhem at a New York City church working for the bad guys, the good guys, *and* herself?"

I tried to get the waitress's attention. The yogurt had thickened into a sort of mortar.

"You mean, does she sometimes trade illegal diamonds on her own? She's a double, Tommy. How did you think that worked? She cooperates because we force her to. Since she's cut a few corners in her life, and is now working for a crook, maybe we could look the other way if she takes care of herself while she's at it."

Tommy immersed himself in his email for a minute. I speared one of his sausages.

In the diamond business it's easy to slip across the blurry line between the maybe legal and the definitely not. Lily had often slipped across it. One time I was waiting on the other side.

It was at Brussels airport. I let the Belgians grab her when she got off a flight from Banjul, the capital of Gambia, with a box of blood diamonds. The diamonds had originated in Sierra Leone. If you stuck a tap into Sierra Leone and turned it on, that's what would come out—blood diamonds. Customs officers know that. So Lily had changed the country of origin to Gambia. Official Gambian government export licenses were stamped all over the parcel in bright red ink. She'd paid for those stamps. Her problem was—there aren't any diamond mines in Gambia. And anyway, we had seeded that parcel with marked stones when it was put together in Sierra Leone.

Here's how I flipped Slav Lily.

The Belgians waited outside the tiny room. It was one of those airless interrogation spaces designed to make the person being questioned feel trapped. A single table and two chairs. On one side of the table there's lots of room. On the other—her side—you have to squeeze into a narrow space between the table and the wall. Lily slid into it as carelessly as if it were a sidewalk café downtown in the Grand Place and we were going to have a quick Kir before lunch. She gazed at me from her still, gray eyes, not even blinking as I dealt out onto the table, like a winning hand at cards, the black-and-white eight-by-tens. Each one digitally enhanced and so crisp you could see the straining muscles on the shackled men who worked the diamond digs.

The photos documented the stones' journey to Freetown, on the Atlantic coast. When I put down the pictures that showed Lily buying the stones from traders in Freetown, and later, in the customs office in Banjul showing the official where to put the phony stamps, she reached out and slid the last two photographs toward her. She cocked her head at the pictures, turning them this way and that, and then fixed me again with her appraising eyes.

"That haircut," she said. "A disaster, no?"

I thought it looked great. We'd been in that room together for a while. It had started to feel as if some hidden machine was slowly winching us closer together. Every time she opened her lips to draw a breath, I had to drag my eyes away from her mouth. In the tight confines of the room, we were barely murmuring. Both of us glistened with perspiration.

Lily didn't roll at the first tap. She tried to bluff. Let the Belgians lock her up, she said. It wouldn't be for long.

But the club I carried wasn't jail. It was the Dodd-Frank Act, which said that companies doing business in the United States had to know all about their customers. If I reported the blood diamonds, the Treasury would threaten the Antwerp banks the Russians used with exclusion from the US banking system. The banks would drop the Russians in a heartbeat.

By the time we left the airport, Lily was my agent. That's how I should have left it.

Tommy and I left the diner and drove to Greenwich Village and parked in front of a row of eighteenth-century redbrick townhouses on Clarkson Street. Nothing about the mellow buildings would make you suspect what was inside—a nest of spies, accountants, phone techs, and hackers working for the US Treasury.

"You know that Chuck is going to make you carry the can for this," Tommy said. "He is going to say that Lily tipped off Lime about you, and that's why they had a plan in place for her to get away."

"Lime doesn't need Lily to warn him about me. I shut down his blood diamonds. I shut down the rough he was stealing from the Russian mines. His Russian partners will eat him alive if he doesn't find another way to get hold of US dollars. So I think you can bet he knows who I am."

We got out and headed up the front steps. No sign identified the building, and you didn't need to knock. The guard had been watching us since we'd parked. He knew us, but he still examined our IDs through the little square of bulletproof glass before he unlocked the heavy door and let us in.

"One more thing," Tommy said when we reached the stairs. His office was on the top floor, mine in the basement. He checked back along the hall. All the doors were closed. "I'm not going to tell you what to do," he said in a low voice, "and I'm not giving you advice. But when you play defensive football, you learn how to read a play. Sometimes it's obvious what's going on, but sometimes you just get a hunch. Like sixth sense. You know something's coming and you know where. I've got that feeling now, Alex. Somebody's running a play. And you know what? They're running it on you."

3

When I got to my office, I stared into the glass panel until the iris scan flashed green. Then I pressed the fingers of my right hand on the black pad. The lock clicked open and I went in.

They built these rooms like vaults. The steel doors would automatically shut unless you propped them open. I kicked a rubber wedge into place, unlocked my window, and opened it a few inches to let in cool air from the alley. My office was small and stuffy. I always left the window open, and security always shut and locked it, even though it was protected by bank-grade steel bars.

In 1990 the US Treasury established the Financial Crimes Enforcement Network, known as FinCEN, to combat increasingly sophisticated money laundering and cybercrime. FinCEN was always secretive. After 9/11, even more. That's when they created Special Audits, the unit I work for. Our assignment was what they called "enhanced data capture." In other words, breaking into secure locations and stealing information. Sometimes, if you have to, shooting people, although you won't find that in the legislation.

I got hired because I knew diamonds. Diamonds are a kind of cash, except without the serial numbers. Criminals and terrorists like that.

Four messages from Chuck waited on my desk. I scrunched them up and tossed them in the waste basket, unlocked the in-tray, and took out the tamper-proof file.

"Oh, you're here," Tabitha said, popping her head around the door. Her auburn hair flew around her head in disarray. "Wow, you look sort of bad," she said, fixing me with her intimidating, sea-green eyes. "Did you know you were leaking?"

She leaned in for a closer look. A lock of hair fell across her eyes. She blew it away with a puff and went clacking out of the room in her slingbacks. She came back with a first aid kit. Her eyes had an eager glint.

"Chuck's been calling every fifteen minutes," she said as she ripped a strip of adhesive from my chin and replaced it with a fresh one. She cocked her head to survey her handiwork, then tore off a second Band-Aid. She dabbed at the cut with a ball of cotton wool and taped on another strip. "Perfect. Even more like a gangster than usual."

I broke the tamperproof clear plastic strip on the agenda folder and examined the list of items.

"What does 'stat review' mean?"

"There's a statutory requirement to review any operation that results in death," Tabitha said. "So that's one thing. Then there's the departmental protocol that stipulates a review when a multi-agency operation fails."

"That's where everybody makes sure the blame gets placed as close to me as possible?"

"Uh-huh. And there was an overnight blue from Washington."

"I thought I was supposed to see all those."

She put a finger on the pale-blue flimsy that was sitting on my desk and pushed it into an even more visible position.

Blues were single-sheet notices from the secretary of the Treasury notifying us when there was high-level interest in an investigation.

"Order to consult," I read out loud. I ran my eyes down the few paragraphs that spelled out the demand. "The secretary wants to be kept up to date on the Lime investigation. Imagine that. A lifelong Wall Street crony of the president wants the lowdown on an investigation possibly linked to Harry Nash, the main threat to the president's re-election."

"Astonishing," Tabitha said.

She sat down purposefully and crossed her slender legs and fixed me with a gaze like a roofing nail.

"Let's just run through that business with the pink last night. It would help if I understood it, especially if you want me to lie to the secretary."

People who didn't know her background made the mistake of thinking that because Tabitha didn't spend much time on her appearance and was impervious to rank, she came from one of the well-connected families that have been inserting their children into the government since they set it up for their own benefit in the eighteenth century. But Tabitha's dad raised pigs in Minnesota. She'd gone to Vassar on a scholarship. She was an intelligence officer who'd been through Camp Peary, the CIA training base in Virginia that spies call "the Farm." Tabitha was way too smart to be seconded to Special Audits as my assistant, but I wasn't complaining.

"What do you know about pinks?" I said.

"That they're worth a lot."

"They're among the most valuable jewels on earth. Take Nash's pink. I don't know what he paid for it, but it could easily be worth hundreds of millions of dollars."

"But it's huge. The one that showed up in the church was tiny."

"Tiny by comparison. But it weighed at least three carats. Say it polished out to a finished stone of two carats. If the color stayed strong, that's a quarter-million-dollar stone. And anyway, the important thing about the pink last night, at least in Washington, is that it might provide some dirt to rub on Nash."

"Oh, that reminds me. I meant to tell you, Chuck was in Washington yesterday."

"That's not unusual."

She sat back and folded her hands in her lap.

"Before he left," she said, "he asked Langley to pull your 906."

OK, that was something else. Personnel 906 files were the top-secret vetting reports for officers cleared to operate under cover. They contained the most sensitive details of an operative's past. The things that you were most ashamed of. A 906 was like a bad conscience copied into someone else's memory. Because I had worked for the CIA before coming to the Treasury my 906 was held at Langley.

There are two ways into the CIA. The most common is straight from university. You download what they call a "Job Fit Tool" from the CIA website. It tells you if you've got a chance. Then you take some tests. If they like the results, you're in.

But there's another way. You don't go to university. You don't download anything. All you do is answer the door one night.

I was twenty-two, with a mountainside condo in Cape Town. Wraparound balcony with a view of Table Bay. In the garage a cream-colored Mercedes 190SL. I was doing OK for a young guy home-schooled in diamond camps in Africa by his mom.

I could see her now. Just managing to keep her desperation at bay with that determined smile, with the good china she always packed and brought along, with the cotton dresses that she ironed in the kitchen of whatever flat-pack house we lived in. Anything to preserve the idea of who she'd been—a New York girl off to see the world with her dashing husband. And a heart that broke every time she realized where she came on his list of priorities.

That wouldn't be in my 906. All they would have about my mother was that she'd died when I was twelve.

For the next six years, until I was eighteen, it was just Dad and me. Then he went to prison for defrauding investors. I was on my own, and became the tough kid who opened his door that night in Cape Town.

I lived by trading diamonds. Some of them were legal, bought from small operators mining the old deposits on the Vaal River. But that was for cover. My main supply was stolen goods. High-end rough from Namibia and Botswana. I ran it up to Antwerp every month, timing my trips to coincide with the big London diamond sales, when Antwerp was full of disappointed traders who didn't get the goods they wanted. The guy who came to my apartment that night in Cape Town knew all about it.

At the time, al Qaeda was financing some of its operations with contraband diamonds. The US government wanted to know how that worked. That night in Cape Town the proposition was a simple one. I could come with him, or wait for the South African arrest team stationed nearby, ready for his signal. Welcome to the CIA.

Chuck had his feet on his desk when I walked in. The desk had appeared two months ago, a massive rectangle of steel that replaced a suite of repro Sheraton. At Chuck's grade, he could pick his own furniture. He'd been fine with the Sheraton until he started visiting art galleries in Chelsea, where he discovered that taste-makers didn't have period furniture from Macy's. They had welded steel.

He wore a crisp white shirt and black jeans. The jeans had that straight-from-the-dumpster look that costs real money. And in case you didn't get that right away, he drove the point home with his $800 Ermenegildo Zegna loafers. His wireless phone headset left both his hands free to clutch at his thick blonde hair as he stared in desperation at the ceiling.

"No, sir," he was saying, "of course I'm not defending it." Pause. "Absolutely, sir. They had a right to be angry." Pause. "Of course it's suspicious. I understand your concern. Yes, sir. Yes. Goodbye."

He took his feet off the desk and leaned forward and banged his head on the steel surface.

"Let me guess," I said. "The secretary."

He groaned. "The NYPD has been on the phone to him all morning, blaming us for that fiasco in the church." He parked his elbows on the table and seized his head in his hands. There was nothing like a bomb dropped from DC to give Chuck real anguish. "Jesus Christ, Alex, it was a diamond swap. In Brighton fucking Beach! It's not like you had to chopper into Pakistan and take out Osama bin Laden. What the hell went wrong?"

I sat down and put my folder on the table. I opened it and took out the agenda and ran my finger down it.

"Is this the statutory review that I've been hearing about? Because if it is," I said, drawing another paper from the folder, "we should start with the memo of execution you sent me."

That was Tabitha's idea. Execution memos were the written authority that detailed an actual field operation. Hit him with the memo, she'd said. He wrote it. He hates being caught in print.

"Let's see," I said. "That's right. Here it is. Operational control, including timing." I tossed the page on his desk. "Me. Yet it wasn't me who suddenly advanced the operation, it was you. And it blew up in our face."

Chuck looked pointedly at my bandages and gave me the display of dentition he thought of as a smile.

"Well, *your* face."

Chuck was Charles Chandler III. He'd got where he was largely by being the son of Charles Chandler II. If Chuck could somehow ooze a little further up the ladder, he would leave the Treasury for one of Washington's high-powered lobbying firms, where he would earn a fat salary advising clients how to avoid bastards like me.

"Let's not squabble over the fine points, Alex. What we should be asking ourselves is if Lime knew about the operation in advance."

"If he didn't before, you sure gave him a heads-up by posting a bonehead in the church who didn't even know how to mute his earpiece."

It was a wild shot, but I saw it hit.

Chuck got up and went to the window and stared out at the summer foliage. "It's the department I'm trying to protect, Alex," he said bitterly. "That pink diamond is going to drag us into the mud."

I wondered where else he thought we spent our time.

He returned to the desk and flicked a switch. A huge pane of thick glass slid into view with a hydraulic hiss. Imprinted with invisible circuitry, it was a powerful computer that performed deductive acrobatics in plain view. FinCEN techs had come up from Washington and hardwired it not only into the government network but also to a streaming system that could suck up data from the entire Web. It could pierce the firewalls of other countries.

Chuck pulled out the keyboard.

"The only entry I'm typing in is the number for the report you filed from Brighton Beach," he said grimly. "Watch."

The lights dimmed, the windows turned opaque. A metallic click from the door announced that the lock had engaged. A red light would now be blinking in the hall to alert the staff that we were not to be disturbed.

Text and images spilled across the glass. The software reached into its vast resources, and with blinding speed, pulled up data and deployed it on the screen.

First the operational target: Sergei Lime. Then a summarized bullet-point account of his business life appeared. A financial wizard, he'd helped Russian investors steal $30 billion in two years by asset-stripping Soviet-era state companies. With the profits, he'd formed a London fund, First Partners. It was only then that the Russians discovered how much money Lime himself had made from the asset-stripping.

They demanded a share. Lime refused.

They waited until he arrived in Moscow for a meeting. Up came a video grab from a security cam at Sheremetyevo Airport. We watched them take him as he came through the gate. He had a dislocated shoulder and a broken jaw before they even dragged him from the building. After a week in the Lubyanka prison, he caved, selling a large chunk of his stake in First Partners. The date appeared.

The second that information flashed on the screen, a red line flicked out and drew a new box on the right-hand side and labelled it NASH. Immediately after that it printed: DATE OF ACQUISITION OF FIRST PART-NERS INTEREST. A line shot out to join the date that Nash bought his shares with the date Lime sold. They were the same.

"Oh, boy," I said.

"I know. He had to have bought those shares directly from Lime."

"Or the oligarchs," I said, "after they beat them out of Lime."

"It gets worse," Chuck muttered.

The system was Chuck's brainchild. He'd worked on it for more than a year, allocating much of our investigative budget to the development. Now he watched with a stricken look as it opened a thread on Nash. Images flowed onto the screen, of Nash as a young naval officer, Nash on the beach at his palatial home on Martha's Vineyard. The machine riffled through a stream of images until it pounced on one of Nash and his wife, Honey Li, at a society ball at the Metropolitan Museum of Art. The huge pink diamond blazed against her skin. Because of online rumors that the diamond had originated in the imperial treasury at the Kremlin, the press had christened it the Russian Pink.

Now a news clip ran of Nash, swarmed by reporters demanding to know if it was true that he owned shares in the Russian fund he'd bought the diamond from.

"Guys, guys," Nash said with his Kennedy smile. "'American businessman scoops Russian treasure.' Is that your story? Hey, that's a headline I can live with."

The screen began to rapidly shed data, refining what was left into a few simple connections. Red lines connected the pink diamond in my report from the church to the Russian Pink, Nash to Lime, date to date, transaction to transaction. Then it made a beep, and a line of print popped out at the bottom of the screen:

DECISION: OPEN FILE ON NASH.

We stared at the screen in a frozen silence. Finally I looked at Chuck. "You programmed this thing to open investigations?"

"For Christ's sake, Alex, it makes *suggestions*," he said. I could hear the panic. "The idea was to make our decisions more data-driven. To remove even the shadow of a suggestion that politics could influence an investigation."

"How's that been going?"

He tapped his keyboard and the screen slid up into the ceiling.

"It's still in the beta phase," he said nervously. "We can override it."

The lights went up, the outside windows cleared, and the lock clicked open on the door.

"Who else knows about this?"

"No one. The searches are logged at FinCEN, but only the searches. Not the conclusions."

I didn't say anything. We both knew how ridiculous that statement was. FinCEN was part of the Treasury. The secretary was the president's friend. It wouldn't take the White House long to find out Harry Nash was tied into an investigation.

Chuck looked trapped. He paced across the office and stared at some prints on the wall. He turned and paced back. Chuck didn't mind the smell of blood in the water, as long as it was someone else's. In the plan for today, it was supposed to be mine. But he had put his fingers into the operation, and he was now understanding where that placed him. Between the president of the United States and the man trying to replace him.

"So I guess we know why the secretary sent that blue," I said.

He seized his hair in both hands.

"We are not investigating a presidential candidate!"

"Tell them at the White House," I said. "I guarantee they already know about the searches. They are going to be asking if the searches are part of an investigation. And while we're on the subject of investigation, is now a good time to tell me why you advanced the operation?"

"I developed my own source."

"Please don't tell me you put an agent in the field without me knowing."

"I asked Amy Curtain to have a look around in Brighton Beach."

I stared at him. "You're joking. Amy Curtain? She's not an agent."

"She passed the Basic Field Training Course at Quantico."

"The BFT? That means she knows how to shoot a gun and read a map. It doesn't mean she's ready to be dropped behind enemy lines at night with a supply of invisible ink and the cyanide capsule in case she's caught."

"She speaks fluent Russian."

"That's right," I said. "She was a trainee officer on FinCEN's Russia desk until they rotated her here to help with the intercepts. She's not a spy. She translates intercepted Russian phone calls. She did Slavic Studies at Yale, so I guess she speaks OK Russian and can tell you about Peter the Great."

"She's missing," he said.

"You mean you had a contact protocol and she missed it?"

Chuck took a file from his tray and opened it.

"Interrupted phone call," he said.

"She was reporting and broke off the call?"

Chuck nodded.

"When?"

"Two days ago."

"The day before you advanced the operation."

"She said that Lime was making what looked like an important contact."

"And she was interrupted?" Chuck just looked at me, so I added the obvious. "You understand this is bad."

"I've notified security."

"Well, now we can all relax." I tapped out a quick message to Tabitha asking her to pull a list of all the operatives we had available in New York City. "You've reported this up to the secretary?"

He shook his head. "I'm afraid it will become political."

"Surely not," I said. "An agent disappears investigating a Treasury target. The target is a business associate of the man most likely to take the presidency away from the treasurer's boss, the sitting president. You can't think our superiors would use that information for crass political motives."

"Heap it on," Chuck said. "But Washington is a dangerous town. The president fears he's going to lose the election. He will try to take Nash down. It's not going to be pretty, and we'll be in the middle of it."

I got up and snatched the file from the desk. "It's Amy Curtain who's in the middle of it," I said angrily, and went back to my office to do what I could. I had an ugly feeling it wasn't going to be enough.

4

That night, thin gray clouds slipped through the sky like thieves, stealing the last of the day. The streets filled with the nylon light of evening in New York.

The crowd flowed along the sidewalk like a serpent, coiling and uncoiling from street to street as it made its way to Lincoln Center. Harry Nash and Honey Li were coming to the ballet. Thousands of people were streaming through the street to see them. And the diamond.

The police were funneling the crowd into a network of steel barricades. White city dump trucks loaded with sand blocked the intersections around Lincoln Center. Not a taxi, not a private car moved anywhere inside the cordon. Counterterrorism cops in black helmets and body armor held stubby submachine guns in their black-gloved hands.

"It's like the Macy's Parade, except a thousand times stupider," my daughter said as she tottered along beside me through the crowd. She's a big kid, and not used to heels. Especially those stilettos she'd talked her mother into letting her wear.

It was Annie's fifteenth birthday. We were going to see Sara Mearns dance the Lilac Fairy in the New York City Ballet's production of *The*

Sleeping Beauty. With the stilettos, Annie wore a shimmery silver dress with spaghetti straps and a ragged hemline that looked as if it had been ripped off between her knees and waist. Last year it was Madison Square Garden for the New York Rangers, this year the Lilac Fairy and the heels. They change. But Annie wasn't talking about the ballet. She'd decided that what I needed most was an enumeration of the assets of my ex-wife's new friend.

"He has a Jaguar XKE. That's a famous kind of English car that's very expensive and they don't make them anymore. They can go very fast. But he doesn't drive it fast because he's a true gentleman. He has a very caring disposition."

It was news to me that gentlemanliness and a caring disposition were high on the male asset list of teenage girls, so I guessed I was hearing someone else's assessment.

"Where did your mom meet him?"

"Miss Harington's summer party. He came over from West Point. That's a famous school where people go for army training."

"And bad haircuts."

"Now *that*," said Annie, sounding exactly like her mother, "is what you always do. You're sarcastic. It's called a 'black sense of humor.' You get it from being a spy."

"I'm not a spy, Annie."

She stopped in her tracks and whirled and grabbed me by the arm. She stared into my eyes with a look that I know was meant to be deeply meaningful.

"Dad, you can be yourself with me."

Then she let go and tottered off again.

"He's called Colonel Tim Vanderloo. That's a very old name in New York State."

"Tim is?"

But she ignored me.

To advance through the police check points and avoid being herded behind the barricades, we had to show our tickets. I got tired of waiting while the cops examined them, and started just flashing my Treasury ID instead. It has a gold shield and the diagonal red stripe that means a top clearance.

The security around Lincoln Center—I'm glad it wasn't my job. Nash had not yet won the nomination, but there was no one in his way. His opponents had withdrawn one by one. The nominating convention was going to be a coronation. People with a chance of becoming president are protected by the Secret Service, and in New York by the NYPD too.

A couple of Secret Service guys were standing at the NYPD check-point where Annie and I entered the plaza on the north side. They were scrutinizing everybody through their shades. One guy seemed to be in charge. Tall and heavyset, with a freckled face and bald head. He took my pass from the cop who was looking at it, and took off his sunglasses. His eyes were colorless. He had a pig's nose, pushed up like a snout, but maybe I just didn't like him.

"Stand over there," he said to me, pointing in one direction. No "sir," and I can tell you I outrank anybody so low on the ladder he's on VIP security. He pointed a thick finger at Annie.

"You, stand over there."

And hey, she's a teenager, but she's still a kid, and suddenly she looked afraid. That's because he meant her to be afraid. So right away things started to go off. I stepped very close to him, into his space.

"She's my daughter," I said, speaking straight at his face. "We're together."

He stared at me with those empty, washed-out eyes, then jerked his chin at one of the agents beside Annie.

"Let me see her purse."

The agent put his hand on her arm, and she stepped back. It was reflexive, a recoil, but he grabbed her. I must have telegraphed that I was going to intervene, because the first agent reached for me. I shot my hand under his nose and shoved up hard. He staggered back with tears streaming from his eyes. I was already heading for the guy with his hand on Annie when six huge NYPD cops just kind of flowed into the middle of the situation like someone had poured them from a drum. They filled up all the spaces so we couldn't move. One of them peeled the Secret Service guy off Annie like picking lint from a sweater. Suddenly I couldn't move. Something hard jabbed me in the ribs.

"One move outta youse, wise guy, and I'll spray your guts into that fountain."

I turned my head to look into Anthony DeLucca's large brown eyes. He blew on the barrel of his finger, twirled it and shoved it back in its imaginary holster.

The Secret Service guy was boiling with rage.

"I'm Agent-in-Charge Rhinelander," he spluttered at DeLucca. "The security of this location is under my direct command."

"I'll be sure to mention that to the deputy commissioner who thought he was running things from his command post inside the Met," DeLucca said.

He was a tall, sad-looking man with curly black hair. He wore a shabby trench coat that smelled of cigarette smoke. He was a detective captain, and had come up through the ranks. After 9/11 the NYPD sent him to the US Army intelligence training center at Fort Huachuca, Arizona, and now he worked in counterterrorism. Terrorists need money, and DeLucca's beat included money laundering. We sometimes worked together on joint operations.

I got my arm around Annie and gave her a squeeze. She was shaking. DeLucca turned to a cop and told him to make sure that Rhinelander could speak directly to the secretary of Homeland Security on the deputy commissioner's hotline.

"That won't be necessary, sir," Rhinelander said.

"Sure it will," DeLucca said.

Then he turned to Annie.

"Wow, honey—don't tell me you're this mug's daughter. Lucky you didn't get your looks from him."

She was still pretty shaky.

"Annie, this is Captain DeLucca."

"Tell you what, honey," DeLucca said. "This nice guy right here," he grabbed a towering cop from the large supply still milling around us, "is going to take you to your seat. He's going to make sure everybody bows and scrapes as you walk by in that knockout dress."

Annie was still biting her lower lip. DeLucca leaned close to her and said in a stage whisper, "I have to keep your dad. It's essential to the safety and wellbeing of the United States, and I need to get him to a phone booth quick so he can change into his Superman suit."

That did it. With a huge grin, Annie wobbled off beside the giant.

The white travertine concert halls of Lincoln Center emit a special glow in twilight. Usually thronged with theatergoers, tonight the great square lay like a gleaming, empty rink. Those with tickets were directed by security to go straight in, and the only people on the wide expanse were uniformed cops and guys in dark coats and sunglasses muttering into their lapels.

DeLucca surveyed the scene. I could see him checking out the spotters on the roof of the Met, raking the crowd with their binoculars. Beside each spotter, just visible at the roofline, the silhouette of a sniper with his rifle at the ready.

People who had paid a fortune for their tickets packed the outside terrace that overlooked the square. A few might have actually come for the ballet, but most of them wouldn't know the Lilac Fairy if she stopped them on the street and asked for a light. They were here for Honey Li. And the pink.

"That Secret Service asshole was waiting for you."

"You know these VIP guys, Anthony. They get carried away."

DeLucca took a pack of Marlboros from his pocket and tapped out a cigarette. He put it between his lips. Then he took it out again and examined it, shook his head sadly and put it back in the pack.

He gave me a cold look.

"You are not a sharing person, Alex. You keep things to yourself. That's fine with me, except when we're working on a joint investigation. Then when you keep things to yourself, I am more inclined to think of it as obstruction."

"I'm not sure what you mean."

"Oh, you're sure. You were blown wide open in that church. You heard something that convinced you to advance the operation. It blew up in your face. Normally my position would be, I couldn't care less. When I do care is when it blows up in my face too."

He had a right to be mad. He was the guy carrying the can for an old lady gunned down on the street right in front of the church where an innocent "tourist" got shot in the head when a drug deal went bad. That's what the NYPD was trying to get the press to swallow: murderous druggies, Brazilian tourist at his morning devotions, old lady caught in the crossfire. They couldn't very well say it was a secret Treasury operation that had gone sour, because the taxpayer wasn't supposed to know that the people who printed their money had guys like me working for them, or that NYPD snipers and tac units would be giving us a hand.

"It wasn't my decision," I said.

"No shit. I sort of figured that out, on account of you looking like a total asshole at the end of it. It seemed more likely to me that it was the brainchild of master spy Charles Chandler III, and that you were simply the dope sent to sit in the command truck so you could have a really good look at how completely Lime had you taped."

A radio crackled. A cop beside DeLucca tilted his ear to the receiver clipped to his shoulder. He pressed the acknowledge button.

"Just crossed Fifth Avenue, captain."

DeLucca nodded. "Nash is on the way," he said. "His motorcade is coming through the park."

Nash lived in a mansion on the Upper East Side. The easiest way for the NYPD to get him to Lincoln Center was straight through Central Park. With a motorcycle escort clearing traffic, he'd be here in minutes. We made our way to the center of the plaza.

"That girl in the church who did the Houdini on us," DeLucca said, "I have a feeling she's not working solely for Lime."

"Who else would she be working for," I said.

DeLucca shrugged. "Fine, have it your way. My bet, that girl is a double. You turned her. Lime thinks she works for him, but in fact she works for you. So tell me, how's that going so far?"

The NYPD helicopter circling nearby shifted its position closer. Nash was almost here.

"You know and I know, Alex, she's a double agent for exactly as long as it takes Lime to figure out you turned her. Once he figures that out, he'll either kill her or turn her again. The dividing line between a double agent and a triple agent is a narrow one, and for all you know, she's already crossed it."

We stopped by the fountain in the middle of the plaza.

DeLucca shoved his hands in his pockets and looked around and shook his head before he turned his sad brown eyes to me.

"Here's what we're not going to do. We're not going to have one of those conversations where I say what's on my mind and you preserve your sphinxlike silence. The scenario tonight is not me the plodding gumshoe and you the uberspook. The scenario is two cops cooperating with each other so that one of them does not have to remind the other of the serious amount of shit he could rain down on your head by complaining to the short guy standing over there with the dignitaries."

He meant Bill Fitzgerald, the NYPD commissioner, an immaculate sparkplug nicknamed Silver Bill for his carefully coiffed gray hair. A former Boston cop, he was a tough policeman with a high regard for his own reputation, and a famously unsparing way with anyone who let so much as a speck of dust land on it. Chuck was too low on the pecking order for Silver Bill, but the secretary had gotten an earful. That was another reason for the overnight blue.

We could hear the distant cheering of the crowd as the motorcade came out of the park onto West Sixty-Sixth Street. The route was packed all the way and the noise built quickly, rolling toward us like a wave as the first motorcycles appeared, followed by squad cars with their roof lights flashing, and at last, the row of gleaming black SUVs with blue and red strobes rippling in their grills.

As the motorcade drew to a halt, the Secret Service detail jumped from the leading SUV and surrounded the Nashes' car. At a signal, they opened the doors.

Nash popped from the car and headed for the rope line, reaching into the crowd, shaking hands and scorching the cameras with his smile. Behind him, Honey Li oozed from the car as if she had been squeezed from a tube, lithe and smooth as paste. She wore a full-length silver sheath that made her skin look lustrous, and against that skin, like a jewel on a cushion, hung the Russian Pink.

Honey Li brought the diamond to life. Her skin awakened it. The diamond poured its radiance into the night. It slung pink photons around the square and into the waters of the fountain. The fountain caught the spray of crimson light and scattered it into the sky. It was easy to see how the diamond had come to stand for the campaign. It was a synonym for the dash and brilliance of the couple themselves—rich, exotic, unmatchable.

Behind Honey Li, a step or two back, the chalk-white figure of Senator Matilda Bolt, Harry Nash's political muscle and running mate.

Nash left the crowd and came striding across the white expanse and put his arm around his wife's waist and swept her into the theater.

"About the church," I said when they were gone. "Lime might have detected surveillance we had on him. That's why the operation was moved up."

"Sadly," he said, "I think I may be a little ahead of you on that."

A look of weariness had crept into his eyes.

"I think we found your girl."

"I'm not following you."

"Ah, come on, Alex," DeLucca shook his head. He swept his eyes around the plaza, checking the disposition of his officers, then turned back to me. "You had a kid out at the beach snooping around in the Russian bars. Then one day she's not snooping anymore. We picked up some chatter that you couldn't find her. Well, I think we found her."

Of course I had to leave. Annie took it well. Maybe not that hard a choice: night at the ballet with dad, or night at the ballet with twenty-one-year-old guy in dress uniform. The deal was the cop would take her home after the ballet. Looking back on it now, I don't blame the cop for what happened. In a place teeming with glittering, powerful people and swarming with protective services, you'd have to expect that maybe for a second, a rookie could be distracted. Bad night all around.

5

Amy Curtain was in Prospect Park, by the boat rental. The stale smell of the lagoon oozed through the dark foliage. Bats flicked through the outer glow of the crime-scene lights. At the war memorial beside the shore, a bronze angel folded her wings around a soldier whose eyes were fixed on his own death. There'd been no one to comfort Amy Curtain.

She'd been concentrating her efforts at Brighton Beach. If that's where they grabbed her, it was only a fifteen-minute drive away. A long fifteen minutes, although the real butchery took place in Prospect Park. According to the medical examiner, the extent of the blood-soaked ground meant she'd been alive when they got there.

In the methodical activity of the crime scene, with the click of cameras and the flash of strobes, the ugly details took on an antiseptic look as the remains of a young woman were transformed into a series of exhibits.

Her fingers lay severed in her lap. Her red hair was matted to the right side of her head. The death blow was a slash to the abdomen. The knife had sliced through her shirt and opened her stomach.

"How much did this kid even know?" DeLucca said as crime scene techs in white suits drifted in and out of the shadows, collecting body parts. "Was she read in at a high level?"

"No," I said. I was going through her pockets.

"Does this look like an interrogation to you? How old was she?"

"Twenty-two."

"Right. Twenty-two."

I could hear the anger in his voice. We'd both seen people who'd been violently killed. Not like this.

"They cut off a finger," DeLucca continued. "Maybe she tells them what she knows, maybe not. Whatever, they cut off another finger. By that time, she for sure spills what she knows, which according to you isn't much."

"Alright if I open the jacket?" I said to the medical examiner. I wanted to check the lining. He nodded.

"These guys know she's not a real pro," DeLucca persisted. He was getting on my nerves. "So why do they keep cutting?" he said. "There's only one answer. It's not her they're working on. It's you."

DeLucca studied the scene for a moment.

"This is some serious psycho shit, Alex."

"I fucking get it, OK?" I snapped.

It was obvious from the moment we'd stepped into the lights and seen what the killers had left for us. It wouldn't have taken them very long to get out of Amy everything she had. It wasn't much. She could tell them who she worked for. That's about it. Chuck hadn't briefed her on the background. He'd given her a simple assignment: nose around Brighton Beach, eavesdrop in bars, see if you can pick up anything about diamonds.

I'd just opened the lining of Amy's jacket when I heard DeLucca's phone. He stepped away to answer it, listened for a moment, then said,

"What do you mean, not in her seat?" And so help me God, my heart stopped beating.

"Could she have got through the perimeter?" He listened, then said in a voice taut with anger, "So she's inside. Get the backup from the buses. *Find her.*"

"It's your kid," he said. I just stood there gaping at him until he grabbed me and we ran from the park.

"Lincoln Center!" he shouted at the driver when we got to the street.

As we raced through Brooklyn I could hear the orders crackling on the radio. They'd already sealed the complex off for Nash. Now they were deploying more cops to the perimeter to stop anyone from leaving.

I called Tommy and told him that unknown operatives had kidnapped Annie at Lincoln Center. I told him to get our Homeland Security contacts to order an airport alert. I didn't realize I was shouting into the phone until DeLucca put his hand on my arm.

By the time we reached the Battery Tunnel, the cops at Lincoln Center had questioned not only the guy assigned to her but all the people in the surrounding seats. So we knew how they worked the snatch.

At the intermission, someone in an NYPD uniform relieved the young cop assigned to Annie, telling him to report to the command trailer. The new cop offered to take Annie backstage. Sure. Get her away from witnesses. It wouldn't have been hard to fool her. She was agog at her surroundings. And the cop she'd been entrusted to in front of her dad was handing her over to another uniformed policeman.

An escort met us as we raced from the tunnel into Manhattan. We were going up the FDR at ninety, a stream of wailing sirens and flashing lights tearing along the East River in the night.

"Whoever took her has to have her somewhere inside the complex," DeLucca said. He still had the phone to his ear. "The officer assigned to her went directly to his sergeant. They knew right away it couldn't have been a cop relieving him. They clamped a lid on the whole site. That took three minutes. We're onto the outside cameras now, running all the tape, and we haven't seen her. She's inside, Alex."

We were coming through the park at Sixty-Sixth when the cops found Annie in a basement room.

She looked more confused than frightened when I got there. One look at me changed that. She must have read the fear in my eyes, because her face just crumbled and she started to shake out big, hard sobs.

The door opened and a woman officer came in. She glared around at the roomful of jostling men.

"Sir," she said to DeLucca, "maybe you could give us girls a sec?" She put her arm around Annie and led her to a quiet corner.

They'd gone through her purse and taken her phone and asked about me. What was I doing there? Had I said anything about Nash? About the diamond? Later, when we put our heads together, DeLucca and I had the same suspicion. The Secret Service.

The agency guarded not only the president but the man planning to replace him. That gave them close access to Nash, while at the same time being under the direct control of the president.

But Amy Curtain's murder—that didn't fit the Secret Service. Slaughtering a young woman to send a message. Just too dark. They don't train that kind of killer.

In the back seat of the cruiser on the way home, Annie took my hand and turned it over and drew an X on the palm with her finger, just as I used to do for her when she was little and afraid of monsters lurking under the bed. It was our secret sign. No monster could harm someone protected by it.

Tell it to the monsters.

Two of DeLucca's detectives went through my apartment when we got there. "I'm putting some guys at the corner," he said when they were done. We both knew there wasn't much point in that. Whoever had grabbed Annie had done what they wanted to. Shown me they could.

As he left, DeLucca stopped in the doorway. "You're going to need protection on her," he said. "At least until we see where this is going. I can handle that."

I shook my head. "I've got some guys." I said.

"Freelancers? Alex, think about it."

"They know what they're doing."

"You'd better be sure."

Anger was the worst emotion I could have. It breathed hot mist on the lens I needed to keep clear. Fear fed the rage that welled up inside me, a toxic fog of images, of Amy's body in the park and of my daughter alone and terrified.

"Anthony," I said, as evenly as I could manage, "I'm on it."

He nodded as he watched me. "Your call."

"Other than that, Mrs. Lincoln," I said to Annie when we were alone, "how was the play?"

The Mrs. Lincoln shtick was our standard post-disaster line, usually spoken when Annie's team, and particularly Annie, got hammered at lacrosse.

She winced as she lay back on the sofa and placed her feet on the coffee table. She'd toppled out of the stiletto heels when the phony cop hustled her into the basement room. Dried blood showed where she'd stubbed her toes.

"I think I can save those feet."

I went into the bathroom and put my forehead against the mirror and iced down my rage until I was a reasonable facsimile of an adult male in control of his emotions. I got a bottle of antiseptic and poured some water into a glass bowl. In another rite from Annie's childhood, I added the antiseptic to the water, turning the liquid milky and stirring it with my finger. I rummaged around for a selection of Band-Aids and laid them out on the coffee table on a sheet of paper towel. I sat beside her and put her ankle across my knee.

I swabbed the scrapes with a cotton ball dipped in the solution. As she leaned back to let me take care of her, she scanned my face and forced a smile.

"Are we a pair?"

"Unfortunately for you."

She watched in silence as I put on the last Band-Aid.

"Where did you have to go?" she said when I was done.

"I'm sorry, baby. It was an emergency."

"Was it, like, a gunfight?"

"Just me and the Brooklyn mob."

"Stop it, Dad," she gave me a shove. "You're always joking. It's your way of avoiding a meaningful conversation."

She had a speech all ready. It came out smoothly, like a script she'd rehearsed until she got it right. So I guess it had been on the agenda.

"I think you should confide in me more," she said solemnly. "I'm your only child. I'm fifteen, and this is the time in our life when we have to build our adult relationship. It doesn't matter that we have a broken home. We need to foster a genuine dialogue."

"Absolutely," I said.

She gave me a pitying look.

"You never talk about what's really happening to you, Dad. You keep your thoughts bottled up inside."

I had a pretty good idea who'd helped Annie with the phrasing. My ex had used the same words to me. More than once. But I wasn't going to blame Pierrette. Annie was a serious kid. With no siblings, she'd spent a lot of time in adult company. She'd become an astute observer. Her parents' breakup had dropped a bomb into the middle of her life. Not surprising she was looking for reasons.

And she was right. Keeping things bottled up inside is part of my professional equipment. I was keeping them bottled up right then. Where else would I keep my thoughts, given what they were. I sat there trying to be a dad while my mind churned with the scene in Prospect Park and a deep and murderous desire for revenge hardened inside me.

Amy Curtain's mutilated body. That was war. But against who? And why?

The entry buzzer sounded. I opened the window and looked down at the street. Double parked as usual. I went to the intercom and pressed the button.

"Come on up, Tommy," I said, and buzzed him in.

"Uncle Tommy!" Annie shrieked. She ran down the hall and out to the elevator, and a minute later came back, her arm draped over Tommy's huge shoulders and her head against his chest. Her eyes were very bright. She was trying hard not to cry.

Tommy shot me a questioning look as Annie curled on the sofa and tried to stifle her tears. He towered beside her with his hands in his pockets, surveying the room. Pale rectangles showed where paintings had hung before they'd disappeared with Pierrette. The décor that remained—maybe a little rudimentary.

It had never really been Pierrette's home. A two-bedroom in the mid-nineties on the Upper West Side. No doorman. "If you must have a pied-à-terre, Alex, let's at least be on the right side of the park." I'd refused to give it up. Furious, she'd come banging in the door one day with some art and a few good lamps. The lamps were gone now too.

On the weekends Annie spent with me she didn't seem to mind. She treated my apartment like that of a big brother who couldn't quite take care of himself. But I wasn't her brother, I was her dad, and at that moment we didn't look like a family that had it all together.

Tommy sat down beside Annie and raked her over against him with a massive paw. She burst like a failed dam and out it came. What had happened. Her sudden discovery that the men who had taken her were not there to protect her. Her fear and humiliation. Tommy didn't say much, just sat there like a big blotter and soaked up all the tears. When Annie had recovered enough to start telling Tommy about the Lilac Fairy, I left them in front of the TV with a bowl of microwave popcorn.

"It has like *zero* calories," she explained to Tommy.

I went into the bedroom, shut the door, and called my ex. I delivered a short account of what had happened that consisted of me talking and Pierrette contributing frosty silences. At that time of night it wouldn't take her much more than an hour to come down from the country and get Annie.

Next, I called Chuck, and told him about Amy Curtain. I knew he wouldn't go to the morgue himself, or even call her next of kin. I suggested it anyway.

"Really, Alex. I'm not very good at consoling the bereaved. This is an operational unit. We have a protocol for these eventualities." He said it as if he were running US Central Command and I'd interrupted him in the middle of the invasion of Iraq.

Last, I called Tabitha. That was the longest conversation. The arrangements I wanted her to make for Annie's security were not illegal. On the other hand, they weren't what anybody would call by the book.

"Make sure it's the twins," I said.

"Hector and Luis. Got it."

"And right away."

"I understand, Alex. They'll start tonight."

"Tell them I'll settle with them later."

"No," she said. "This is operational. You were working. This is on the department. But we can keep it low profile. I'll put it through as an intelligence provisional. That way it comes out of a special budget. It won't go into the dailies. It goes into a folder with a limited circulation."

"Limited to who?"

"Me," she said.

When Tabitha and I were finished, I sat on the bed and went through what had happened, looking for connections. I included everything. Grabbing Annie. The failed operation at Brighton Beach. Amy Curtain's death. Where were the links? Brighton Beach was a center of Russian gang activity. Lime had Russian criminal help running illegal diamonds. Now he was switching to rare pinks. Harry Nash bought a pink, possibly from Russia. If you drew a line from each of these, there was one point where they all met.

Me.

The air seemed heavy with a sense of failure as I sat there in the bedroom, as if my ruined marriage lived on here, its pain rooted in the place where Pierrette and I had shared our deepest intimacy. I was still sitting there ticking through my sins when the buzzer sounded.

"My God, Alex," Pierrette said when I opened the door. "Even for you, this is bad."

She stepped past me into the hall and waited for me to shut the door. You could rescue Pierrette from a treehouse in the middle of a typhoon and she'd look exactly as she looked at that moment—her lipstick perfectly applied and her ice-cold eyes peeling off my skin in strips. Her face was bathed in a golden haze from her lamé bomber jacket. She'd tossed it on over one of the boat-neck T-shirts that she liked: a hundred bucks at Saks and worth every penny. The cut showed off her beautiful throat and left plenty of room for the silver choker with the single square-cut emerald.

"Can this go on, Alex?" she said in an urgent undertone, holding me by the arm to keep me in the hall. "The life you lead—that's your business. It's already wrecked our marriage. I'm not going to stand by while you let it wreck our daughter too."

"Pierrette," I began, but she shook her head.

"I know how you feel," she said coldly, "so don't try to explain. You feel guilty. That's how you always feel." She let go of my arm and stepped back and looked intently at my face.

"You think you have to drag the problems of the world around, that somehow it's Alex Turner's job in life to solve them. It's not, and it never was. You were not responsible for your mother's death, and you have to find that little boy and let him know that, or you will never be free of this obsessive, self-destructive life."

Pierrette didn't have to rehearse a speech like that. She had an instinct for the killing cut. She knew that my mother's death when I was twelve haunted me. She knew, and she'd gone straight for it, finding the old wound and making sure she opened it again.

She had sublime self-confidence. That's partly what I'd fallen for. I found it powerfully attractive. It starts with a beautiful young woman seated beside you at a dinner party, putting her lips against your ear and murmuring, "Angel, the fish fork is the little one with the three tines," and it ends sixteen years later with your childhood grief draped like an albatross across your whole life.

After Annie and Pierrette had left, Tommy stood peering into my fridge, holding the door open with one hand and sliding mostly empty cartons of Vietnamese food around with the other. He grabbed a plate and dumped some spring rolls onto it, and added what was left of the vermicelli noodles with pork and sweet-and-sour sauce. He sniffed at a Styrofoam container of pho, shoved it back, and slammed the door. He found chopsticks in the cutlery drawer and stood there at the counter keeping a steady flow of cold Vietnamese food going from plate to mouth without so much as a single strand of vermicelli slithering to the counter.

"I don't want to make you feel any more like a washout than you already are," he said. A noodle swayed back and forth as he waggled the chopsticks at me. "But just for the record, where do you think you rank on the scale of coping dad in tune with the needs of active, growing child?"

It was better to just let him get it over with. I hoped it wouldn't take too long. The sooner he got it out of his system, the sooner I'd find out what he really had to say.

"One of these days you're going to wake up and that girl will be a woman," he said, turning to rummage in the fridge again. He found the foil container with the chicken satay and the little tub of peanut sauce. "She'll be grown and you'll have missed the whole thing," he said through a mouthful.

This theme occupied Tommy as long as the satay. When he'd cleaned out the container, he put it back in the fridge and assumed the expression that meant he was going to demonstrate how much more he knew than I did.

"There's something I need to tell you," he said. "I didn't think it was that urgent, but I'm changing my mind."

He'd been at a meeting in DC, a regular meeting of lawyers from the Treasury and the Department of Justice. There was a man at the meeting Tommy hadn't seen before. He sat beside the deputy secretary, who chaired the meeting. The deputy didn't introduce him.

"Deputy starts pressing me about the Lime investigation. I clammed up. Said I couldn't discuss it in an open meeting. The deputy looked pretty steamed, but what could he do? I had him in a corner."

I recognized my cue. "How's that?"

"If the deputy challenged me on calling it an open meeting, I could insist he identify the guy, which clearly he didn't want to do. So he gave me a dirty look and moved to the next item on the agenda."

Tommy leaned back in his chair and stared at the ceiling. He was enjoying himself, but I didn't want to wait all night.

"Can we get to where this is going?"

"I kicked it around after the meeting with FinCEN's senior counsel. She used to work at the FBI. I asked her who she thought it was. She said she didn't know, but that a unit of MI had been sniffing around FinCEN asking about Russia investigations."

"Military Intelligence? MI's job is battlefield preparation," I said. "They develop intelligence for tactical commanders in the field."

"So I learned. But according to the FinCEN lawyer, and she's been around the block, MI has a National Security Agency connection too. Their responsibility is what they decide it is."

Military Intelligence. If that were right, we had fallen through the wormhole and come out in a different universe. In this new universe the most powerful organization in the world, the United States military, had a sudden interest in our case.

We sat in silence for a while, until Tommy said, "If you think that's bad, read this."

He handed me a note. I recognized the thick paper embossed with his title that Chuck liked to use to show off his elegant handwriting. It was only a few lines. I read it quickly, then read it again in disbelief.

"I have an appointment with Honey Li."

"In the morning."

I stared at the note for a moment.

"This stinks, Tommy."

"Watch out for those fuckers, Alex. Chuck is serving you to them on a plate, but they're the ones who placed the order."

6

At five o'clock I gave up trying to sleep. I pulled on my old shorts and walked to Central Park and hit the Bridle Path for a run. When I got home I climbed into the shower and stood under full cold for three minutes. I put on my best summer suit, dark blue, and a Turnbull & Asser shirt Pierrette had bought me back when she still thought I could be improved.

The calls I needed to make took half an hour. I still had an hour before my appointment, so I cut into the park at Eighty-Sixth and walked around the Great Lawn a couple of times.

I thought about Honey Li. The file Tabitha had couriered over was pretty thin. Mostly newspaper and magazine profiles, stories that got longer and more frequent as the odds of winning the presidency began to tilt to Harry Nash.

Honey's father was Li Wenjun, the Harvard mathematician whose work in number theory had won him a Fields Medal, the Nobel Prize of mathematics. Li had met his Finnish wife while in Helsinki for a conference.

Honey Li took after both of them. She had her father's ivory skin and her mother's blonde hair and sky-blue eyes. Not only beautiful but smart too. While still an undergraduate she wrote a ninety-page book called *The Social History of Zero* that made the best-seller list.

All the articles had the same story of how she'd met Nash. So either they had good message discipline or it was really true that Harry had fallen for her at a Roaring Twenties party when Honey, in a fringed dress and with strings of beads wound through her golden hair, gave the cheering mob a perfect demonstration of the Charleston, tossing her heels and stretching her arms above her head.

The scent of money rises from the pavement as you leave the park, cross Fifth Avenue, and enter the Upper East Side. The streets are cleaner and the people slimmer. Hermès scarves bloom like weeds. Even the professional dog walkers wear Burberry sneakers.

The apparatus of power was already reaching out to Harry Nash. Manned police checkpoints closed off the block where the Nashes lived. Police in full tac stood in clumps at the Madison Avenue and Park Avenue corners, and Secret Service agents checked IDs and directed visitors through a scanner.

The limestone crawled with carvings of serpents and creatures with scaly wings. According to my file, the house had been built in the 1800s by the Stuyvesants, an old New York family, and ridiculed by Edith Wharton as "a medieval nightmare from which poor Mr. Stuyvesant can never wake."

"Ugliest house in New York City," Nash had cheerfully agreed when reporters quoted the line to him. "We're nuts about it."

I mounted the steps to the gleaming black door. Before I could touch the buzzer, the door swung inward. A young woman with a crewcut and a silver stud in her nose said, "Sir?"

"Turner for Ms. Li," I said. She was wearing full-dress tails and a white tie. She opened the door and stood aside as I stepped into a black marble foyer with facing mirrors. A white earpiece perched on her ear, and I guess she had a mike too, because she said, "Mr. Turner, ma'am."

A few minutes later battered tennis shoes squeaking across marble announced the arrival of Honey Li.

She was wearing jeans and a man's dress shirt with the sleeves rolled up and a thick swipe of dirt across the front. She wore gardening gloves and held a trowel in one hand. "Mr. Turner, please come in. Nicky," she said to the butler, "can you bring some coffee to the garden?"

I followed Honey through an anteroom and into a long gallery. The walls were painted a creamy yellow and the lighting showed off the Nashes' collection of art and furniture.

Honey stopped in front of a throne-like armchair covered in brocade. "French, late seventeenth century." She waved her trowel at the chair. A clod of mud flew off and splatted on the floor. She fixed me with her eyes. They were extravagantly slanted, beautiful and calculating.

"Louis XIV, the Sun King, used this chair," she said. Then she leaned toward me, close enough for me to smell her perfume—gardenias— and said in a conspiratorial tone, "Upstairs it's all IKEA." She put her head back and laughed. I already knew she liked that line. Every magazine profile of her had it.

We reached a set of tall French doors that opened to a courtyard. A yellow marble fountain splashed in the sun. Water spouted from the mouths of fish clutched by cherubs who stared around with wild expressions, as if they had been snorting coke and had only just managed to scramble back into place and grab the fish before we came through the door.

Nash had created the courtyard by tearing down a glass conservatory and putting in the fountain. Balconies opened from the bedrooms onto the little plaza. A marble Venus held a swag of drapery across her body.

Honey led the way to a wrought-iron table. The butler came out with a silver tray. China coffee pot, matching cups, basket heaped with croissants.

"First of all," Honey said, leaning forward with a grave expression, "I want to tell you how upset Harry and I were to hear about your daughter. I gather there was some awful security mix-up last night."

"There was something last night," I said.

I didn't mean to make my voice as hard as it came out. But it made me mad, the way she tossed off her sympathy, as if what happened to Annie was some minor glitch in the Nashes' smooth operation. She picked up on my tone and sat back in her chair.

"Well, I'm sure it will all get straightened out."

"It certainly will," I said, and maybe that was a little icy too. "But this is your meeting, Ms. Li. I'm here because I was told to be here. If I had to take a guess, I'd say it's because of a case I'm working on. You could only know about that if somebody committed the crime of telling you, but I'm all ears."

A flash of something glinted in her eyes, quickly suppressed. She wasn't used to being spoken to that way, but it wasn't going to rattle her. She gave herself a moment to think, pouring us each a cup of coffee and putting a croissant on a plate and sliding it in my direction.

"You're not happy. I get it. But Harry already gets top-secret security briefings every day, to prepare him for the presidency, if we win. So please, don't start breathing fire. The fact that the Treasury is investigating Sergei Lime and that pink diamonds have come into the picture is not the closest-held secret in Washington. You'll be reading about it in the *Post* soon, served up with a good helping of slime from the president's friends."

She plucked a croissant from the basket and tore it in half, spraying the table with pastry flakes.

"We expect that," she said, waving a chunk of pastry before she popped it in her mouth and washed it down with coffee. "Slime is the *plat du jour* in politics. I'm not complaining. What I hope you'll understand is how remote a jewel like the Russian Pink is from whatever seedy machinations Sergei Lime is involved in."

The butler came out with a light gray leather box and put it on the table. Honey waited for a moment, her fingers on the box. She drew a deep breath, her expression tense, then opened it. A pink mist gushed onto her face. The soft light of the diamond seemed to saturate the air. A rosy haze enveloped us.

The cut diamond was the size of a small plum. It smoldered and pulsed in its satin nest. She placed a loupe beside the box. "I thought you would want to look."

I lifted it out and held it in the fingers of my left hand and brought it to the loupe. I knew it weighed 464 carats. That had been in every story. So I expected the weight. But until my eye accustomed to it, the color overwhelmed me. Colored diamonds are called fancies in the trade. They're graded according to a strict assessment of the depth of color. This one was the highest grade, Fancy Vivid Pink, sometimes called a Fancy Deep.

When my eye got used to the color, I saw what a risky stone it was. A single fracture plane slashed diagonally through it. Not all the way, or the stone couldn't have been polished. The fault seemed to lie deep in the center of the jewel. And when I turned it in front of the loupe, something else appeared: tiny cloudlike flaws, like threads, along the fault. They looked like microscopic jellyfish frozen in a crystal sea.

I placed the diamond carefully on the table.

It was cut simply. At a glance, maybe sixty facets. Unlike white diamonds, where cutters aim for brilliance, or "fire," colored diamonds call for restraint. The cutter's object with a stone like the pink wouldn't be to make it blaze but to calm it, to preserve the depth of color.

"I find it profoundly moving," Honey said. "It's quite sad, really, that some sordid little crime could touch the reputation of such an object."

"The only reputation it has is that Harry Nash bought it and you wear it."

Her face lit up in a dazzling smile. She leaned toward me. "Exactly," she enunciated, delivering each syllable in its own tiny case, as if they too were jewels she'd discovered. "The secret sauce of a famous name!"

She shoved the coffee things aside and parked her elbows on the table.

"Last year a Hong Kong billionaire paid almost $30 million at auction in Geneva for a sixteen-carat pink. Sixteen goes into 464 twenty-nine times, so by simple arithmetic this stone should be worth $870 million." She caressed the diamond with her fingertips. "But large diamonds don't progress in value arithmetically. They grow exponentially, because the larger they are, the rarer. Not only that, but the fame of their owners makes them more valuable still, like the diamond Richard Burton gave to Elizabeth Taylor. I wrote an algorithm that takes all that into consideration," she said, leaning back in her chair and spreading her fingers. "The price came out at well over a billion dollars."

She'd been shopping that algorithm pitch all over New York, but nobody was buying. That's what I'd learned on the phone. She'd also been testing the waters with the imperial-Russian-treasure theory, confirming the suspicion in dealers' minds that the Nashes were the ones who planted the rumor in the first place. Because, please. A 464-carat pink diamond owned by the Romanovs? It's not like they kept their jewels secret. How come nobody's heard about it.

No, the dealers had their own thoughts about where the diamond came from. They suspected it had been polished from a fifteen-hundred-carat pink that came out of the Chicapa River, and then disappeared from view. Until they knew for sure, and could examine the stone with scanners and microscopes and learn what had happened to the rest of it, they wouldn't touch it with a bargepole.

Honey tilted her head and arched an eyebrow and let me have a few seconds with her bewitching eyes before she shaped her lips into a siren smile and said,

"I've run the algorithm on previous known outcomes, and it's bang on every time. Still, I'd like to be sure I'm right."

"Yes," I said.

"Yes what?"

"Yes you'd like to be sure."

Her eyes flashed daggers at me. She was one of the people who inherit the earth—brilliant, beautiful, powerful, and rich. She'd thought the pink would be like any other thing she and her husband owned and ran. Now she was learning that no one ran a diamond. It ran you.

She put it in the box and closed the lid and scraped back her chair. The butler appeared and Honey thrust the box into her hands.

"Do you mind staying for a moment?" she said, standing up. "I'm afraid you have another appointment."

I thought it might be Nash himself, but it was Matilda Bolt.

Tall and spare, she had lank black hair and chalk-white skin and eyes the color of straw. A harelip corrected in childhood had left a faint scar above her cruel mouth. She wore a plain white sleeveless shirt and black jeans and thin gold sandals on her narrow feet. She took a hungry drag on a vape and blew out a stream of smoke.

"You're the Treasury dick," she said. "Don't blame Honey for this. I'm the one who told that Chandler moron to send you over."

She gave me an arid smile and sat down at the table.

"I know all about your secret little black-ops outfit, Commander Bond," she said, waving the vape. "I helped write the legislation that split it off from FinCEN, and I OK'd the recruitment from the CIA when we decided to put a few people like you in with the accountants. I know your history. You're a devious person, Mr. Turner. That's what makes you so useful to those of us who love and cherish the deep state."

At least now I didn't have to wonder who Chuck had pulled my 906 for.

A two-way radio crackled as her Secret Service detail positioned itself just inside the door. Her yellow eyes bored into me.

"I'm saying this so we don't waste each other's time. Our nominating convention is thirteen days away. That convention must nominate Harry Nash. If it doesn't, you and I may not have a country left to work for. It can't have escaped your notice that the president is dismantling our republic. Harry Nash has the best chance of beating him. You know the country we're turning into, because that's the country you met last night at Lincoln Center."

Editorial cartoonists always made Matilda Bolt look haughty. She wasn't. She was menacing.

She took another pull at her vape and let the smoke float from her mouth. She studied me carefully through the haze.

"You reading me?"

"You mean the message that my kid's in danger? How long did you think it would take me to figure that out?"

She nodded coldly.

"Fine. Cards on the table, then. We have a problem with Harry's diamond and Sergei Lime. Your idiot boss has been feeding searches into his Wizard of Oz machine. He may try to sit on the results, but they're already leaking. I heard last night that the software actually recommended an investigation of Harry, and if I heard, so has the White House. They are determined to find something to compromise Harry."

"It probably won't be that hard," I said. "And try to understand how concerned I am about Harry Nash when I tell you that last night I identified the body of a twenty-two-year-old murder victim who was investigating your candidate's former business associate."

"Mr. Turner," she said impatiently.

"Her right cheek was shattered and her teeth dislodged," I said in a louder voice. "There was a gaping wound in her stomach. She'd bled to death, probably knowing she was dying."

"Look," she said, "things like that, they're horrible."

"They snipped off her fingers and stuffed her in a ditch in Prospect Park." I wasn't shouting, but one of the agents in her detail appeared in the door again and frowned at me. She motioned him back.

"Her dad is a seventy-two-year-old retired teacher in the Bronx. Widower. No other kids. He had to come down and confirm the ID."

Matilda Bolt had wielded power for a long time. She had chaired the Senate Armed Services Committee until her party lost the majority. Even out of the chair, her military ties were deep. She'd sent men to war, and had heard the ugly things you have to hear when they die.

"That's a terrible death," she said. "I grieve for that girl. So let's find out who did it."

"I'm not laying off Harry Nash."

She gave me a wintry look. "You're not understanding me. I'm not asking you to lay off Harry. I want you to investigate him and his moronic bauble. Because you won't find a killer. You won't even find a criminal. You'll find the shameless schemer that voters have already fallen for. In other words, the perfect president."

Another crackle of radio noise came from the house. She glanced at the aide leaning anxiously out.

"One last thing," she said. "It wasn't hard to find you, and as you've learned, I'm not the only one looking." She had a hawk's-beak nose, and her pale eyes stared down it. "But I find I need you, Mr. Turner. So lucky you. In a friendless world, you've got me."

She didn't wait for a reply.

7

The mint-green Mini Cooper was waiting at the corner of Madison Avenue. As soon as I clicked the seat belt into place Tabitha popped the clutch and shot into the traffic.

"The whole world seems to know about Chuck's new toy pointing the finger at Harry Nash," I said.

"FinCEN techs wired it up. He should have known. But that's not what's really bothering him. Chuck has friends in the West Wing," she said. "Apparently they have private polling that says the president's headed for a train wreck in the next election."

That would account for Chuck's hesitation to open a file on Nash.

We went through the park and took the West Side Highway downtown.

"The computer guy, is he there now?" I asked.

"He's waiting."

"And he's worked for us before?"

"The Russian diamond-smuggling network. He wrote that program for tracking the diamond flows from the Russian mines so we could tell how much Lime was laundering for the oligarchs."

I remembered him now. Patrick Ho. PhD from Stanford in computer science. He had worked for the Office of Tailored Access Operations, the team of NSA hackers that penetrated the Chinese military's Shanghai-based hacking operation. For weeks, the team at Fort Meade had logged every keystroke that the Chinese made in their campaign to penetrate the US government's computer defenses. Finally, when they'd got all the information they wanted, Tailored Access had snapped pictures of the Chinese hackers, using the cameras on the hackers' own computers. The first the Chinese knew they'd been hacked was when Tailored Access posted their faces online, with their names.

Patrick had later joined a unit at the Treasury that was modelling some kind of big-data weapon to help the United States bludgeon other countries with the power of the dollar. I mean, more than we were bludgeoning them already. Tabitha had managed to get him temporarily seconded to me when we launched the original operation against Lime.

Her window was open. Her hair flew around her head. The car smelled of her shampoo.

"Patrick Ho," I said. "His dad is Ho Wang Wei. Used to run a big mahjong game in Chinatown."

"He still does," Tabitha said.

That was true, but since I'd never put it in a file Tabitha must have developed sources of her own. Strictly speaking, she should have told me first. I filed it away in the corner of my mind where I store suspicion. It's a large corner.

We turned off the highway into a parking lot beside one of the cavernous old freight terminals that survive on the west bank of Lower Manhattan. They stick out into the Hudson like fingers clawing at the past. Around them the waterfront blazes with glass condos and outdoor restaurants and parks where people walk their tiny dogs. Against this, the old piers mount a crumbling rearguard of boxing gyms and doomed businesses that ebb and flow like the murky waters of the river.

As we got out of the car, I waved to the black man who was sliding the chain-link gate shut behind us. Augie Treacher ran the pier. He did me favors because I was Tommy's friend. Tommy had arranged a no-contest plea deal with suspended sentence after Augie had walked into a Queens restaurant with a rivet gun and fatally interrupted two members of the Capezi crime family in the middle of the pasta special, which that night was spaghetti carbonara. Two months before, they had cut out Augie's tongue in a dispute about who said what to whom.

"And you've explained the problem?" I asked Tabitha as we climbed a narrow flight of stairs.

"He understands," Tabitha said.

"And his clearance?"

"It's current."

The narrow passage smelled of damp metal and oil and old timbers. The steel stairs echoed as we climbed. On the top floor, cracked linoleum added the odor of old wax to the smell of the river. At the end of the hall was a tiny office cut in half by a wooden counter. Behind the counter hung a rack of golf clubs. I grabbed a driver, and we pushed through a steel door onto the driving range.

After the dim interior the light was blinding. Across the river the towers of Hoboken blazed in the sun. The driving range stretched before us, 350 yards of Astroturf surrounded by nets hung from pylons. Beyond the netting, white hydrofoil ferries went skimming down the river to the Battery. In front of us a tanker the length of a football field plowed slowly up the Hudson.

We stepped onto the driving platform. I placed a ball on a tee and handed Tabitha a driver and stood back to watch the most beautiful swing I had ever seen that was not on the PGA. The ball lifted in a lazy arc, following a perfect line. It bounced onto the green carpeting around the 225-yard marker. We'd been here before. We both knew that I would follow with a vicious slice, so I got it over with while Tab tried not to look.

Patrick Ho was waiting in the glassed-in booth to one side of the tees, where the golf pro kept his bookings, his whisky, and his despair. I don't know why he was always so morose. If he wanted to remind himself that things could be worse New Jersey was right there across the river.

Augie had closed the range for a few hours, and the rickety pro shop was a handy place to sit. The glass rattled and wind whistled through cracks and water lapped at the old black piers. I shut the door behind me and sat down.

Patrick Ho was short and compact, with a crewcut and black-framed glasses. He wore a gray turtleneck, black chinos, and brown suede ankle boots, an attire that managed to be monastic and stylish at the same time, as if he belonged to an order of monks that ordered its habits from J. Crew.

"Tabitha says you think you can help us."

"Maybe. The problem, as she explained it, goes roughly like this. Nash bought into First Partners when the Russian oligarchs forced Lime to sell. Later, Nash bought the Russian Pink from the fund. Question: Are Lime and Nash in some kind of partnership, and is the Russian Pink part of it?"

"That's right. I don't know why Nash would buy shares in a Russian fund and then immediately buy an asset from it. But he had a reason, and I think it's a reason he shared with Lime."

"Do we know how First Partners bought the pink? I'm assuming it's not a normal kind of business acquisition for a fund."

I told him that all I had was a tip from a South African source that Barry Stern, a Johannesburg dealer, had paid $12 million for a large pink.

"If we take that as the start of the money trail, can you follow it?"

"Maybe later, when we have more data," Patrick said. "But there's something else I'd like to try first."

The wind was rattling the glass so hard I was leaning across the desk to hear him. We left the pro shack and made our way down to the end of the range. A Circle Line boat loaded with tourists wallowed through the waves.

"Shoot," I said.

He hooked his fingers through the netting.

"It's something I've been thinking about for a long time. I'd like to create a program that thinks like the person we're targeting."

"And how do you do that?"

"By using a new kind of computing system called a neural network. The problem with most computers is that they only know how to do what we tell them to do. They don't think, they follow rules."

He warmed to his plan. As he explained it, a computer following rules never benefits from its experience. It doesn't get smarter with each successive operation. A neural network actually got smarter. Through a process called machine learning, the computer absorbed data and learned to draw conclusions from it.

"But how do you know its answers are right?"

He took off his glasses and polished them carefully. He held them up and squinted at them before he put them back on.

"Do you ever know someone is lying to you? You have no proof, but you're certain anyway?"

"Sure."

"That's because many people have lied to you, and you've discovered they have, and now you're able to recognize the lie as it's happening. You don't follow rules, you've just learned to know. A neural network works like that."

He used medicine as an example. Neural networks were already making complicated diagnoses. Instead of writing rules to tell the computer what a lung tumor looked like, programmers created data sets of hundreds of thousands of images and scans of lung tumors. They fed them into the machine. The computer learned what lung cancer looked like the way a doctor learned: by seeing it.

"The computer looking for a tumor knows what it's looking for," I said. "This time it won't."

"It will learn," Patrick said. "It will sift through emails and phone logs and bank records, and eventually, if I'm right, it will figure out how Lime did business, not only with Stern but with Nash."

A bright red chopper from the heliport near the Battery appeared in the sky and headed for the Statue of Liberty with another load of tourists. Two hundred bucks apiece for a seven-minute spin. Huddled masses, welcome to New York.

"Earlier you mentioned computers we have access to. You've probably gathered that what I'm asking you to do is off the books. That's why we're meeting here. You wouldn't have a Treasury contract."

"I know that," Patrick said.

"I want to make this clear. When I said off the books, I meant way off."

Patrick nodded, took off his glasses, and polished them again with the bottom of his shirt.

"You cut my dad a break. There were some aspects of his business that were not one hundred percent legal." He held his glasses up to the sky again. "If you had gone strictly by the letter of the law, my dad would have been deported as a felon. And anyway," he said with a sudden grin, "the Treasury will never catch me. When I go into the network, they won't know I'm there."

Even with the river lapping at the pier and the deep thrum of a tugboat as it chugged upriver, the *ping* from my phone sounded loud.

I could count on one hand the people who have my cell number. Unrecognized sender—right away that's bad. No message, just a link to a live stream. It took me a moment to recognize what I was looking at, and when I did a block of ice formed around my heart. It was a stretch of highway I knew well. That's how the horror starts. Something mundane. It's your life, and now someone else is driving it.

That highway was the road to Annie's school.

8

My mouth filled with an acid taste. My heart pounded as chemicals surged through my body to prime it for violent action. But what action? I was forty miles south of Annie's school. Bolt had warned me I'd be targeted. Here was the attack. On my daughter.

The Convent of St. Mary at Croton-on-Hudson was a girls' high school. Like every school in America, they had a lockdown protocol for shooters. I didn't know the intentions of the people streaming to me, except to do harm.

"Lockdown. Please, lockdown," I said, and even to me my voice sounded like the snarl of a cornered animal.

"Alex?" Tabitha put her hand on my arm. I had walked back up the length of the range with the phone gripped in my hands.

I shrank the image and called the school. The line was busy. I stabbed redial. Still busy. The call didn't bounce to voice mail. I knew right away what was happening. Whoever was streaming to me had tied up the number. It's not hard. You can hire a call-flooding company online.

Services in India will bombard a number with so many calls that the phone is effectively out of service.

I must have groaned. Tabitha's fingers tightened on my arm. "What's wrong?"

"Where are the twins?" I said.

"They'll be where Annie is. One of them will. They've split the job into twelve-hour shifts. Alex, what's going on?"

"There's an attack on Annie's school," I yelled, rushing for the stairs. "Call the twins' number. Tell whichever one is at the school to alert the school security guard. Tell them there's a call flood on the school, so I can't call the guard direct. They have to go to lockdown."

We ran down the stairs and out of the building. Augie read the urgency at a glance and dashed for the gate. We shot out onto the West Side Highway, took the left-hand lane, and were running the light at Twenty-Third Street as Tabitha finished the call.

"Tell him we're on our way, Luis. I'll keep you posted as soon as we know more, but you should treat it as an armed attack."

"Call DeLucca now," I said, as soon as she was finished. "Tell him to get the state police to send cruisers to St. Mary's School at Croton. There's a back entrance that they have to cover too. Tell him somebody's after my kid again."

Tabitha had the department's private switchboard on speed dial, and asked the operator to get hold of DeLucca.

The view on my screen was across the steering wheel to the road, so I guessed the driver had a GoPro strapped to his head. In the foreground, his gloves gripped the wheel. Tight leather gloves fastened at the wrist with straps.

DeLucca was on an operation with restricted communications. Tabitha had the call on speaker. I listened as our operator made her way implacably through the succession of closed doors.

Now the black gloves framed the familiar strip mall a quarter mile from the school. I gripped the phone so tightly my hands were shaking. I was only dimly aware of how fast we made it up the length of Manhattan and left the city behind. We were racing along the twisting parkway that goes north through Riverdale when my phone pinged again. Another unknown number. I tapped, and another stream began. I recognized the narrow bridge that crossed the Croton River and led to the back entrance to the school.

"Tell Luis they're coming from two directions," I said, forcing my voice under control. "Tell him to get down to the back gate. They're about five minutes away."

The school occupied a large, wooded property. It was three-quarters of a mile from the main building to the back gate. Luis and his brother had been Army Rangers. Luis would understand that it was better to move toward the attack and neutralize it than let the attackers get into the grounds.

The feeds ran side by side. The slow pace made the action feel unstoppable. The second car drifted along the suburban lane that ended at the property. The first car reached the white gates of the main entrance. Agonizingly slowly, it turned in through the gates and started up the road that climbed through woods to the hilltop school.

From Tabitha's phone I heard the NYPD dispatcher snap a code word at someone in a command trailer.

The school appeared, a three-story redbrick house with tall, white-trimmed windows and a cupola topped by a weathervane. The shot jiggled as the car went over the speed bump where the driveway loops around to the front door.

Then the camera jerked as the black gloves left the wheel and the driver opened his door. The lens pointed at the ground as he swung out of the car and planted his dirty Reeboks on the gravel.

Cyril, the retired cop who ran security at the school, would be alone inside, watching the approach.

"Don't come out, Cyril," I said out loud. "For Christ's sake, don't come out."

He came out, placing his feet carefully, his pistol held straight out in both hands as he kept his eyes on the men. I knew there were two of them, because he kept swinging his aim back and forth from the camera to a point beside the camera. Cyril was a tough old guy. He'd made his sergeant's stripes in the NYPD before he'd bailed for a softer job upriver. He'd spent the last ten years of his service running the desk at the Fortieth Precinct in the Bronx, the one they call Fort Apache. He was no pussycat, but in addition to his age he had one more serious disadvantage: there was only one of him.

The guy on the passenger side must have been standing behind his open door, to conceal his weapon. He waited until Cyril was swinging the gun away from him and back to the driver, and gunned him down point blank. He must have let the whole clip go. Cyril wore protection, but the burst blew him off his feet and tore his arms to rags.

DeLucca's voice crackled from the speaker.

"We're just getting onto the Saw Mill River Parkway," Tabitha told him. "Escort should look for a green Mini Cooper."

"Anthony," I roared. "One team just killed the guard. There's a second team coming in the back way."

Cyril had secured the door when he came out. The driver fired a few rounds into it. The lock must have been set into a steel frame. It held.

The second camera had almost reached the back gate. I had a clear view from the dashcam when Luis stepped from the trees and raised a Heckler & Koch MP7 machine pistol. I saw the windshield disintegrate and then the feed went black. At the same time, the first team shot out a window and entered the school.

They headed down the hall. They seemed to know where they were going. There was a central atrium beneath the glass cupola and a broad flight of stairs leading to the second-floor classrooms. They were almost at the stairs when the nun who ran the school, Sister Gene, came hurrying out of the narrow hall that led to the offices at the back, raising her arms. She disappeared from the frame.

A siren made a single whoop beside us as a New York State trooper pulled up and signaled Tabitha to follow. The trooper switched on her roof lights and siren.

"The escort's here," Tabitha said into her phone.

"Anthony," I shouted, "two victims, one fatality and one probable fatality. They are going up the stairs right now to the classroom floor."

I heard him yell to someone nearby, "Scramble a chopper!"

We hit heavy traffic a few miles south of Croton-on-Hudson. The highway was at a dead stop. The trooper pulled a U-turn. We raced back to the closest exit and headed east. She was making for the same bridge that the second team of attackers had crossed.

I tried to keep my hands steady as I gripped the phone and watched the screen.

The men mounted the stairs. Not hurrying. Giving me plenty of time to watch their assault unfold before my eyes. A blaze of multicolored light appeared as they reached the landing halfway up the stairs and the camera tracked past the stained-glass window. The deliberate advance up the broad stairs, the unhurried pace, gave the display the feel of a ritual enactment in which Annie and I were the only participants who did not know the end. My stomach heaved as I watched the approach.

Nothing could stop them. That was their message. They were going to reach my daughter. They would do what they liked.

At the top of the stairs they turned right. Slowly the camera advanced along the hall. At every classroom door they paused to show me the rows of girls crouching beneath their desks. They didn't linger. They knew where Annie was.

"Where's that fucking chopper?" I said into Tabitha's phone.

DeLucca came on.

"I'm at the UN. We were doing emergency drills on the East River. I've detached a chopper. They're on their way. Ten minutes to Croton."

"Tell Luis to get back to the school!" I yelled at Tabitha.

She put DeLucca on hold and tried the number. She knew, and underneath my terror I knew too, that he wouldn't have his phone.

Tabitha's knuckles where white on the steering wheel as we followed the cruiser fast into a blind corner. The trooper had her siren going. An SUV sailed out of an intersection, the driver's head bent to his phone as he texted. The cruiser's steel ramming grid caught him on the rear fender. The SUV spun a full 360 and dumped into the ditch as we gunned past him up a hill and shot across the bridge.

Annie's teacher had blockaded the door with her desk. They forced it easily, grabbed the nun, and slammed her into a wall. She slumped to the floor.

Annie's desk was in the row against the windows. The silence of the picture intensified the horror as the men crossed the classroom and went down the aisle. The windows provided plenty of light to illuminate my daughter's face as she understood that they had come for her.

Where was her tough dad now?

I will find you and kill you I will find you and kill you I will find you and kill you, an animal sobbed in my throat.

The guy wearing the camera reached down and grabbed her hair and yanked her to her feet. The camera held on her face so I could feel her terror and see the last moment of her childhood before he seized her blazer and shirt in his hairy fist and struck her savagely on the side of her face with the back of his free hand. Her head snapped sideways with the force of the blow, and she fell across the desk and into the next aisle. The camera let me have ten seconds of my girl with her knees drawn up, her arms folded above her head and her body wracked by spasms. Then it panned away and they walked calmly from the room.

The camera shooter hung his GoPro on the newel post at the top of the stairs. The last pictures on the feed were the two of them walking down the stairs, then a few minutes later Luis tore by, followed five minutes later by the first cops and the paramedics. Then a shot of me with my eyes popping out of my head like a madman as I stormed up.

Annie was on the floor, collared and strapped to a board. An IV dripped into her arm. The doctor was a young guy with a crew cut. His glasses kept slipping down his nose. He looked harried, but in control. He knelt beside Annie with his fingers on her wrist. With the other hand he shone a light into her eyes.

I took her fingers in my hand and whispered her name. She gave me a faint squeeze.

"We're taking her to the ER," the doctor said. "I need to assess her. She received a very hard blow." He lifted her hair to show me the bruise that had started to creep onto the side of her face.

Cyril was dead. Sister Gene had a broken jaw. They'd clubbed her with a gun butt. Annie's homeroom teacher was going out on a stretcher.

The grounds were swarming with the sheer numbers that police commanders order to a scene when they have no idea what to do. Police and dogs poured through the woods. I don't know what they thought they'd find. The attackers were long gone. We passed their abandoned car at the main gate, where they'd apparently switched vehicles. Crime-scene techs in hooded white overalls were taking swabs from the steering wheel and going through the car with powerful lights. Good luck with that.

Luis had killed one of the team at the back gate and captured the other. He'd shot him in the leg, secured his wrists with plastic ties, and put him in the trunk, where he screamed until he passed out.

At the hospital, the ER doc ran tests to make sure Annie was not concussed. Her blood pressure had dropped, and he ordered a CAT scan of her spleen because she'd fallen so hard across the desk. She checked out OK. He wanted to keep her in for observation, but I knew that if he did, we'd have another trauma to take care of—Pierrette. I'd only managed to keep her from coming by promising that things would go more quickly if she waited at home.

"OK," the young doc said. "She has no fractures, but she has suffered a technical trauma. Her blood pressure is low. She's not in shock now, but she was, and that's a very dangerous condition that can come back fast. You really have to watch her."

His glasses slid down again as he peered at me.

"*Will* someone be watching her?"

"Yes," I said.

He looked at me doubtfully. "I gave her Dilaudid for the pain." He held up a pill container and rattled it. "If she needs another in four hours, OK, but she's young and healthy so it's better if she just gets through it. This is an acutely habituating drug."

Something about the way I looked made him stop talking. He handed me the pill container. I went away with my daughter in my arms.

9

Maybe it's true what they say about revenge. That it's a meal best eaten cold. But you can plan the menu anytime.

As Annie's head rocked against my chest I rummaged through the possibilities of violence.

It had to be Lime. Lime could have put together a Russian team with a phone call. Russians bring a special viciousness to their work. But the streaming. I understood its purpose—terror—yet it came at a price. Even if they'd engineered the traffic jam and arranged to divert the state police, which we now knew they had, they should have scouted the school first to assess security. They might have spotted the twins. And anyway, a straight attack on the school, without warning: That would have accomplished the aim of throwing me off balance without the mayhem.

Unless they wanted mayhem.

Tuxedo Park, where Pierrette lived, is a private village for rich people. Mansions dot the wooded hills around three lakes. A private police force keeps out non-residents. A state trooper was parked in front of the stone gatehouse when we drove in.

The property Pierrette inherited from her grandmother was a 4,000-square-foot cedar-shingled house. It had big verandas and an English garden that took a gardener two full days a week to keep in shape, but her grandmother had left enough to cover that too.

Pierrette was waiting in front of the house. Beside her stood a Ralph Lauren ad in dark brown cords and a beige turtle neck. His hair was short and neatly parted at the side. He looked like what he was: a soldier trying to look like a civilian. Those aren't good reasons to hate a man, but you have to start somewhere.

Pierrette clasped her hands tightly when I climbed from the back seat with Annie limp in my arms. A single wrinkle cracked the porcelain smoothness of her forehead. She was holding herself in check by sheer willpower.

She kissed Annie gently and put the back of her hand against her daughter's forehead and said we'd better get her upstairs right away.

"Alex, Tim Vanderloo," she said distractedly. He put his hand gently on her shoulder.

"I think I'd better leave you and Alex alone with Annie," he murmured.

"Please don't leave," she said.

"Of course not. I'll be here as long as you need me."

"On the other hand," I snapped, "we might be a while."

"Oh, Alex," Pierrette said, in a voice that really did sound heartbroken. Shaken awake by my hard voice, Annie started to heave as if she were fighting for breath, and then broke down into awful, rasping sobs. I carried her into the house and upstairs.

Her bedroom occupied a corner with a view of Tuxedo Lake. It had been her grandmother's room. French doors led to a terrace that faced across a side lawn to the water and the forested hill beyond. A sofa and two chairs huddled before a fieldstone fireplace. Annie's desk with her laptop sat in a bay window bathed in sunshine. The feature of the room that Annie liked best as a child was a door concealed in the paneling. It opened to a servants' staircase connected to the kitchen at the back of the house. The summer weekends we'd spent there as a family were punctuated by endless ambushes when Annie, having crept from her room and made her way downstairs, would spring out at us, shrieking and laughing as we feigned surprise.

"They had a TV in the hospital that showed the inside of my brain," Annie said as I tucked her in. The familiar surroundings had calmed her.

"Try to rest now, darling," Pierrette said.

"Dad, are you going to catch them?"

"Try to be quiet," Pierrette said, sitting beside her and putting her hand on Annie's cheek.

Annie lay back but didn't take her eyes from me.

"Don't go, Dad."

Pierrette stroked Annie's hair. "Now, sweetheart," she began. "You know Mom and Dad love you very much."

"He can *stay*," Annie said vehemently, squeezing my fingers with all her strength. "He can sleep in my room. On the couch!"

She put her head back then, but kept my hand firmly in her grip. After a few minutes I felt her fingers loosen. Her breathing was even.

"They picked me, Dad," she mumbled.

That dagger stayed firmly embedded in my heart as Pierrette and I sat there on either side of Annie. Finally I gave her a pill. Screw the habituation. Five minutes later she was fast asleep.

Pierrette and I went onto the balcony and sat on the wicker sofa.

A hawk was riding a thermal along the chain of hills. On the lake, a canoe with a single paddler dragged a widening *V* of ripples across the glassy surface.

Some women stake out real estate in your heart and own it forever. It didn't matter how bitter the breakup. Pierrette could still freeze me solid with a glance, and maybe that's what made her moments of tenderness so devastating. Her eyes could express a warmth that melted me, and that only changed to pity at the end. Now, with our broken daughter sleeping in her bed behind us, I longed to take her hand and hold her and press my face against her fragrant skin. I made that thought go away.

"I'm not going to blame you," she said. She was wearing a sapphire ring that she kept twisting, the only sign of how upset she was. "I know that can't have been your fault."

"Of course it was my fault," I said harshly. "Who else's fault would it be?"

She put her hand on my knee to remind me to keep my voice down.

"Please, tell me what's going on. What does this mean for us? Are we safe? I have to know, Alex. Who is behind this? What have you gotten into?"

"It's an attack on me."

"Obviously," she said, suddenly bitter. "But why not you directly? Isn't that part of your job, to be attacked?"

"I can only say that it won't happen again," I told her, a promise as feeble as it was ridiculous. Pierrette shook her head.

"You look terrible. Your face—it looks so, I don't know, *ravaged*. Maybe that's because you know that you can't really promise anything. But that's the life you chose to lead. You never would give it up for us."

"Let's not go there, Pierrette."

The canoeist had reached a wooded point and was disappearing out of sight around it.

"That's Miss Harrington," Pierrette said. "She does that every day, and she's done it every day for eighty years. Am I going to be here when I'm old, too? Doing the same things that I do now for no better reason than that I've always done them?"

"Yes," I said.

She gave her head a brisk shake. She wasn't going to make that mistake again.

"I won't keep you," she said, standing up and leading the way out. We went down the stairs into the main hall.

"State police are putting a permanent detail here until further notice," I said.

We stopped on the veranda. She cocked her head at me.

"You know, you're very clever and tough, Alex, but I often wonder how much you really understand about the world."

I doubted that Pierrette wondered about me at all, never mind often.

"Your world view is cynical because the people you have to deal with are criminals," she said. "But not everyone is a criminal just because they have money. Being rich is not inevitably bad."

"Now you tell me," I said. She shook her head sadly and opened the front door.

Vanderloo was waiting on the porch. He gave Pierrette's hand a squeeze. She repeated the introduction, this time adding Vanderloo's rank and referring to him as "our friend." Annie had used the word "boyfriend," but I wasn't sure he'd been hired for the position. He looked like a candidate still in the application phase. The XKE would help, black and polished to a gleam.

"And you're from West Point," I said.

"That's where I'm posted at the moment."

"What do you teach?"

"I'm not really what you'd call a teacher."

"Is that right. What would I call you?"

"Colonel," he said.

And you know, fair enough. I didn't like him, but in the circumstances, who would I like?

Tabitha was waiting by the Mini. Pierrette looked at her and arranged her face into one of those smiles women learn in combat training. I thought she was at least going to come off the porch and say hello, but she turned and walked back into the house. Vanderloo lifted his eyebrows at me, then followed her inside.

Tabitha and I stood there for a few minutes, looking at the lake and the hills and the mansions peeking from the trees. We got into the car. The Jag was at the top of the circular drive, and I snapped a shot as we rolled by.

"I'm forwarding this to you," I said. "When you get back to the office, run the plates."

Tabitha pulled up in front of my apartment. I'd just put my hand on the door handle when she reached across and held me by the arm.

"Would you like to talk?"

"No," I said.

She didn't let go of my arm.

"We can sit here for a minute."

"Why?"

She looked at me with a grave expression. "You're crying."

I moved her hand from my arm. I got out and shut the door and went inside with nothing to console me but the murder in my heart.

10

At 4 A.M. I got out of bed, climbed into the shower, and let it run cold. I had a coffee and some toast, then opened the little gun chest in the closet and took out the Ruger. Lightweight, compact, five rounds of .357 Magnum. I laced up the brown suede desert boots with the steel toes. Before I left I grabbed the extendable baton.

The Santa Clara is an ornate fairy tale of a building on what New Yorkers call the Gold Coast—a stretch of Central Park West lined with expensive real estate. John Lennon was assassinated a few blocks from the Santa Clara in front of his own famous building, the Dakota. Celebrities and tycoons shell out fortunes for the views from the Gold Coast's private terraces, and the Santa Clara is the reigning princess of the strip. Sergei Lime had paid $100 million for the three-story penthouse at the top.

I parked and sat on a bench on the Central Park side of the street and watched the dawn unfasten clumps of darkness from the trees. The feelings churning in my chest settled into an icy ache. I had no plan except to get close to Lime.

In the strengthening light I studied the building. Not the trade entrance, I decided. In buildings like the Santa Clara the trade doors have more security than the main entrance, where the presence of staff provides the illusion of safety. I got up and headed across the street.

A doorman in a scarlet coat with a double row of polished brass buttons stepped to the door and pulled it open. He'd spotted the bill I had folded in my hand.

I followed the crimson carpet into the lobby, an expanse of rose-colored marble. Dark, old chests and antique chairs. A chandelier glowed with a soft amber light. At the far end of the lobby, near the bank of bronze elevator doors, a sleepy concierge in a dark gray suit came out from behind his desk.

"Sir?" he raised his eyebrow in the signature expression of gatekeepers everywhere.

"Lime," I said, flipping open my Treasury ID with the gold shield and holding it beside my face for a quarter-second before I snapped it shut.

"I'll call up," he said, picking up the phone.

"Let's make it a surprise," I said, and took the phone from his hand. I put it back in the cradle, gripped his upper arm and pulled him into an open elevator.

I pressed the penthouse button. The car began its dignified ascent.

"Will the door open when we get there?" I had the baton in my hand and he was staring at it. Wide awake now.

"No," he said. "You have to punch in the code."

Beside the floor buttons was a small numeric keypad.

"What's the sequence?"

"I don't know," he stammered.

I gave him a jab. "See if you can guess."

The elevator eased to a stop. I punched in the code he gave me and the door slid open with a loud *pong*.

The elevator closed behind me. I was in a large atrium. A staircase rose along one wall to a gallery that surrounded the entrance hall. On the floor where I stood, an archway led into a series of connected rooms. Even in a huge apartment, someone would have heard that elevator sound. A door slammed somewhere nearby and I heard footsteps coming, fast.

I opened the nearest of two doors and stepped into a closet full of coats, and got the door shut just as the footsteps arrived. He was breathing heavily, so probably a big guy.

I put my ear to the door. No more footsteps, but he was moving. I could follow the sound of his breaths. Silently I extended the baton and listened.

I put myself in his position. Had somebody come out of the elevator? His working assumption had to be yes. Where were they? Not enough time to get up the stairs, and he had come through the only other way into the apartment. If there was an intruder, he was behind one of two doors. He picked the wrong one.

The second I heard him yank the other door open I burst from the closet and took a swipe with the baton. He was fast for a big man. I just grazed him, drawing a bright red line across his forehead.

He was taller and heavier than me, and from the way he placed his feet, with a quick, agile step, I thought he might be faster too, so I came in right away and took another cut at his head. While he was grabbing for the baton, I got a good, hard kick at his knee.

The steel toe caught the bottom edge of his kneecap. He roared with pain and fell back. Instead of throwing myself on him and going for a neck hold and choking him unconscious, as I should have, I tried to stamp his face. He dodged it, got hold of the baton, and wrenched it from my hand.

He rolled aside, taking a savage strike at my ankles. I lost my balance and crashed into a table, shattering it and smashing my head against the wall. He was on me like a spider, pinning me, punching, digging at my face with the grip of the baton. I felt my lip tear open. I got a thumb in his eye, but he still had the baton. He was cocking his arm for a strike when a voice boomed, "Vasily!" A stream of Russian followed.

He punched me again on the side of the head, frisked me, and found the Ruger. He got to his feet, grunting with pain. He gripped the baton in one hand and with the other leveled the Ruger at my stomach.

Lime stood halfway down the staircase, posed like a figure in a painting. I couldn't see too well, my vision blurred from the punch. Was that a dressing gown? He came quickly down the stairs. It floated out behind him in a stream of peacock silk.

He flowed across the room. Under the dressing gown he wore pajama bottoms and a T-shirt. Bare feet. He had a battered, handsome face with bullet-hole eyes. Thick hands with knuckles that looked like rocks under the skin.

He almost managed the look of unruffled composure he was struggling for, but anger ate into the veneer like acid. My ID had fallen out. Lime snapped another line of Russian at the guard. He picked it up and handed it to Lime, who flipped it open and studied it. His face hardened. He extended his arm toward me, the leather folder held between two fingers.

"Tell your guy to put the gun down and back away," I spluttered through my torn lip. "You're both under arrest for attacking a federal officer. Don't make it worse for yourself."

He looked at me with contempt.

"Really, Mr. Turner. Is that the best you can do?" He forced a bitter smile onto his face. "One man. Armed with a pistol and a fighting stick. Government ID. Yet strangely you appear to be alone."

"You're not stupid enough to bet on that," I said, spraying drops of blood.

The smile flaked from his face as he studied me. The Treasury badge had stung him. We were hounding him, closing his accounts and freezing his assets. Even the palatial apartment, the property of a numbered company—we were coming for that too.

He shook his head slowly. "It's not my stupidity that's at issue here. It's yours." He kept his eyes fixed on me while he calculated what to do. "There is no one with you. You have no warrant, or you would have shown it." He frowned. "This is personal."

Lime had a thin, slightly crooked nose with a scar across the bridge. In a story that appeared when he bought the penthouse, *Vanity Fair* had called him "dashing." They'd also described him as a "passionate collector," making a big deal about the $80 million he'd paid at auction for a foot-long Hans Voortlander sculpture of an erect penis, cast in lead crystal and studded with 5,228 tiny diamonds. The reporter either had to say he's a whack job or a connoisseur, and ticked box number two.

He barked a word at the bodyguard and went swirling off across the room, the dressing gown rippling in his wake. The guard jammed the baton into my ribs. I struggled to my feet, trying to look even more pathetic than I was. He wasn't buying. He stood far enough away to give himself room to swing the baton. Plus he had the Ruger.

I followed Lime through a hall with cream-colored walls. Illuminated by tiny spotlights in the ceiling hung Lime's collection of Russian icons. Saints in bejeweled robes gazed out at the twenty-first century from mournful eyes. The Virgin Mary clasped a chubby Christ. The child stood with his feet planted on her lap and regarded the world with an irritated expression. Maybe it was the Voortlander penis that bothered him. It sparkled like a pagan fetish on a table in the center of the room.

Lime crossed the gleaming parquet, ran up a flight of stairs, and pushed through a door that seemed to lead straight out into the sky. The clouds were right there, coasting above New York City on their way to sea. The room wrapped around two sides of the penthouse. Central Park and the Manhattan skyline spread out like a tourist poster. Glass doors opened onto a brick terrace. A boxwood hedge ran inside the iron railing.

Cool morning air flowed in through an open door. The dressing gown billowed as he made his way to a sofa. His anger wrestled with confusion in his face.

"What is this? I get that you are vengeful, dull-witted people. That's what fits you for your work. But this," he waved his hand at me in a gesture of revulsion, "this is something else." His face was pale. "There's nobody with you. You have no authority. I know who you are. You are a lawless person." His eyed burned.

"Call the cops," I sputtered. My mouth was a rubbery mess. "Let's see how they treat you when I tell them I came up here to investigate the murder of an agent and an assault on a school, and your goon attacked me."

His eyes were hard and unblinking, like a snake's. He was clenching and unclenching his fists. The knuckles were swollen. At the end of the room were punching bags and a steel frame with weights. Lime was a devotee of mixed martial arts, a cage fighter. That had been in *Vanity Fair* too.

"I don't know what you're talking about," he said in disgust. "Is this about Slav Lily?" His lips curled into a sneer. "I know about you. I know how you trapped her. You think you're her protector now? She'll betray you." He clenched his teeth. He was holding himself in. He wanted to strike, but he also wanted to understand. "Or is this to protect Nash? Is that what this is about? You want to implicate me falsely in a crime so I can be taken out of the great man's path." His hands were balled into fists. "I'm an American businessman who made my investors a fortune by buying undervalued foreign assets. Nash became one of those investors. Now he's the great white hope and I'm a criminal?"

He leapt to his feet. His voice had risen to a shout. I was waiting for the guard to shift his attention to Lime. You can make a weapon out of anything. I had a hand on the back of the sofa, beside a heavy cushion. But the guard didn't take his eyes off me.

"You've come here to attack me," Lime growled. "To assault me in my home."

Fencing swords, daggers, pistols, and other weapons hung around the room. Lime stormed to the wall and yanked a six-foot-long curved blade from its hooks. It had a worn leather grip. He grasped it in both hands and swished it back and forth in front of me. The polished steel glinted. He handled the heavy blade as easily as a table knife.

"Russians call this kind of saber a *shashka*," he waved the blade back and forth. "Cossacks used these swords to terrify their enemies."

He cut the blade above my head in a lightning stroke. I felt the swish of air.

"But I'm a fair man," he smiled. He put the saber on a table. "I'm going to give you better odds."

The guard must have spotted the words *grab the big sword* in the thought balloon above my head, because he ditched the baton and grabbed the shashka. He held it like a giant cleaver.

I'd delivered myself on a platter. Even if the concierge called the police, what would he tell them? A guy with Treasury ID might possibly be hassling a resident? They'd send a car, but it wouldn't be right away.

"Find what you need in here," Lime said, kicking an equipment box toward me. "And lose the boots."

He tossed his dressing gown aside and changed into boxing shorts and pulled on a tight pair of fingerless leather gloves. His torso showed signs of the treatment he'd got in the Lubyanka. He approached a heavy bag slung from the ceiling and delivered a rapid combination of punches followed by a lightning blow with his foot.

"This is a country that worships wealth. Yet I'm the bad guy."

Let him talk. I took off my boots and found a pair of fighting gloves. I watched carefully while Lime demonstrated his prowess, raining blows and terrific kicks on the bag. I learned to fight from an Irishman who worked at one of my father's bush camps. He'd had his moment in the ring in Cork, but he wasn't preparing me for the ring. *Remember this, Alex. Always box a fighter and fight a boxer. If he's a street scrapper, hang off and pick his face apart for him. But if he fancies himself with the fists, come in close and tear his nuts off.*

Even cage fighters have rules. Combinations they like. Lime's was punch-punch-kick. Punch-punch-kick. I waited until he started again. I launched myself at him in the middle of the second punch, when he was already shifting his weight for the kick. I hit him in the ear twice. He roared with pain. I grabbed his hair and yanked and tried to smash him into the wall. He managed to twist away and cushion with his shoulder when he hit. I was cocked for a throat punch when the goon stepped in and jabbed me with the sword. A searing pan shot up my arm. He had the sword poised for another stab. Lime sprang to his feet and kicked me hard in the ribs, sending me sprawling through the door onto the terrace.

"So, you're a coward too!" he screamed, storming out after me and driving his foot into my ribs again. "Get up," he shouted. "Fight!"

When I staggered to my feet he pointed to an octagon laid down in tape.

"That marks the dimensions of a fighting cage. Stay inside the lines or Vasily will cut you again."

He had his fists up, but this time he didn't start with a punch. His foot shot out and caught me in the stomach. I reeled backward gasping for breath. He leapt on me and drove a series of elbow punches at my head. I managed to turn my face away and rolled out from under him. I scrambled out of the octagon and looked around for something to throw. The sword tip caught me in the calf. A red-hot pain shot along my leg.

"Inside the lines," Lime snarled.

I put my hands up and came in carefully.

He kicked at me again. This time I dodged it. I had longer arms, and landed a punch to the side of his head. I thought I'd rocked him, but when I followed with a roundhouse, he ducked it easily and took advantage of my loss of balance by stepping in close and trying to knee me in the groin. I lurched back, and he drove his fist at my throat. I turned away, but a seam on his glove ripped the side of my neck.

"Go ahead," I panted, backing away, "but you're finished. We know what you and Nash are up to." It was a shot in the dark, but I saw the hit go home. He flicked his eyes away from me, only for a fraction of a second before he recovered, but that's a tell.

He came in fast and jabbed at my face. I protected, and he hit me hard in the stomach. I bent with the pain and he rocked me with an uppercut. I was still protecting with my fists, but his blow smacked them back against my chin and jarred me. He jabbed again with his left and kept his right locked and loaded.

He boxed me steadily back. I saw his eyes flick behind me, followed a second later by a piercing jab from the sword. It caught me behind the hip. I grunted with the pain and reeled out of the octagon. I crashed into the wooden planter where the hedge grew, and would have gone right over if I hadn't clutched a fistful of branches.

"Oops," Lime said.

He growled a command to Vasily, who shoved the Ruger into his waistband so he could grip the saber in both hands. That took his eyes off me for a second. I yanked the bush I was holding from the planter and flung it at Vasily's face. A clod of dirt exploded on his forehead, blinding him for a second. I threw myself at his legs.

He delivered a hammer blow between my shoulders as I collided with his knees. His mistake was trying to hold onto the sword instead of using both hands to break his fall. His head smacked on the bricks. *My* mistake was grabbing the sword instead of the Ruger.

I scrambled to my feet and hacked at Lime. The long blade was hard to control. I gripped the hilt in both hands and held the blade in front of me.

Lime circled slowly, gauging my awkwardness. He made a feint, and I stepped back and raised the blade high above my head. Too high. The momentum of the heavy blade toppled me backward. The planter caught me behind the knees.

Over I went.

11

I heard Tommy's voice booming somewhere in the distance. That answered the question: could things get any worse.

A door opened.

"The bodyguard's got a depressed skull fracture," DeLucca said. "He's in bad shape. Lime's lawyer is screaming attempted murder."

"I'll take care of that shyster," Tommy said. "A Treasury agent in the lawful execution of his duty? By the time I get through with him he'll be begging to plead out."

I was face down on a table. I produced a sound to let them know I was conscious.

"Lawful?" DeLucca said.

"He had a warrant," Tommy grumbled.

"You mean a FISA warrant?"

Tommy ignored him. The Foreign Intelligence Surveillance Court is a secret tribunal, and he wasn't going to tell DeLucca what paperwork we had.

I was in a back room of the Twentieth Precinct on West Eighty-Second Street. A police surgeon had spent an hour on my mouth, repairing the cuts and injecting me with something that had taken down the swelling. The medic finishing the patch-up was the same one who'd treated me after the Brighton Beach operation.

"All the other cuts are superficial," he said. "I've closed them with glue. This one," he prodded my butt with a blue-gloved finger, "I put a stitch in this one. I think the blade just grazed the sciatic nerve. It'll hurt for a while."

"Incontrovertible proof that you are a pain in the ass," Tommy said.

The design of the Santa Clara had saved my life. Lime's apartment was on three floors, but the top two were stepped back, the architectural detail that gave the tower its famous wedding-cake silhouette. When I went over the railing I'd landed on the terrace below. I stumbled inside, found the elevator, and hobbled out into the lobby dragging the six-foot blade just as a swarm of cops were coming in the door.

When I'd left her, Tabitha had worried about what I might do. In the morning she'd tried calling, but couldn't reach me. I'd left my phone in the car. She ordered a GPS location search, and when she saw that it came from just outside Lime's building, and wasn't moving, she called Tommy. He called DeLucca, who scrambled a tac squad.

They arrived just as a bleeding crazy man came rushing through the lobby with a sword. They screamed at me to drop the weapon and get down. It had taken DeLucca an hour to get to the precinct and spring me from the holding cell. Tommy was now here to take care of the paperwork and see if he could make my day a little worse.

"You want to talk to the concierge?" DeLucca said to Tommy. "His cell phone shows he called Lime to warn him about Alex. I got him in the cage. Here's his sheet."

He tossed a thick wad of pages on the table.

"Let me see that for a sec," said Tommy. He scrabbled in the breast pocket of his citron-colored bowling shirt. This one had lime-green piping and the name "Cato" stitched on the pocket. He fished out his reading glasses and glanced quickly through a few pages.

"I'll have a chat with him later," he said, placing the file on the table and giving it a pat. "I need the exercise. In the meantime," he turned to me, "where are we with your sparring partner? It would be nice if you actually learned something. Other than that you're an idiot."

"Nash and Lime are connected," I said, getting slowly off the table.

"What, did he give something up?"

"I pretended I'd discovered their plan. It hit home."

"That's the takeaway? You faked him and he blinked?" Tommy shook his head and looked at the medic. "You didn't tell me about the severe brain injury and delusional complications."

I paced gingerly around the room. It felt as if an electrified wire ran from my hip to my ankle. Every time I moved, the wire delivered a shock. The medic had left me with ten days' worth of fentanyl. I pretended to study a notice on the wall and swallowed one of the pills.

When the medic left, DeLucca closed the door and glanced at Tommy. They both looked glum.

"Want the bad news first?" Tommy said.

Washington was taking us apart. The attorney general had found cracks in the legal structure that kept the operations of our unit confidential, and was busy hammering in wedges.

Nash had been baiting the president, ridiculing his business past. Ridiculing his physical appearance. He played the president's game, but dirtier, until the president was incoherent with rage. The president was going to use whatever weapon against Nash he could, and he had a big one: the government of the United States.

"How can we protect the files?" I said.

"Jesus Christ," Tommy snapped. "Are you not paying attention? There is nothing we can protect. The president runs the administration. There is no such thing as a file he can't see once he knows about it."

I tried to sit, but the pain shot down my leg again and I leaned against a wall.

"If that's the bad news, what's the good?"

"Yeah, well, that's where maybe I misstated," Tommy said. "There's bad news, and then there's worse."

I had a hard time concentrating. The sword cuts still burned beneath the fentanyl, just enough to let me know they would be waiting when the drug wore off.

I bit the inside of my cheek to help focus. Tommy had something important to add, and it would be best to actually hear it.

"I'm listening."

"There's an order for you to report to DC to be debriefed at the Treasury."

"Debriefed? There's a statutory restriction on who can question me."

"I think you'll find they've got that sorted out."

What it came down to was this: Chuck was only nominally in charge. The treasurer had started running things. He would send marshals for me if I didn't come.

Unless I ran.

And that's what we agreed on. I had a legitimate reason to leave the country: to pursue an existing investigation. Anyway, that was going to be the story.

When Tommy left, DeLucca and I worked out the details. He would be my contact. The NYPD was the largest police force in the country, and the city of New York, the fortress that protected it. Any communications with DeLucca would be safe.

For the next two hours we talked about what I would have to do. He made some calls and so did I. The pain was giving me trouble. It roamed around inside my body. It chewed at the places where the sword had cut. Fentanyl is a short-acting drug, but the medic had given me some patches too.

By the time we left the precinct, it was night. We drove downtown and stopped outside a condo tower on Chambers Street. A block away, where the Twin Towers had stood, the spire of the World Financial Center soared above ground zero. An NYPD squad car idled at the curb nearby.

"Your car's in the garage," DeLucca said. "Parking level two. My guys packed the bag exactly as you asked. It's in the trunk. I'll give your apartment keys to Tommy."

A thin stream of exhaust dribbled out of the tailpipe of the squad car parked ahead of us.

A stab of pain shot down my leg. I was feeling nauseated.

"One more thing," I said. "I know you've laid on a lot of protection, and I'm grateful. But I'd like somebody I personally trust at Tuxedo Park. Augie Treacher. You probably know who he is."

He shrugged. "Sure I know. He's a killer."

I took the Holland Tunnel. No tail that I could see. I picked my way carefully through Jersey City, Paramus, and Ridgewood, doubling back on myself, exiting suddenly, parking. Nothing.

I got on the I-87 and six hours later crossed into Quebec with a Canadian passport in the name of Alan Ryder. I reached Montreal airport in time for Air Canada's morning flight to Brussels.

12

The plane landed in heavy rain. It was still coming down in sheets when I cleared immigration and emerged from the terminal. She was waiting in a lemon-colored Porsche. It was all I could do to toss my bag in the back seat and climb in.

"You look terrible," Lily said as the rain drummed on the roof. She put her hand against my forehead. "You have a fever."

"It's only some cuts."

As she drove out of the airport and took the fast route into Brussels, I told her about Lime. She shook her head.

"He's very expert. He could have killed you."

I swallowed some antibiotics. The medic included those too. He'd said there was a chance of infection. Maybe that's what was making me feel nauseated.

Lily got off the expressway and took a winding route, checking for a tail. The rain had strengthened into a monsoon by the time we circled the park in front of the royal palace for the sixth time and Lily decided there was no one following us. Even so, she didn't head for either of the two main highways that go north from Brussels. She picked her way through the

99

scrapheap of suburbs that ring the administrative capital of the European Union. Finally, we cleared the city and drove out onto the central plain of Flanders.

My body felt as if it were running some special software to destroy itself. My vision blurred and cleared and blurred again. A tiny arsonist patrolled my arms and legs, setting fires.

Out among the farms, Lily visibly relaxed. She no longer drove with one eye on the rearview. In her cream-colored sweater and black jeans she could have been any stylish young woman who liked to accessorize with bandages. One covered the back of her right hand. She must have injured it when the motorcycle slid out from under her at Sheepshead Bay. Another dressing bulged beneath the tight denim of her jeans, and I remembered the limp as she hurried onto the footbridge. But the bruise on her face?

I hadn't seen Lily since she'd blown a load of splinters into my face three days before. We'd kept our communications to the bare minimum. There had always been the likelihood she'd be suspected of betrayal after Brighton Beach.

"Lime?" I said, eyeing the bruise.

"Not the worst thing he ever did to me."

I let that go. There was a blade buried deep in Lily, and Lime had put it there.

Lily started stealing diamonds in her teens. She was working as a sorter at the huge facility in Mirny run by Russgem, Russia's state diamond company. Russian oligarchs with friends in the Kremlin were stealing about 15 million carats a year from Russgem's 40-million-carat production. Lily's scheme was modest by comparison, but it managed to extract 150,000 carats a year.

The goods she stole were at the lower end, but even at $125 a carat, she was grossing almost $20 million. She had to pay some people off. She could afford to.

Here's how it worked.

Russgem's diamond scales expressed weights to five decimal places. Because rough diamonds poured through Mirny in such high volumes, recording every parcel to such a fine degree wasn't practical, and they set the machines to report to only two decimal places. The scales still weighed to five, but only reported to two. Lily took a cut from the unreported weight.

Say a parcel weighed 100.22314 carats. The system reported a weight of 100.22. The .00314 unreported carats still existed. The weight had disappeared only from the books. Lily inserted a program that kept track of the actual weight as opposed to the reported weight and helped herself accordingly. Because the volumes were so high, even such a tiny cut quickly ballooned.

Russgem understood that rounding off the decimal places left unreported diamonds in the production stream. They ran a quarterly check designed to pick up the unreported rough. Lily's genius lay in designing her theft so that it left behind enough loose weight to satisfy her bosses.

There was something elegant to this colossal theft and, as Lily saw it, fair. She made regular cash gifts to the Orthodox cathedral in Mirny. That covered God. Unfortunately, the local Orthodox patriarch was in the pocket of one of the oligarchs already robbing Russgem. When the patriarch realized that Lily's generosity had reached a level beyond her apparent means, he informed his patron.

Mirny was a brutal place. Lily had no protectors. She was nineteen and beautiful. Lime had just arrived in the city, humiliated, bruised, seething with hate. The oligarch who owned the priest was one of the investors who'd ripped off most of Lime's shares in First Partners. To recoup that loss, Lime had been offered a chance to help the oligarch find a new way to launder the rough diamonds he was stealing.

Lime sent for Lily. He demanded to know how she stole the rough and, as importantly, how she sold it. Lily wouldn't tell him. She still had a few million dollars in rough in the pipeline. She knew she might not get out of Mirny alive, but if she did, it was going to be with her money.

What Lime performed on Lily was a kind of surgery. He raped her, and with care and deliberation, he damaged her. At the end of three days there was little left of her but a core of hatred. By then Lime understood that he would have to either kill her and learn nothing, or compromise.

In the split they worked out, Lily got the diamonds still in the pipeline and the job she specified at Russgem's St. Petersburg office. Lime got the information he needed to move rough through Lily's contacts, plus a few tips on how to cheat the oligarchs.

The rain intensified. The road turned into a frothing stream of brown water. The Porsche's windshield wipers flailed back and forth. We could barely see. Lily pulled to the side of the road.

"I take it Lime doesn't know you have the pink," I said.

"I told him you must have it," she said, unsnapping her seatbelt and digging her hand into a pocket of her jeans. She handed me the neatly folded rectangle of paper.

I flicked it open with my thumbs. The pink dagger-shaped stone flared against the crisp white paper. In the aqueous interior of the car, the diamond flowed with crimson light. The rain thrashed against the window and a heavy gust buffeted the car. The stone shone with unearthly power. The only other pink I'd seen with that knockout punch was Nash's.

"Where do you think the Brazilian got this, Lily?"

"He was one of the Sousa brothers from Minas Gerais. Some very good fancy colors come out of the rivers there, and the Sousa brothers get them all."

"If it's a river stone, why no frosting?"

Lily had dealt in river stones. The trade calls them alluvials. They have a frosted appearance. Rolled along in the gravel for millions of years, the surfaces get scratched and pitted until the skin of the diamond is opaque.

"Alex, let's speak plainly. You're not up to playing games. Neither of us thinks the stone is Brazilian. It's a fragment of the Russian Pink. Lime wanted to conceal that from me. Using the Brazilian was the way he tried to do it. So I would tell our buyers the source was Brazilian. He wants to see what the market is without saying where it really came from."

I folded the diamond back into the paper. The torrent thundered on the roof. It had been raining the night I'd turned Slav Lily at Brussels airport. Later, when I came out of the airport, she was waiting in the Porsche. You bet I got in. It rained all the way to Paris. We holed up in a crooked little house in Montmartre that Lily owned.

The rain let up and we drove on. Soon we were entering the Antwerp suburbs. An idea was struggling to form in my head but I couldn't hold onto it. Why would Lime want to smuggle a piece of the pink into the United States? There was an answer to that question. I could almost see it.

The pain from my cuts returned in a sudden rush. I fumbled in my pocket for the plastic bottle, but I couldn't get the top off. I wrenched at it until Lily took it from me and tapped a pill into my open palm. I made an impatient gesture and she tipped out another. I swallowed them and put my head back and waited for the drug to unhook the talons from my brain.

The diamond city of Antwerp lies on the river Scheldt. In the old quarters of the town ancient mansions glower at the present. In the sixteenth century Antwerp was the richest city on the continent. Its main cathedral has four works by Rubens, the Flemish master whose commissions from the kings and queens of Europe paid for his own palace in the city. The swaggering civic buildings that line Antwerp's main square show how highly the Flemish burghers thought of themselves.

The rain had swept the tourists away. We turned onto the quay beside the river and drove to a shabby hotel. It faced the water with a look of hopelessness. Faded green paint peeled from the stuccoed walls.

We left the car in a shed at the back and pushed through a door into a dim interior that smelled of damp carpet and sausages. The front desk was abandoned. Rain drove against the dirty windows. Through the glass, the blurry shapes of dockside cranes loomed across the river. A threadbare gray cardigan hung on a nail beside the row of empty mailboxes. I dinged the bell. The slap of footsteps approached and a fat young woman in a dirty tank top appeared, stared at us, snatched the cardigan from the nail, and dragged it on over her bulging breasts.

"Full," she said, wiping something from her mustached lip.

The hotel had not been full in fifty years, so I guess that was the recognition word.

"Room five," Lily told her, stepping up to the counter. She slid a brown envelope across the scarred surface.

The woman sniffed and wiped her moustache again. The smell of cooking was stronger now. She dropped the keys on the counter, wiped her fingers on the sweater, plucked up the envelope, and disappeared in the direction of the sausages.

We climbed the narrow stairs. The top step had a strange, high-pitched double squeak, like a bow drawn back and forth on the string of a violin. The room was painted a color that had long ago given up the fight against the damp and joined the general spirit of despair. The worn, candlewick bedspread had once been white. On the desk stood a yellowing card with the name *Hoge Raad voor Diamant*—Diamond High

Council—emblazoned at the top. Below was a list of telephone numbers dealers could call to get the latest details of the London diamond sales.

It had been a long time since any diamond dealer had stayed in this hotel, and the London sales had dried up like the company that ran them, slowly gnawed to bits by the increasing cut taken by the countries where the diamonds came from. While London withered as a diamond center, Antwerp boomed. The horde of Gujaratis, Israelis, Russians, and European Ashkenazim who made Antwerp the world capital of diamonds were still here, haggling their way through $16 billion worth of rough every year. But not at this hotel.

The back room overlooked a cluttered courtyard. Directly below the window, the rusty tin roof of the parking shed shuddered in the gusts. A storm of paper and loose dirt eddied in the narrow space.

"You told Davy I wanted to see him?" I said.

"He refused."

I looked out the front window. The line of cranes stretched down the river. The wind moaned and shrieked in the steel lattices. The water thrashed in a tormented chop. A stubby, orange pilot boat with a rounded bow pitched and rolled as it made for the harbormaster's pier.

"Does Davy still get to the restaurant at the same time?"

"Seven."

I put my forehead against the cold windowpane. The rain struck the glass in a steady hail. I hadn't slept since leaving New York.

The gale clattered against the front of the hotel. Everything shook and shuddered in the wind. I heard the squeal of ships yanking at their moorings and the tormented cries of seabirds flung downwind.

I sat down on the hard bed. The sound of the storm receded. The dirty gray light at the windows formed into a serpent and crawled down the wall and across the floor toward me. My head felt huge. My right leg stuck out straight in front of me. It wouldn't bend.

"Alex," said a distant voice, "I think you need a doctor."

She knelt in front of me and took my hand.

"Just tired," someone mumbled.

She pushed me gently back onto the bed and took off my shirt. She unbuckled my belt and tugged off my pants and sucked in her breath in dismay.

"Where did this happen?"

"Lime."

I managed to raise my head. The leg was swollen and had a grayish tinge.

I let my head drop back onto the cheap foam pillow. The room rolled and lifted as it met the tossing sea. I heard Lily unzip her jeans and the bed sagged as she slid beneath the covers. Her body was cold. I breathed the scent of her soap. She pushed one leg between my knees and the bandage on her leg rubbed against the inside of my thigh. It reminded me the leg was sore, but I didn't care. I searched my mind for something I needed to ask her. My head was whirling with fragments of images.

"I need to see Piet Louw, Lily."

"Yes, darling," she murmured in my ear. "You've been raving about it."

"The stone, Lily," I mumbled.

She poured her gray gaze over me.

"Go to sleep," she said.

"Davy," I protested.

"I set your alarm."

She was gone when the alarm went off. I felt as if someone was scrubbing the inside of my skin with sandpaper. I needed to be alert, so the fentanyl would have to wait. I found a drugstore and got some Tylenol and swallowed four.

I stood in the shadows in an arcade on the east side of the Grote Markt and watched the corner of Blauwmoezelstraat. The leg that I'd managed to calm for a while started to claw its way through the Tylenol. If I kept it straight it wasn't so bad.

Davy appeared just before seven, walking with that slouching gait I knew so well. With his cowboy boots and long white hair he looked like a Jewish Wild Bill Hickok. The toes of his boots curled up like skis. He wore a cashmere coat that fell to his ankles like a cowboy's duster. The storm had moved on northward into the Netherlands. All that remained was a fitful, soggy wind.

Davy sloshed across the square. The statues of Justice, Prudence, and the Virgin Mary followed his progress from their places high on the ornate facade of the Stadhuis, the old town hall. After he disappeared around the corner of the building, I waited five minutes. No shadows on his tail, so I followed his path across the square.

The last of the clouds blew away and the moon flashed silver light onto the mullioned windows. I made my way around the building to an alley at the back. Davy was already sitting at his favorite table in the window when I came in the front door of the restaurant. The waiter, a sour, doddering Belgian who'd been there for decades, was banging a glass of clear liquid onto the table hard enough to make sure some of it spilled. Davy wrapped his massive workman's paw around the tiny glass and tossed it back. He caught sight of me as I stepped in.

He shook his massive head slowly and raised one of his calloused hands in a gesture of refusal. I put a hand on his shoulder. He had hoisted me onto that broad shoulder many times when I was a boy.

"Hello, Davy."

"I told the Russian girl I could not see you," he said wearily.

I signaled the waiter to bring another glass of Holland gin. I hated the stuff. It tasted like gasoline. But it was Davy's fuel.

"Can't a kid come and see his *feter*?" I said, using the Yiddish word for uncle that I'd used as a child. He waved his hand dismissively.

"That boy has not been around for a long time. That boy used to visit with his lovely papa. Now there is this different boy, the hunter, always hunting, always looking. You want to talk about the big stone." He shook his head. "I have nothing to say about it. I am bound by confidentiality. I cannot even say whether I have seen this stone."

"Nonsense," I said. "Who else would they take it to?"

Davy made a gesture of dismissal, but the compliment struck home. The diamond cutter has not been born who doesn't think he's God.

The waiter tottered over with the bottle and another glass, muttering to himself. He slopped some into Davy's glass. I took the bottle from his hand and gave myself a quarter inch.

"And bring us some hennepot and black bread," I said as the waiter turned to go.

Davy lifted his glass and drained it. When he thumped the glass back down, I saw that his hand was trembling. Davy had been swimming lengths in Holland gin for a long time. It's the diamond that decides how it will be cut, Davy liked to say, not the cutter. I don't know. Ask a dealer how he feels if his stone craps out on the wheel. It's not the diamond he gets mad at. I'd heard they were getting mad at Davy more often, and maybe the gin had something to do with it.

"This is all under the radar," I said. "Nothing you say goes anywhere."

"Bah," he said. "Nothing is under their radar. You can hide nothing from these people."

Even with my leg straight out it was sending electric stabs of pain along the nerves.

The waiter arrived with the hennepot and a plate of thickly sliced black bread. He moved the bottle of Holland gin to one side, arranged the food, and left.

I spooned some of the hennepot onto a slice of bread and shoved the plate to Davy. They've been making this terrine of chicken, veal, and rabbit in Flanders for six hundred years. It was the specialty that had been bringing Davy to the smoky little restaurant behind the Stadhuis ever since he could pay for his own meals. But he ignored it now.

He finished his glass and filled it again and took a long swallow.

"A stone must have a story," he said. "Like a person. To understand a person, you must know his story. Where does he come from, who are his parents? But the pink, it had no story."

"I heard it came from the Chicapa."

Davy spread his hands. "Where is the frosting? Where in the river did it come from? Who found it, and when, and who else was there?" He leaned forward. "Who attended the *birth*?"

He studied my face for a moment, as if he had recognized something in it he was trying to identify. The boy I'd been.

"Remember that big white your papa found in Botswana?"

"At Letlhakane." How could I forget? We had lived there for a year.

"Everyone told your papa that little diamond pipe was barren, but he did not think so. He drilled it and found the little mineral grains that only your papa knew about. They were his secret science."

"Indicator minerals," I said.

"And from these tiny minerals," Davy said, his eyes shining, "your papa knew the pipe was rich with diamonds."

A pipe is a type of extinct volcano. Diamonds come up from the deep earth in such volcanoes. Most are destroyed by the violent forces of eruption. The trick is to find a pipe where the diamonds survived the journey.

"He invented a technique for analyzing the chemistry of the minerals," I said. "He knew certain minerals were formed in the same part of the earth where diamonds are formed. He could tell from these minerals what the odds were of recovering large diamonds."

I was feeling sicker, but the story was helping me keep control. The familiar facts, arranged in the right order.

"And he was right," said Davy. "He found that 602-carat white. And do you remember how he announced it? The release gave everything: what time of day they found the stone. Who found it. Where it came from in the pipe. The age of the diamond. He called it the Star of Letlhakane. By the time the stone arrived in Antwerp, it was already famous!"

Davy was a great diamond raconteur. He loved the lore of diamonds and his place in it. Davy's stories often featured the queen of England wowing over some great stone he'd cut. Or maybe it was the former empress of Iran telling Davy how fantastic he was. For a moment I caught sight of the old Davy, the swashbuckling diamond cutter. Buoyed up by the gin, but still Davy.

"The big pink arrived like it had a private shame," he said. "In Antwerp, we had heard about it. Who had not? We heard the rumors of this fantastic pink, more than a thousand carats. Who can believe such a thing? Surely it is false." He leaned forward and his eyes glittered through his shaggy eyebrows. "But no! Not false. True!" He slammed his board-like hand on the table. The glasses jumped and I reached out to steady the bottle.

Davy came from an illustrious diamond family. His grandfather, the mathematician André Deich, invented the brilliant cut in 1914 when he published a treatise describing the exact proportions and angles of a fifty-seven-facet, polished diamond that would produce the maximum possible light return, or fire.

"My first sight of the diamond was in Russgem's building," Davy said.

They brought him to an empty room on the sorting floor. On a table lay a plain gray metal sorting box. He opened it, and there was the stone.

"I have never seen a stone like this," he said. "Fragments from the deep earth are still clinging to the diamond."

"You mean it wasn't cleaned?"

"It has been cleaned," he said, "but the earth where it has been born, the mother earth, she does not wish to release her child."

That's just how Davy talked.

"It was like a deep lake with a fire burning inside the waters. And the whole appearance—I didn't dare touch it. It was observing me! When I took it in my hand, I was scared to crush it."

"Who owned it, Davy, Russgem or Lime or who? Had Nash bought it by then?"

But he was back with the diamond.

"Inside this turbulent stone lies a calm center: the truth of the diamond. An equation lies inside the diamond waiting to be solved. An equation written by God."

"I'm not writing a newspaper feature, Davy," I said impatiently. I wasn't sure how long I could stand the pain. "How many polished stones did you get from it?"

"How many?" He stared at me in amazement. "One!"

"One? But I heard the rough weighed something like fifteen hundred carats."

"It was a monster! I started to put a window in to examine the interior. It shattered! Into pieces! There was the single large stone at the heart of the diamond. An amazing stone! The rest was thin slivers like daggers."

When a stone is deeply flawed, the heat from the friction of polishing can cause the diamond to blow up on the wheel. Shatter into tiny pieces. Its value destroyed in a second. If the stone Davy had cut from the surviving rough was the 464-carat Russian Pink, a thousand carats had blown into chips.

I got up and waved the waiter over and threw some money on the table. With the rain gone and the skies clearing, more people had wandered down to the old part of the city and the restaurant was filling up.

"Let's finish this outside, Davy."

The night air had softened. Davy stamped across the square and we came out at the cathedral. Couples with selfie sticks posed in front of the Gothic stonework, crowding their heads together in the frame to make sure that whoever was checking out their Instagram would not have to waste time looking at the most beautiful mediaeval tracery in Flanders.

"I miss your beautiful papa," Davy said with a sigh. "He was a great diamond person. I loved him. He was very badly treated in America. He should never have gone back."

That's what he thought too. They'd had to extradite him.

A string of white trolleys came rumbling along the brightly lit ring road. We crossed the tracks and strolled up past the smart shopfronts toward the glass dome of the central railway station. Waves of dizziness washed over me. My legs were so swollen they hit each other as I walked.

"It was not your papa's fault. That other pipe he found—investors always take a risk. Nothing is guaranteed."

"He cheated them."

We loitered at a dealer's window near the diamond quarter. Davy examined the jewels on display.

I could hardly stand. I put my hand on the plate glass window and waited for the nausea to pass.

"The pink blew up on the wheel, Davy. What happened to all the pieces?"

"She took all the pieces."

"Who?"

"The Chinese one with the blue eyes."

"Honey Li? She was here?"

He kept staring into the window, his face bathed in light from the display.

"That woman will be more famous than Cleopatra."

Somehow I made it back to the river. My head was screaming. Near the hotel I stepped into a shabby bar and drank two double gins.

The front door was locked at the hotel and no one came when I rang the bell. I pounded on the door with my fist. I stood back and would have kicked it off its hinges if the fat woman hadn't finally come.

When I got to the room I shut the door behind me, found the fentanyl, and swallowed two. I got under the covers and lay there shivering. Slowly the fentanyl pried the fingers from my nerves. I lay there in a state of exhaustion, wanting sleep but unable to escape the hyper-alertness of my mind. I heard every sound on the river, the squeal of a hull against a dock, the long, drawn-out sound of a mooring cable stretching taut as a ship strained against it. I heard the other sound too. The high-pitched double squeak, like a bow drawn back and forth on the string of a violin. Someone had put a foot on the top step—someone who had otherwise climbed silently.

I struggled out of bed. What felt like a load of mud shifted in my brain. I almost passed out. As I made it to my feet, pain flooded up my leg. The right leg of my pants looked ready to burst at the seams. I lost my balance, stumbled hard against the wall and somehow got myself behind the door. A key went in. The door eased open. I summoned the last of my strength, stepped around, and threw the hardest punch I could. An enormous Hassid with red earlocks caught my punch in his hairy paw. Then I passed out.

13

I swam up to the surface of a tepid sea to find myself lying flat on my back on a bed. A room came into focus. Through a window in the opposite wall I could see the branches of a tree, fringed with tiny leaves that shivered in the breeze. Then a thick mist floated in and concealed the tree. When the mist blew past, as if a magician had snapped his cape to complete a magic trick, a lilac-breasted bird with an iridescent turquoise belly sat on the highest branch. It tilted back its head and opened a jet-black beak and delivered a harsh noise—*raak raak raak*—into the wooly air. Then the magician passed his cape across the window again, and when it snapped away the bird had gone.

Now I heard the distant boom of surf. Then, much closer, the sound of a machine that made a steady *whir-thunk, whir-thunk*. I turned my head to see an IV bag on a shiny metal stand release a drop of red liquid into a tube that led somewhere out of sight behind my head. I tried to reach for the tube but my hands wouldn't move. Something was holding my wrists against the bed. By curling my fingers, I could feel the leather manacles. They were lined with a soft material. Identical restraints held my ankles in place.

I struggled. My limbs felt leaden. Sounds drifted into the room—the cries of seabirds and, somewhere closer, a closing door. Human voices exchanged muffled sentences. When I tried to shout, an animal whimpered in my ear, as if it were being tortured by the same fingers that were rummaging inside my head. They could not find what they wanted and began to scratch more fitfully, in bursts of panic. The animal whimpered on my pillow.

A door opened and I heard the sound of rubber flip-flops slapping on the floor. Lily came into the room with a young black man who bent over me. He took out a pencil light and shone it in my eyes, then checked my pulse.

"I'm a doctor," he said. "Can you hear me?" He had a strong accent that was familiar but which I couldn't place.

"Head," I said.

"You have pain in your head?" He touched my forehead with his fingers. They were long and delicate and cool.

"Scratching," I said.

He nodded.

"You went through a week's fentanyl supply in two days, so you're having withdrawal symptoms. I'll give you something. It won't be an opioid but it will help you sleep."

He sat on the edge of the bed.

"We had to restrain you because you were violent and we needed to get started right away on filtering your blood. You had thallium poisoning. Those cuts you received, the blade that made them must have been dipped in the poison. Are you following me?"

I opened my mouth and made a croaking sound.

"I'm cleaning your blood by means of a process called hemoperfusion. There's a pump behind you. It contains a filter made of artificial cells that are filled with activated carbon. Thallium is a metal, and the thallium molecules get trapped in the carbon."

Suddenly he gave me a radiant smile, and I could see how young he was. He patted my hand.

"Got all that?"

I recognized the accent. South African.

He gave me the shot. Before I drifted off, Lily took his place on the bed. She studied me with her grave eyes. An errant breeze came in the window and stirred the black coils around the tips of her ears.

She twitched a corner of the blanket into place and left.

I woke to sunlight beating on my face and the lilac-breasted bird with the turquoise belly practicing his lyrics in the tree. A thorn tree. I recognized it now—acacia. I moved a hand to shield my eyes and the bird flew off with a harsh cry—*raak raak raak*.

They had taken off the restraints while I slept. The pump was gone. My body felt as if everything in it had been taken out and scrubbed with a brush, put back roughly, and stapled into place. Pain nibbled here and there like tiny mice. I felt drenched in chemicals.

Clothes hung neatly over a chair. I crawled out of bed, pulled on a pair of jeans and a T-shirt. At a sink in the corner I splashed water on my face. It failed to improve the puffy, patched-up mug that stared back from the mirror—dark bags under my eyes and a three-day beard.

A pot of cold coffee sat on the stove in the kitchen down the hall. I poured a cup and walked outside, sat on the sagging porch, and watched the Atlantic Ocean roll onto the beach. Judging by the sun it was mid-morning. I thought I knew where Lily might be. We both knew this place well.

Port Nolloth is a biscuit-colored town in Namaqualand, the slab of desert that forms the northwestern corner of South Africa. The frigid Benguela Current scrapes along the coast. Every morning the cold sea rolls a dense band of fog onto the land. It had burned off by the time I set out along the seafront.

The diamond fleet tugged and jingled at its moorings in the anchorage. Fierce riptides battled at the harbor entrance. The ocean boiled in a fury around the offshore reefs. Every now and then a towering sheet of spray exploded from the breakwater as a huge Atlantic comber smashed itself to bits.

The sea was too rough for the tubby little diamond boats that locals call tupperwares. Usually they put to sea at dawn, trailing their suction hoses behind them. When they reached the inshore diamond ground the divers would go over the side. They vacuumed the diamond gravels for hours at a time in the freezing water. Today the wind was up. The surge would turn the shallow seabed where the divers worked into a storm of rocks and sand. The fleet stayed bottled up in port while the crews languished in the bars or headed north for a few days to steal diamonds in Namibia.

I found Lily in the front pew of the Church of the Immaculate Heart of Mary. Morning Mass had just finished. Other than Lily only a few elderly parishioners remained behind, gossiping in whispers in the pews. An old woman with a bright length of calico wrapped around her head and her nylons rolled around her ankles padded up to the altar and began to rearrange a vase of gladioli. I slipped in behind Lily. She knelt with her hands joined in front of her and her eyes closed, her head bent forward so it rested on her hands. I breathed in the faint scent of incense. Under the pale blue vault of the ceiling, a deep silence reigned. The boom of surf crashing on the beach only made the church more peaceful.

We knew each other the way lovers do. Through our skin. That searing, electric surge of information, that animal exchange of scent and sweat. And later, the murmured confidences in the soft parts of the night. When the urge to be known wrings out the past in fragments.

She was the only child of an elderly musician and a teacher. Her father played first violin in Mirny's tiny orchestra, padding his meagre salary giving lessons at home. Her mother taught English at the Polytechnic and ran the gun club.

Every year in July the family packed supplies, loaded their old, tarred boat, and went putting up a muddy river into the endless forest Russians call the taiga. They would spend a month at their cabin. Lily's mother showed her how to make ammunition—carefully measuring out gunpowder at the kitchen table and reloading cartridges.

"Economy," her mother would enunciate, making Lily repeat the English word. "Thrift."

Mother and daughter would smear their faces joyfully with mud and stalk off into the forest after deer. Her father stayed behind to play Tchaikovsky to the weasels.

She loved the winter too. On Christmas Eve they would leave the apartment before midnight and walk through the snowy streets to the Cathedral of the Holy Trinity, ablaze with candles and shimmering with the golden images of saints. The massed choir, the vaulted ceiling spattered with stars, and the priests in gorgeous robes. And just inside the church, a nativity scene with the infant Jesus lying in the manger, warmed by the breath of animals and adored, as Lily herself was adored, by rapt adults.

That world came to a cruel end when the plane carrying her parents on a visit to the regional capital crashed in the taiga. Lily was sixteen. The criminals who ran the town took one look at her and ate her up.

Her parents' savings evaporated in a sudden tax claim. Men from the local government came one day to the apartment and shouted at her to get out. They waved a paper in her face. Lily discovered she had no legal right to the only home she'd known.

A friend of her mother's at the Polytechnic got her a job at the Mir diamond mine. A menial position. In the sorting room. Lily brought to the task a shattered heart and ice-cold hatred. The heart healed. The hatred remained. Only the diamonds soothed it.

In church, I think she brushed all that away. In church it was always Christmas Eve, and she was the girl she'd been. In church she reached back into that lost world where devoted parents cradled and protected her. As I watched her pray, her head bowed and her hands joined, I felt a powerful urge to reach forward and touch her. But I didn't.

Before we left, Lily folded five hundred-dollar bills into a neat wad and shoved it through the slot beneath the votive candles. She lit a large candle near the top. It flamed into life behind the ruby-colored glass. She made the sign of the cross and genuflected to the Virgin. We walked down the side aisle and out the door.

The sea had started to settle. Crews were moving around on some of the diamond boats. I doubted they'd put to sea. The swell would last for another day. Not far from the harbor entrance, the ocean ground its teeth on the reefs. We sat on a bench above the harbor while Lily brought me up to date.

While I was meeting Davy, Lily had sold the pink to Dilip Gupta, whose Bombay family ran the biggest diamond polishing company in the world. Dilip paid her $1.5 million on the spot—a steal for the Guptas, but they knew she was in a hurry. While they were in his office waiting for the wire to clear into Lily's Zurich bank account, Dilip's nephew, who handled security, came in to report that hard men were in Antwerp looking for us. Lily got hold of Meier Lapa. It was Meier who'd come to collect me from the hotel.

Meier's crew got me to the airport, where Lily had a Gulfstream ready to go. Sofia, Cape Verde, Port Nolloth—that was the route, never mind what the flight plan said.

While I was lying lashed to the bed, Lily had tracked down Piet Louw, the South African who'd found the big pink and brought it to

Barry Stern. Not surprisingly, Piet was no longer working in Angola, having neglected to share the news of his discovery with the government.

"When will he get in?" I said.

"Tonight."

"He may not come in this rough sea."

"It's calmer at night."

"And he's coming from the offshore fleet?"

"He bought a small ship with the proceeds of the pink," Lily said. "Now he buys from the crews of the Namibian diamond fleet. He brings in his rough tonight."

"What time?"

"Any time. We should be ready from sunset."

She sounded low. The onshore breeze ruffled her hair. The tips of her ears peeped through the curls. The bruise was a livid yellow shading into purple.

"I'm sorry, Lily."

She took a deep breath. The smell of seaweed saturated the air. An old man with a stick and a mangy dog made his way along the beach. A cloth bag hung from his shoulder. His sparse white hair blew around his head. When an object caught his eye he stopped to poke it with the stick, prying it out of the sand for a better look, then walking on. Lily leaned forward with her elbows on her knees and watched him scan the beach.

"Really, Alex, sorry for what? That I'm caught up with you again? That your hold over me is so profound that I charter a jet to fly you to the diamond coast? Poor Lily, forced into a helpless life."

The beachcomber stopped and dug his stick into the sand. Then he crouched and wrestled with something until he freed it from the sand. He held the object up to his eye and examined it. He waded into the shallows and swished it back and forth to remove the sand. When he held it up again it glowed dully in the sun. He tossed it back in the water, returned to the beach and plodded off along the shore.

"You're not responsible for me. I chose my life. I waited for you that night at the airport. I knew what you were."

My body felt empty. Hollow. The sun beat down and the breeze came off the ocean and I tried to take in both the warmth and the freshness of the air. A pair of kelp gulls flashed their black backs in the sun as they hung on the wind, calling back and forth.

Suddenly she sat up and locked her arm around my neck and pulled my face in close and kissed me. Her lips tasted of salt. "You're a mess, aren't you, darling." She put her hand against my cheek. She smiled tenderly and got up. There were tears in her eyes.

We walked past the boatyards and along a crooked street to a garage I knew, where we rented a pickup with four-wheel drive. It had seen better days. So had the guy who ran the garage, but he took cash and didn't ask for paperwork.

Half a mile out of town we turned off into a small, dusty subdivision carved out of the desert. I followed a rutted lane that skirted the houses. It ended at a compound surrounded by a wall of concrete blocks topped with a coil of razor wire. A peeling sign identified the premises as XHALI SECURITY SYSTEMS. A slot in the steel gate slid open and a pair of dark brown eyes examined us. The slot slammed shut and a moment later came the screech of a metal bar as two young black men pushed open the heavy gates. Each had a Chinese AK slung from his shoulder.

We parked beside a black Range Rover and entered the dim interior. A thin, elderly man with a scarred face and aviator glasses stood behind the counter watching us come in. He had a clipped gray moustache and neatly combed gray hair and wore a spotless white shirt buttoned at the cuffs. The wall behind him was covered with a display of electronic sensors, surveillance cameras, and examples of the kind of steel-mesh fencing that snips your fingers off if you try to climb it. He also had a rack with throwing knives and the short stabbing spears that Zulu warriors taught their enemies to fear. The main stock in trade was out of sight.

The powerful smell of steel and gun oil filled the room. The aviator glasses panned back and forth between us.

"I'm looking for one of your security systems," I said. "One that can provide maximum coverage."

"A portable system?" he said.

"That's right."

He pursed his lips. "For a situation where a dispute might arise?"

"Well, that can happen in any interaction, can't it."

"Yes, it can," he said sadly, shaking his head, as if the contemplation of the human condition had caused him many disappointments in his life, and he didn't think it was a situation likely to change. "Would the dispute be with one person, or more than one?"

"Impossible to say."

He spread his wrinkled hands on the table and examined them. The tip of a tattoo poked out from a snowy cuff. It looked like the point of a dagger. He drummed his fingers on the counter, shot me a quick glance from behind the dark lenses, then reached down and brought out a narrow wooden crate. He removed the top and placed it carefully to one side. He took out a brand new Chinese Type 56 assault rifle, removed the plastic sleeve, and placed it before us. Same model as the guards on the gate were carrying, so I guess he'd bought a large shipment.

"Special this week," he said.

You can tell the Chinese version of the classic Russian machine gun at a glance. It comes with a short bayonet folded back against the barrel, which the Russian guns don't have. Anyway, I didn't want a gun that was a yard long and weighed ten pounds fully loaded.

"Something smaller," I told him.

The aviator glasses stayed aimed at me until he said, "I think we've met before."

"It's possible."

He nodded and fished out a ring of keys and unlocked a cabinet behind him. The gun he put on the counter was just what I was looking for. Czech, four-point-five-inch barrel. A sweet little gun with a beautiful, light-wood pistol grip.

"I'll take it."

"Ten-round or twenty-round magazine?"

"Two mags of the twenty."

Lily needed ammunition for her Glock. He shook his head when she asked for Fiocchi Extrema, her favorite bullets, and slid a box of a cheaper make across the counter. Lily glared at him. She snorted in disgust, snatched the box from the counter and stuffed it savagely in her purse. When we were through she paid in cash.

"Christ, Alex," she said as we drove out through the gates. "How many people are we going to have to deal with?"

"I don't know. Piet will have some kind of back-up. He won't hesitate to kill us. He's tough. He fought in Angola when the South African army was trying to push the Cubans out. He was in the 32nd Battalion."

"The Buffalo Battalion." Like all diamond traders, Lily knew the stories of Angola's diamond wars, and those who'd fought them.

"The Angolans called them *Os Terríveis*," I said. "The Terrible Ones."

"I get it," she snapped. "What other kind of person could run a diamond barge on the Chicapa? I know he's a savage bastard." Her eyes blazed at me. "After all, I know the type."

Lily was a whirlpool I had fallen into long ago. After I'd turned her, we had torn a year to shreds, flying off to places like the north coast of Iceland. Think about it: private geothermal pool plus frenzied Russian girl plus zero chance of surveillance. But she could flash from affection into anger in a blink. You bought the whole package with Lily, and there was often a surprise inside.

We stopped at a grocery on the highway. It was after noon by the time we got back to the house.

A wooden picnic table stood on the brick patio out back. A tall fig tree with smooth, pale bark and tortured limbs shaded the table. Lily found plates in the kitchen and a faded tablecloth and we unpacked the lunch—packaged ham, pickles, and a hunk of something identified as cheddar. I unwrapped the stale baguette, cut it in half and sliced it open lengthwise. Lily found a jar of mustard in the fridge, and two ice-cold bottles of Castle beer.

"This is the kind of food I detest, Alex," she said, regarding the table with revulsion.

"Yes." I fit three slices of ham into my half of the baguette, slathered it with mustard and added cheese and pickles. "It was thoughtless of me to pick out this instead of the fresh imported Black Sea caviar so abundant in Port Nolloth."

The pain still came and went. My limbs felt like cement. But as we sat there in the sun and I ate the sandwich and drank the beer, I felt strength seeping into me. Lily tasted the mustard on the tip of her tongue, then shoved her plate away and stuck to the beer.

The breeze from the ocean stirred the leaves. Jigsaw-puzzle shapes of light and shadow shivered on the tablecloth. A pair of small gray birds made piercing cries as they rummaged in the fig for bugs. Their calls reinforced the heavy silence of the afternoon. Neither of us spoke for a while. I suppose Lily was thinking about the night ahead. I was thinking about Lily.

The long-range jet she'd chartered in Antwerp. Those planes start at $10,000 an hour. Lily would have had to pay a premium on top of that because she'd wanted it right away, needed the pilot to file a false flight plan, and the destination was a strip on a cutthroat coast. I doubted she'd paid less than $12,000 an hour. Say thirty-hour round-trip before the crew gets the jet back to Antwerp. Tab comes to $360,000. On the other hand, she had cash from selling the pink, so she probably got a discount for that—straight into the owner's offshore bank account when he had a moment to fly out. Call it an even $300,000.

Lily didn't get rich by throwing money away. Why had she agreed to such an expense? Because she loved me? That's not the way it worked. Our love was framed by calculation. Maybe all love is. I'm no expert. What I know is that Lily would not have considered herself bound to grant the wish of the plainly half-demented, feverish man in the hotel in Antwerp when I told her I had to see Piet Louw. I'm not saying she would have abandoned me. But there were lots of places she could have taken me to hide from my pursuers that did not involve a flight down the length of Africa to certain danger. Why had she done it? Only one possible answer. She had her own reason for being here.

Fear of Lime was one explanation. If that's what it was, staying close to me might be her best option. She'd stolen the small pink from him. That might have damaged the plans of people she feared even more—the diamond oligarchs. If I discovered something important about the Russian Pink from Piet, Lily could trade that information back to the Russians in exchange for her safety. I wouldn't blame her. I'm the one who'd put her in the danger in the first place.

How long had we been sitting silently? Lily watched me speculatively. "You're working through your dark suspicions, aren't you, darling. I can see the black clouds swirling in your head." She stood up and took my hand. "You'd better come inside. You need to rest."

The setting sun was splashing the surface of the sea with molten copper when we left Port Nolloth and drove north along the diamond coast. Just before the Orange River, a range of dark hills between the highway and the sea marked the last of the South African beach mines, a government-run operation that chewed dispiritedly through the depleted sands. Once the sun set, the desert would come alive with the figures of thieves streaming like an army of shadows across the highway and through the porous fence.

At the village of Alexander Bay we left the highway and dropped down into the delta of the Orange River. We bumped along a potholed gravel road that wound its way through tall marsh grass and clumps of shrubbery. As we rounded a bend, a dense cloud of flamingoes erupted from the surface of a pond, rending the night with their panicked cries.

The road ended at a small parking lot where a jetty poked into the sluggish current. Just west of where we stood, the Orange River ended its 1,400-mile journey from the Drakensberg and flowed into the ocean. Seals barked on the sandbars at the river mouth. Only a small channel pierced the barrier. Piet Louw would come through that.

On the north side of the river the low, black shape of a bluff showed where Namibia began. You can cross at a bridge upriver, but unless you have a special permit you won't get further than the border post. Inland and along the coast lies a 10,000-square-mile control zone called Diamond Area 1. When Namibia was still a German colony, the area was called the *Sperrgebiet*—the Forbidden Territory. The beach mines of South Africa are all tapped out, but in Namibia, towering bucketwheel excavators the size of Ferris wheels strip the richest coast in the world. Far offshore, much further out than the little tupperwares of Port Nolloth venture, the red ships of the Namibian diamond fleet smash up the seabed with drills and suck the diamond-bearing gravels up into shipboard recovery plants.

Like schooling fish, thieves and smugglers swarm this rich feeding ground. Every night a stream of stolen diamonds makes its way across the Orange River and down the old pathways of the diamond coast to Port Nolloth, where middlemen supply it with the paperwork for the onward journey to the diamond bourse in Johannesburg.

We heard the sound of tires crunching on gravel. Piet's flunkeys. We'd been expecting them. I slipped into the tall marsh grass. A white Ford F-150 with its headlights off came into view and stopped. There were two of them. They kept the engine idling, and can't have been happy to find an unexpected complication waiting at the rendezvous in the form of a parked SUV and a woman walking toward them. The driver rolled his window down and stared at Lily.

"I seem to be lost," said Lily in her throaty accent.

The driver turned and said something in Afrikaans to his companion. They both had a good laugh. I had moved around through the pampas grass. While they were distracted by Lily, I was supposed to step out of the grass and put the barrel of my Czech machine pistol into the passenger's ear. And here's how fast things can go wrong:

The driver grabbed Lily by the arm. He was fast, and very strong. His hand clamped her above the elbow and he yanked her against the door so hard her head banged the frame. At the same time, the passenger opened his door, climbed out and walked around the truck. He yanked up Lily's shirt. The Glock fell out and clanked on the gravel.

The passenger swore angrily and kicked the gun away. The driver had her tightly held against the door. His accomplice drew a knife and held the blade in front of Lily's face. Struggling to pull her face away from the knife, she caught sight of me coming out of the grass and approaching the open passenger-side door. I made a sideways gesture with the barrel. With all her strength she managed to lean away from the driver. I stretched across the cab and shot his head away.

The explosion of automatic fire and the bits of the driver's skull spattering his face made the other man fling himself away in blind terror. He uttered a high-pitched scream and started scrabbling on the ground looking for the Glock. I came around and kicked him in the throat.

Lily's face was frozen. Her eyes seemed adrift, unable to focus. She shook uncontrollably. An awful, tearing sound came from her chest as she gasped for breath. I put out my hand and she dug her fingers into it.

"It's OK, Lily."

I bound the knife guy hand and foot with plastic ties. I handed Lily her Glock. She stared at it.

"Now we have to listen," I said quietly.

She stood stock-still. The delta was noisy—wind rattling in the reeds, spooked flamingoes, the distant boom of the surf. But the wind was blowing onshore. I doubted anyone approaching from the sea would have heard the gunfire. The man on the ground made gagging noises. I loaded him into the back of the F-150.

A line of black clouds straggled up the coast. There was just enough moonlight to dab a strip of pewter onto the tops of the clouds and add a few highlights to the immense, heaving presence of the ocean. A wild pig snuffled and grunted somewhere in the grass nearby. I heard the buzz of Piet's outboard before I saw the Zodiac. He came through a narrow slot in the sandbar and slowed to navigate the channel. I stood at the end of the jetty, watching him come. The shred of moon was behind me. He hailed the dock in Afrikaans. I raised an arm and shouted back a garbled string of syllables that I hoped would do the trick, what with the wind and the engine and the swish of water on his boat. Piet came straight in. He cut the engine and nosed the rubber dinghy into the dock. There was an AK-47 on the seat beside him.

"Hey, Piet," I said. "If you touch the AK, I'll kill you where you sit."

Piet sat there staring up at me for a minute while his head churned through the possible courses of action available to him and arrived correctly at the number zero. Even somebody as stupid as Piet could see that he was trapped.

"Ditch it in the water," I said, "and the .38 in the ankle holster too."

When the guns splashed into the river I stepped back and told him to get out.

He pretended to have trouble balancing the boat while he tried to push a small canvas bag out of sight with the toe of his shoe.

"Toss the rough to my partner," I told him as Lily stepped out of the shadows.

I cuffed him, shoved him into the back seat, and climbed in beside him. Lily drove. Piet didn't say a word as we bumped past the F-150. Even in the feeble light you could see the cloud of mosquitoes around the slumped, headless driver and the figure in the back. If their fate bothered Piet, he kept it to himself.

The airport at Alexander Bay stayed open 24/7 to handle the big helicopters that ferried South African crews back and forth to the offshore diamond fleet. I gave the lone security guard 1,000 rand to find something needing his attention. So we sat in the empty, brightly lit departure lounge like three ordinary people waiting for their flight, except for one wearing handcuffs. Lily had come up with the location.

"He won't like it there," she'd said. "It will make him afraid we have a plan to fly him out."

Piet's eyes were bloodshot and his dirty hair hung to his shoulders.

"We're not here to mess with your game," I said, lifting the bag of rough on the plastic chair beside me and then putting it down again. If I had to guess, about a thousand carats. The average price for those ocean diamonds was running around $250 a carat. A quarter of a million dollars in rough.

"We know you have people stealing for you on the diamond fleet. We don't care. We want to talk about Angola."

Piet hadn't said a word since I'd put him in the back seat and he didn't say anything now. His face was roadmapped with a network of burst blood vessels. A scar went across his right ear where he'd been hacked with a machete. He looked at me with his hard, blue eyes. Piet expected everyone to be as mean and crooked as he was. Considering his acquaintances, he was usually right.

"I don't do Angola now," he said, a drool of saliva leaking onto his chin. "You so smart, you already know that."

"It's the pink I'm interested in," I said.

"What pink? No pink. You crazy? Who find pink?"

"You did. You found it just before you bought the big boat you've got offshore. That would coincide with when you left Angola, having killed your partner Denny Vorster, explaining why you are the sole owner of the boat and Denny has vanished from the earth."

"Fucked-up hose kill Denny!" Piet screamed. He could no longer keep his fury in check. It wasn't being accused of murdering Denny that enraged him. His eyes were on Lily and the bag of rough. A quarter of a million dollars was a lot of money to Piet right now. He had overpaid for that mothership of his. While I was still recovering, Lily had put together a good snapshot of Piet's financial condition. She had bought rough from every corner of the continent, and she had contacts. That's how I knew Piet was not getting the amount of rough he had counted on, and sure as hell he was not getting this parcel.

I held up my hand.

"I don't care what happened to Denny any more than I care about what will happen to you if you don't answer my questions. But just so we're clear, I will take you back down to the river and hogtie you and open shallow cuts in your arms and legs and roll you into the grass. The pigs will do the rest."

The tip of his tongue appeared between his dirty teeth as he thought through his options.

"Start with what the diamond looked like, Piet."

"It covered in mud and rock. Not like river stone."

"Where did you take it?"

"Barry Stern."

"How exactly did Barry pay you?"

Piet snorted. "Long time ago. How you think I remember?"

"And the account numbers too," I said. "I need your banking details."

He displayed his brown, crooked teeth in an ugly smile.

"I hear he sell to Russians. You think you make trouble for these guys? They chop you and your Russia pussy into pieces and feed you to the crocodiles."

There's always this little to and fro. You have to be patient. I let Piet think about the pigs for a while.

"He pay cash," he said at last. "You can't trace it, because he paid cash. That how it work now."

He watched me with glittering eyes.

"That's how it's always worked, Piet. But he didn't pay you all cash. He paid you part cash and the rest by check. The check amount was his declared value for tax purposes. So take another run at this, and it better add up to the number I already have."

I didn't have any number, but I was guessing Barry Stern had screwed Piet, and I was right. Piet wasn't the brightest guy, and he had to stick his tongue between his teeth a few more times and think very hard to recall the order in which the payments had come, which ones were cash and which were wires. I led him through the deal until

I had it right—one million cash as a down payment, and a week later a bank draft for $11 million. I got Piet's banking details.

Dawn was still an hour away when we heard the powerful *thwack-thwack-thwack* of helicopter blades as a big Sikorsky came in from the diamond fleet for the crew change.

"Hey," said Piet. He looked frantic. "You leave me for those guys, they take me out to the fleet and drop me off the side. They bastards."

"Relax," I said. I led him outside, shoved him in the back of the SUV and clambered in beside him. The bus from Alexander Bay with the daytime crew was just turning off the highway as we drove out of the airport and headed back down into the delta.

The herd of pigs clustered around the F-150 scattered into the bamboo as we pulled up. Only the massive boar, who'd managed to get his hooves up onto the tailgate, showed a reluctance to move, his attention divided between the bloody, tied-up guy in the back of the truck and us. Not until Lily gave him a bunt with the front bumper did he drop his legs from the truck and trot off into the thicket with an angry grunt.

I dragged Piet out of the SUV and shoved him into the truck bed and cuffed his ankles. Lily took a handful of small rough from the bag and stuffed it in his shirt pocket and gave it a friendly pat. Piet said he would kill her and she was a cunt and blah blah blah. Sure, he was mad. If the pigs didn't get him first, the cops would take a turn when they found the rough in his pocket. In South Africa it's a criminal offense to possess rough diamonds without proof of where they came from. The law makes the presumption that anyone with rough who can't account for it has stolen it. They would put Piet in an overcrowded jail where the other inmates mostly had a different color of skin and personal histories that had not taught them to love Afrikaners. Piet would try to bribe his way out, but guess what: He would discover that there was no money in his bank account.

Piet was a killer. He wasn't the only murderer on the diamond rivers, but he was the one I had right now. He'd killed his partner, and his accomplices would have raped and killed Lily. If the cops found Piet first, fine. But I was pulling for the pigs.

A saffron dawn walked her fingers up the sky as we drove back down the highway to Port Nolloth. The wind had died in the night. In the strengthening light the ocean blazed like a pane of stained glass, changing color by the moment. The tubby little diamond boats paraded out past the breakwater. They threaded the reef and headed south for the inshore diamond grounds. The suction hoses swam behind the boats like faithful serpents, carving fantastic arabesques on the tangerine surface of the sea.

We drove along the ocean until I found a strong signal. While Lily examined the rough, pulling out the larger stones and holding them to the morning light, I sent a message to Patrick Ho. It detailed what Piet had coughed up on how the early diamond payments were structured. He would pay particular attention to the wire for $11 million. Barry had obviously waited until his buyer paid before making the deposit for Piet. Connected to what we already knew, Patrick could start to tease apart the strands of the money trail.

Then I tapped out another message, to Tabitha. I asked her to see if any strand of payments went to a research facility, and to look for a bank connection on Long Island.

The messages didn't take long to send, but longer than I liked. The kind of people looking for me probably had access to the supercomputers at Fort Meade. They ransack the world's message traffic around the clock. If they're looking for you, you'll eventually be found. But you can make the search take longer.

A dark net is a place that normal search engines don't have access to because they don't have the code to get in. Most people who want to hide use software like Tor, an acronym for The Onion Router. Tor is a network of subscribers who provide their own computers to construct the onion's layers. Instead of a message going from sender A to receiver B, it will go from A to C and from C to X and from X to Y. It will eventually get to B, but not until it has slipped from layer to layer through the onion long enough to shake off most pursuers.

The system Patrick had set up had no subscribers. It was a private dark net, much harder to access. Even so, if people in Washington were looking hard, we could only slow them down, not elude them altogether.

We went back to the shabby bungalow, made coffee, and took it onto the sagging porch. The sun was higher now and the ocean had turned light green. A pair of giant petrels with black wings and white wingtips wheeled above the beach. We sat side by side in ancient canvas deck chairs and gazed at the Atlantic.

It's an evil coast. In places they call it the skeleton coast because of the wrecked ships and the desolation. The first diamonds were discovered when Namibia was under German possession. A railway worker found wind-blown diamonds in the Namib desert. The Germans sealed off the entire southwestern corner of the country. It took them years to find that the diamonds were not in the desert but on the beach and in the ocean.

"Didn't Lime have a diamond ship he kept here?" I said.

"*The Benguela Queen*. It was an old mining vessel he bought. He established a base at sea and put down the drill and made a mess in the water so the South Africans would think he was mining. Actually, he was buying stolen Namibian rough. He thought he could compete with Fonseca."

Portuguese colonists, driven from Angola after independence, ran the Port Nolloth trade in stolen rough, and they ran it for João Fonseca.

"Lime thought he could outbid Fonseca," Lily said, "and still make big profits."

"What happened?"

"After one month, Fonseca sent boats out at night. They boarded the *Queen* and took the crew on deck and tied them together, even the cook, a girl of sixteen. Then they sailed the ship close to shore and ran it on the reef, so everyone in town would see what happened next. Then they set the ship on fire and burned the crew alive."

We could see the reef from where we sat. The screams of the dying would have come clearly to those on shore, their relatives and friends.

The misery coast.

"What time do we meet Fonseca?"

"Seven," Lily said. I looked at my watch. It wasn't even noon.

As the sun rose, the heat of the desert clamped on the town like an iron lid. Lily wore cotton shorts and a linen shirt with the sleeves rolled up to her elbows. In spite of her pale skin the sun didn't burn her. It brought out a golden blush. The smell of her skin and hair seeped through the heavy air. Her fragrance. She fingered the hem of her shirt and turned her eyes to me.

Consider who we were. Old lovers on the run in a seaside town in Africa. We bore marks of violence. Where else would we turn. In the garden of the knowledge of good and evil, we had eaten the apple long ago.

14

The bird with the lilac breast sat at the top of the acacia tree, its feathers polished into gems by the setting sun.

We packed, left the house, and drove to a despondent seaside restaurant decorated with fishing nets and lobster pots. We sat on the concrete terrace. Lily frowned at the menu, as if by concentrating hard enough she could make something more appetizing appear. A young woman in a black T-shirt and black jeans appeared from the kitchen.

"Try the fried kingklip," she said. "It's always fresh."

Her hair was plaited into tight braids and coiled around her shapely head.

Far out on the rim of the ocean a ship was steaming south to the Cape. A drill rig identified the vessel as part of the Namibian diamond fleet. Heading for a refit. The crew would take the opportunity to dispose of whatever diamonds they'd stolen and not already sold.

"You booked the flight to Cape Town?"

"Stop fussing, Alex. We're confirmed."

I looked at my watch again. I guessed someone was checking us out. Fonseca would make sure we had come alone. He knew Lily; they'd done business when she ran Russgem's foreign buying out of Antwerp. I'd never met him, but I assumed "information of interest," as his message had said, meant he wanted to betray someone.

João Fonseca bought most of the rough stolen on the diamond coast. Everything from Namibia came through him: Piet's diamonds from the offshore fleet; the steady trickle of stones from the sorting operation at Oranjemund; the rough that made its way from the beach and along the myriad smuggling routes across the Orange River. All of it passed through João's hands. As rich and powerful as he was, Fonseca had come a long way down from what he'd owned before.

Basically, Angola.

In 1975 Portugal lost a bloody war of independence in Angola. When they lost the war, they lost the diamonds. João's family had owned the diamond rivers. They had ranches and yachts and private planes. They had mansions in Lisbon and Luanda, a languid city often called the Paris of southern Africa. In those days, rich South Africans swarmed the beaches and casinos of Luanda, finding in the elegant Portuguese city an easy sophistication absent from their puritanical, race-obsessed homeland. And not just South Africans: Aristocrats flew down from Lisbon for the legendary blowouts at the Fonseca palace on the beach. In the end, the Fonsecas had to leave it all and run for their lives. They came to Port Nolloth.

"The Paris of Namaqualand," I said.

"Diamonds were their life," Lily said, guessing at my train of thought. "If they couldn't get them one way, they'd get them another."

They settled in Port Nolloth and began to rob the diamond beach. There was theft before the Fonsecas took it over. João scaled it into an industry.

The bottom edge of the sun touched the horizon. Crews from the diamond boats came in and filled the tables on the terrace. Pitchers of beer and plates of boerewors, South African country sausage, clattered onto the tables.

I saw our contact arrive. He stood at the entrance and looked at us. He was short and stocky. His bright green palm tree shirt billowed around him in the onshore breeze. He stared at me with black, unblinking eyes. I nodded and threw some money on the table. Outside he stopped at a black Mercedes and held the back door open. We walked by and got in our SUV. He shrugged and shut the door and we followed the Mercedes up the hill from the harbor.

At the north end of town, the ramshackle houses straggled to an end at a stretch of dunes jumbled between the highway and the shore. A suburb of concrete villas nested in the dunes—the Portuguese colony. BMWs and Range Rovers sat in the driveways. Mastiffs with bloodshot eyes glowered through the fences. Fonseca's lieutenants and relatives, their lawyer, the guy who ran the Portuguese grocery—all huddled here in this cantonment on the coast, gorging on diamonds and dreaming of Luanda.

We stopped at a tall, wrought-iron gate. The letters JF, painted in gold on a heraldic shield, shone in the floodlight. A pair of rampant lions held the shield in place. With their long red tongues, they looked like they were dying of thirst. Green Shirt punched a code into a panel, and the gate creaked open.

João waited for us by the pool. He was tall and thin, with the gaunt face and sallow skin of the malaria sufferer. He wore a white terrycloth beach robe and a look of bored bemusement. With a flap of his yellow hand he waved at lounge chairs.

"Thank you for coming," he said. His words ended in a long, racking cough. He held a folded handkerchief that he pressed to his mouth. When the coughing subsided, he examined the handkerchief.

He sat with care, arranging himself in a wicker chaise and crossing his bare feet on a cushion. His ankles were swollen. An inhaler lay on the table beside him. I could hear the wheezing in his chest.

"Something to drink," he said, lifting his hand in the direction of the house.

A servant came out with a silver tray. On it stood a frosted pitcher of water clinking with ice cubes.

"Very important to stay hydrated," he observed sadly as the girl filled his glass with water.

"We're interested in what you wanted to tell us," I said.

"I did not think you would bring the Russian." He didn't even glance at Lily.

Terracotta tubs filled with frangipani and azaleas surrounded the terrace. Beyond the flowers and a thicket of rubbery leaves rose a high wall topped with broken glass and razor wire. I pulled my chair around so I could see anything happening behind Lily; she would have me similarly covered. João closed his eyes and gave his head a shake of resignation. He'd spotted the shape of the machine pistol beneath my shirt. I didn't think he had invited us there to kill us, but the Fonsecas had murdered people on the diamond rivers and they'd murdered people on the beach and they'd murdered people at the crossings on the Orange River. Kill enough people, it gets to be a habit. In the long view, two more bodies wouldn't make much difference, but I wasn't taking the long view.

"I will come to the point, Mr. Turner. You want to know about the stone they now call the Russian Pink. That is why you're here. You have learned what you wanted from poor Piet." He shook his head again, as if the cares of the world were weighing heavily on him. "Piet has suffered enough."

He produced a scrap of smile that stopped well short of his eyes. Probably the bag of high-end rough we'd taken from Piet had been destined for João, and João's people had gone looking for it. If Piet was still alive when they found him, I doubt they'd have thought that whatever he'd suffered was enough.

João's concave chest whistled and clanked like broken plumbing. He inspected his handkerchief and found a dot of blood, and refolded the white linen until he had a spotless square again.

"Lime has deceived your Mr. Nash. He has made a fool of him. You know about the Camafoza Pipe?"

"The largest diamond pipe in the world. You managed to hide your continued ownership from the Angolans. They wouldn't have been too curious about the Camafoza because the pipe has disappointed everyone who's ever drilled it. How am I doing so far?"

"Yes," he said. A hairline scar ran from his left eye to the corner of his mouth, like the track of a tear, if the tear had been made of acid. His eyes burned with a feverish brightness. "That is true as far as it goes. What you may *not* know about the Camafoza is that a loop of the Chicapa River crosses a corner of the pipe." He looked at me expectantly.

"OK," I shrugged.

A bright green gecko flashed from a crack in the terrace and froze.

"It is important," João said, leaning forward, "because the river exposes an edge of the pipe. As you know, a diamond pipe is an extinct volcano shaped like a funnel. It extends deep into the earth, to the place where diamonds are formed. In the geological past, it was the eruption of such volcanoes that brought diamonds to the surface. Each pipe has its own peculiarities."

His eyes blazed even more brightly.

"I expect you know this very well, because it was your father who described the suite of minerals that enable us to understand the individual chemical signatures of diamond pipes. That is what tells us whether a given pipe is worth the expense of exploration. From that analysis, we concluded the Camafoza was rich in diamonds."

A shiny blue beetle trundled into view and the gecko flicked forward and seized it. With its prey in its mouth the lizard froze. The only movement was the beetle flailing its blue legs.

"The problem was the size of the pipe. The Camafoza has a surface expression of 150 hectares—almost 400 acres. That is a vast area to explore. We could drill many holes and still miss the diamonds. But," a bony finger shot up, "we were lucky. The Chicapa River cuts across a corner of the pipe. The river has washed away all the soil around that part of the pipe. To explore this large section, all we had to do was dam the river and dig directly into the pipe."

A sheen of perspiration covered his face. He reached for the inhaler and clutched it in his fist. The gecko's body twitched as it swallowed most of the beetle. Only the beetle's bright blue head remained in sight, its antennae waving frantically.

"As soon as we penetrated into the pipe, we made an astonishing discovery—huge xenoliths!"

"Stranger rocks," I said.

"Yes!" he rasped. "Geologists call them that because they are not like any other rocks found on the planet. They have not been fused with other rocks in the normal process of geological formation. They are as they were when formed in the depths. What geologists know from long experience," he leaned forward, his body shaking, "is that a diamond pipe that has carried up large xenoliths may also have carried up equally massive diamonds!"

A tawny blur shot from the leaves, snatched the gecko in its mouth, and sprang into João's lap, where it crouched and stared at me with enormous amber eyes. The gecko clawed wildly at the air and the beetle in the gecko's mouth waved its blue antennae. The Sokoke cat made a soft, snarling sound deep in its throat. It pinned the squirming lizard with a paw against the snow-white robe and bit off its head.

João seemed hardly to notice the cat, or the spreading bloodstain in his lap. His eyes showed a momentary glint of panic and he opened his mouth and took a greedy gulp of the inhaler. Relieved, he closed his eyes for a moment and stroked the cat.

"If the diamonds were, as we believed, as massive as the xenoliths," he said, regaining his breath, "we should find them where we were digging, at the edge of the pipe, where the centrifugal force of the rising lava would have pushed such heavy stones."

The hand that stroked the cat stopped and João watched me, waiting for the question.

"And did you find them?"

"Atílio!" João called, and Green Shirt emerged from the house with a leather attaché case. He snapped the catches, opened the case, and placed it on the table beside João.

João took out an enormous diamond, at least 500 carats, and held it reverently. It was roughly egg shaped, flat on one side, and pale brown. He handed it to me and gave me a loupe. I peered in through the flattest surface. Even in the weak light of the poolside lamps, the brown tint was apparent. Some miners have successfully marketed browns. The Australians invented new color names, calling them cognacs and champagnes. But color was not the biggest challenge of the stone. Even if you could accept the color, the diamond I held in my hand would never get to a wheel. It was cobwebbed with fracture planes. I tilted the stone this way and that, straining to penetrate the blizzard of flaws and find, if it was there, some part of the diamond that was clean. And then I caught sight of it, just a glimpse. I made a minute adjustment in the angle, and caught it again. A pool of stillness deep in the center of the stone.

I took my eye from the loupe for a moment. To rest it. Then looked in again. This time I found the pathway to the center more quickly, and there it was. What I'd glimpsed before. A tranquil pool in the eye of the storm. Unruffled and serene—but not unmarked. It swarmed with tiny inclusions, as if an alien horde had invaded the diamond and been captured there for all eternity. I had never before seen such strange inclusions. Except once. Less than a week before. As I sat with Honey Li.

I handed the diamond to Lily. She inspected it briefly. "Hopeless," she said.

João snatched the stone back. "A Russian would always say that," he spat. Scarlet patches appeared on his cheeks and he was seized with a violent spasm that ended in a long, racking cough. He dabbed at his mouth with the handkerchief. Slowly he mastered himself. His face softened as he put the jewel back in the case and stared at it.

"When we recovered this diamond from the edge of the pipe, it weighed almost 4,000 carats. It was larger than the mother stone of the Great Star of Africa."

"The biggest stone in history," I said.

The Sokoke finished the last of the gecko, closed its eyes, and began to purr like an idling truck.

"Four thousand carats. Can you imagine? I was going to call the color 'umber.' Cognac and champagne—they are not names for a jewel. This would be pale umber," he placed a finger on the case. "Others would polish to a deep, vivid umber." His voice had taken on a dreamy tone. "I thought it would restore the glory of Angola." He turned his ruined face to me. "Was that so wrong?"

He was infected not just by his disease but by the stone. The diamond ravaged his imagination.

"We tried to cut it."

"And it blew up on the wheel," I said.

João closed his eyes and let his head sink back. At last I understood. It should have struck me sooner. Browns and pinks were companion colors. They could exist together in the same deposit. In Australia's giant Argyle Pipe, eighty percent of its eight-million-carat-a-year production were low-grade browns. Yet also present at the mine was a small population of fabulously rare and sought-after pinks. The presence of one color could indicate the other.

"You're saying the Russian Pink came from the Camafoza Pipe," I said.

"Where else," he murmured hoarsely.

I played it out. The pink would have got into the river the same way every diamond gets into a river: by washing in from its primary source, a pipe. In this case, the pink would have been dislodged by the mining at the edge of the pipe, and the machinery had failed to capture it. It rolled in the current until it was vacuumed up. Unlike other river stones, its placement in the river had not been millions of years ago, but recently. That explained why it still had pieces of rock clinging to it.

The Sokoke licked at the bloody patch in João's lap, then laid its chin in the gore and glared at me. João paused to summon his strength, drawing in deep, rattling breaths.

"Lime stole my pipe. He found out that I owned it through a nominee and told the Angolans." Another wrenching cough shook his body, ending in a string of violent spasms. He shoved the handkerchief hard against his mouth until the shaking stopped.

"When the world learns where the Russian Pink came from, the shares in the company that owns the pipe will rise to many times their present value."

"What's the company?"

"Great Pipe," he gasped, groping for the inhaler. His eyes alight with fear, he drew two puffs deep into his disintegrating lungs. The last of his strength was bleeding away into the viscous night. He closed his eyes and waited for his body to calm itself.

"It's all in here," he said in a whisper, handing me a manila folder. "I even put in your father's conclusions. He believed in the Camafoza." He fixed me with a gaze as full of hopelessness as hatred. "Lime is using your Mr. Nash. I ask only that you ruin Lime."

"Why did no one see it?" I said to Lily as we drove away.

"The reputation of the Camafoza," she shrugged. "Every previous exploration failed."

We left Port Nolloth behind and headed north up the highway to Alexander Bay.

"What's the pipe worth now?" Lily said, breaking the silence with what we'd both been thinking.

"You tell me. Hundreds of billions? In Australia, brown and pink diamonds exist in the same deposit. Obviously they do in the Camafoza too. Even if a lot of them are badly flawed, they might still yield large stones. Look at the Russian Pink."

Lily nodded. "And now we know why Lime was smuggling in that small pink."

"That's right. If he could show that those bits and pieces left over from the shattered stone could be polished into jewels, then the value of the deposit explodes. If Lime revealed that all at once—that the Camafoza had produced not only the Russian Pink, but other smaller pinks as well, polished from the same stone—the share price would skyrocket."

We left the car at the airport in Alexander Bay and caught the hopper that goes through Springbok on its way down to the Cape. Springbok is the capital of Namaqualand. It has a Dutch Reformed Church, a post office, and a road that ends at the abandoned copper mine. You wouldn't normally expect to find the local cop poking his head into the once-a-day Beechcraft and carefully checking out the passengers against a photograph he had. He held it up and frowned at it and turned it this way and that before he decided that, yes, it was me, folded the image away, and left. So I wasn't surprised to find someone waiting for us in the terminal at Cape Town, but I didn't expect it to be Chuck.

15

Chuck's disguise was a tailored safari suit, brown-suede English chukka boots, and $500 sunglasses—an outfit that would have marked him as a seasoned Africa hand as long as he'd stayed in the two or three blocks of Madison Avenue where he'd bought it all. Lily had never met Chuck, but she had no trouble recognizing him. She gave him a sour look. I had a sarcastic remark ready for the handoff until I realized how bad he looked.

I shook my head when he opened his mouth to speak.

"Not here, Chuck."

He clamped his jaws shut and we went straight through to the parking lot. The harsh lights didn't improve his appearance. The purple edge of a black eye was creeping out from under the sunglasses. We skipped the American car-rental chains and went to a local company in a corner of the lot. Lily paid cash.

We took the N2 motorway that leads around the black mass of Table Mountain. The city came into view: a blazing cluster of hotels and office buildings straggling up the mountain. On Table Bay ships rode at anchor, their lights reflected in the polished mirror of the sea. Floodlit cranes festooned the busy docks.

I drove down to the shore and took Beach Road past the Mouille Point lighthouse. At the Sea Point traffic circle I pulled into the driveway of a concrete bungalow with peeling paint. A dilapidated sign swinging from an iron bracket identified KENSINGTON VILLAS. A maid answered the door and, as always, Sylvia Gold shuffled out a few minutes later from the back of the house. A stained kimono flapped around her scarecrow frame. Her hair was dyed bright red. A cigarette hung from her carmine lips and her thin wrists jangled with bracelets. The fistful of keys was never out of her grasp. She peered at me from watery eyes.

"How many, luv?" she said in the cockney accent that fifty years in South Africa had not dented.

"Three of us, Sylvia. One or two nights." I handed her a wad of thousand-rand notes. She pocketed them without a glance.

"Number twenty, luv," she said, handing me a plastic ring with two keys. "It's on the water. Lovely view, number twenty has. I've just put in a new hotplate. You can make a proper breakfast. Go down to the market at the corner and tell them you're a friend of Sylvia. They'll do you very nice bacon at the corner, and the eggs are fresh. Tell them you're a friend of Sylvia."

A repeated phrase meant the police had been around. I'd been using Sylvia's for years. She could provide a number of services, including false IDs and, in a pinch, a gun. Just don't bet on the eggs. They haven't had fresh eggs at the corner for a decade.

The main street at Sea Point has been going downhill for a long time. Impoverished migrants who find the Cape burning like the last candle on the continent haunt the road looking for the flame that brought them here. They come up against the cold Atlantic and locked gates.

A cluster of luxury hotels with ocean-view terraces and private whirlpool tubs huddled for mutual protection in a gated enclave on the headland. I turned onto a street that ran beside the seawall. In a fenced compound of their own, Sylvia's weather-beaten townhouses looked like an English suburb that had been banished to a penal colony.

We sat on the damp veranda. Across the road the South Atlantic rolled ashore after an unbroken run from Antarctica. The waves thundered against the seawall and filled the air with cold salt spray and the smell of seaweed.

"A pleasure to meet at last," Chuck said, giving Lily his best sardonic smile.

"Oh, for Christ's sake," she muttered.

"Chuck," I said. "Spit it out."

He took off his sunglasses. It was going to be a great shiner. He was exhausted, but he held himself together while he told his story.

Two men showed up at the front door just as Chuck and his wife, Natalie, were getting ready for bed. Chuck had never been door-stopped by pros. They flipped badges in his face and said they were from military intelligence and barged past before he had time to react.

The one who seemed to be in charge rattled off the terms of an order to investigate a breach of national security. He started peppering Chuck with questions about me and where I was and under whose authority.

While this was happening the other one went into the den and started yanking open drawers and tossing papers around. When Chuck tried to stop him, he caught a jab in the eye. Natalie went after the guy with a table lamp, so he punched her too.

When they were through, and Chuck had his arm around Natalie, more to restrain her than comfort her, they ordered him to report to the federal marshals' office in Manhattan the next morning to face a formal charge of conspiracy to subvert the government of the United States. Chuck knew there was no such crime, and that if there were, it wouldn't be MI who came around to announce it. But he realized that things were not going the proper-process route. They were going the punch-in-the-face route.

After coaxing Natalie to go to her parents' in Vermont, he packed a small bag, swapped his passport and driver's license for the forgeries he wasn't supposed to have, and walked to the subway at Twenty-Third Street. He watched the platform carefully and didn't get on the northbound train until the doors were closing. That trick wouldn't have brushed off a pro, but at least he was trying.

At Thirty-Fourth Street he got off the subway, went through the tunnel to Penn Station, and caught a New Jersey Transit train to the stop for Newark airport. There, he boarded the AirTrain shuttle from the train station to the terminals. At Terminal C he got off, went straight downstairs to the arrivals level, and hopped a cab. He had the taxi drop him off in downtown Newark, walked around the crowded streets for ten minutes, then ducked into a department store. In a restroom, he ditched his old clothes and changed into the safari gear, bought the year before for a holiday in Kenya. Near the train station he rented a car and drove fifteen hours straight to Miami.

From Miami, he flew to São Paulo and caught the South African Airways flight to Johannesburg with an onward connection to the Cape. The only thing I hated more than finding myself saddled with Chuck was how easily he'd found me.

I could understand him picking up the trail to Antwerp. Someone else already had. But Namaqualand and the plane to Cape Town?

"How did you get our flight information?"

"I had a contact in the South African police."

"Oh, man," I said, glancing at Lily. She got up and left the balcony and I heard the door to the apartment close softly as she went outside. She moved like a cat. Only because I was listening for the sound did I hear it: the barest *snick* as she shut the security gate behind her and left the property.

"Congratulations, Chuck. Someone was hoping you would run. They wanted you to lead them to me."

I saw a movement in a patch of shadow below the balcony. Lily emerged and crossed the road, slipped between two cars, and disappeared in a clump of trees.

"No one knew I had that passport," Chuck said, "not even you."

"Please. If the NSA facial-recognition system was asleep when you went through Miami, believe me, someone would have woken it by the time you reached São Paulo. Who's been pulling your strings in Washington? Because they're getting impatient."

Between New York and Cape Town, Chuck had spent lonely hours mulling over this hard fact himself. He'd been trying to steer a middle course between Nash and the president's allies, afraid that Nash would win and equally afraid he wouldn't.

"I was called to a meeting with the secretary," he said. "He told me there was bipartisan concern that the Russians were going to compromise Harry Nash."

"Bipartisan. And that made sense to you?"

"Of course it didn't," Chuck said, flushing. "I'm not a fool, Alex. These are sophisticated people. Some of the president's party now believe they're going to lose this election. They know that voters are sick of the president. Their view is more nuanced than win or lose."

"Well that's a weight off my shoulders. They're taking a nuanced view. Thank God. For a while it looked like they were taking the view that involves violent assault and murder." I gripped the railing. "I mean, Jesus Christ, Chuck. Will you *fucking* wake up?"

"I'm not trying to say they have altruistic motives," Chuck bristled. "I think the cooler heads are evolving a new strategy. They think that if Nash is going to win anyway, they shouldn't squander any dirt on him right now, but use it to wreck his presidency. That way they regain power in four years."

I could picture Chuck expounding this thinking in the office, his legs crossed on the desk so the interns could admire his jeans. Chuck was seduced by his own imagination, a fertile garden that he'd never learned to weed. I have a less nuanced mind. As long as it's dirty enough, I favor the explanation right in front of me.

"They don't *believe they're going to lose*, Chuck. Where did you get that, MSNBC? They *fear* it. That means they will use whatever dirt we can dig up for them. They won't hold it for four years. They'll use it when they get it. See if you can remember a last-minute slime job turning a presidential election on its ear."

I heard the gate again as Lily came back.

"I circled the block," she said when she was back on the balcony. "Two cars, both unmarked. They're not even bothering to hide."

I leaned over the railing and looked along the street. There was one about six cars away, on the far side of the road. The driver took a drag on a cigarette, the orange dot glowing in the shadows. The one riding shotgun sat there checking his email, his face lit by the glow of the screen.

We didn't have to wait long to find out what they wanted. The car pulled up in front of us. The driver got out and placed a flashing blue light on the roof. His partner climbed out too, and they took up position under the balcony, not even bothering to glance at us. Down the street another car slid out of a side street to block the intersection. A minute later a car flashed its lights at the cops in the intersection, drove through, and stopped below us.

A short, slim figure hopped out of the passenger side, said something to the policemen, and followed them up the sidewalk.

The escort came in first. They gave us the hard look that said, I hope we understand each other. They checked the apartment quickly, sweeping their flashlights around the bedroom and opening the closets. Then they stood aside.

She wore the same black jeans and T-shirt that she'd worn when she'd waited on us in the restaurant at Port Nolloth.

"I hope you're not going to complain about the tip," I said.

"Mr. Turner," she said, "whatever you're involved in is above my pay grade. Basically my job tonight is to airmail you off to someone who has more important friends than you do."

She gave me a warm smile.

"While I'm at it, though, I'm hoping to do a swap with you. I think you found out something about how that big Angolan pink got paid for. That's something I'd really like to know. In return, I have something for you. Isn't that how our business works?"

"I'm the ranking officer," Chuck interjected. "We're not authorized to disclose information about a US government investigation."

A long pause followed while she studied Chuck.

"Wow," she said finally. "Did I just hear someone mention a foreign government operating without permission in South Africa?"

"We're just here for the beaches," I said.

"I'm so glad," she replied, her eyes still on Chuck.

She stepped to the railing and looked out at the ocean. The black shape of a container ship, marked by its running lights, sailed slowly eastward on a course that would take it around the Cape of Good Hope.

"Barry Stern and people like him are bleeding us," she said, her gaze fastened on the ship. "They declare only a fraction of the diamonds they buy and sell, and smuggle the rough out, sometimes on ships like that one," she tiled her chin at the distant shape. "We don't care so much about the diamonds. Most of them are Namibia's problem. But they smuggle gold too."

"Theft from your mines," I said.

She nodded. "Stolen ore means the mines lose at least a fifth of their production every year, probably more. We've managed to track some of it. Most of that stolen ore goes to a refinery in the Persian Gulf. First Partners runs it."

"And you want to find out how they pay for it."

The container ship was almost out of sight around the headland. Two more ships had appeared behind it, sailing the same course. An endless convoy steamed past the Cape on its way to ports in the Gulf and China. From Africa they took copper, steel, chrome, oil, timber. Gold and diamonds. Behind they left poverty, corruption, and despair.

I sent a message to Patrick. Using the information from Piet, he'd already started mapping a trail of transactions by First Partners. I read off to her the account number of every wire that had a South African banking code.

When she'd entered the last number I gave her, she put her phone away and pressed a flash drive into my hand.

"I think you'll find that interesting. Now, you have a plane to catch. Henny Botha has the flight plan. You know how to find him. I believe he was your pilot of choice when you had that great apartment on the mountain."

She gave me another dazzling smile, and a moment later I heard the car doors slam and the sound of their engines fading down the road.

I followed the coast to Hout Bay, then cut through the mountains. An hour later we were picking our way through the leafy streets of

Stellenbosch. I found Henny Botha in the tiny living quarters attached to the back of his hangar at the airstrip on the edge of town.

"Ach!" said Henny when I appeared at his door. "After all these years! Still flying around in the night?"

"Can't let bats have all the fun."

Henny's leathery old face split into a grin. He put his head back and sent a roar of laughter up to rattle among the stars. "Bats have all the fun," he repeated, shaking his head in appreciation. He wiped a tear from the corner of his eye, chuckled again, and shoved a cigarette into his mouth. He lit it with an ancient Zippo, inhaled deeply, and led the way to the apron where his sixty-year-old Antonov single-engine biplane stood. A ladder leaned against the open hatch.

"Ach!" he said in disgust, "I tell the boy—don't leave the ladder and the open door. Last month I was halfway to Mozambique. Puff adder dropped from hole in overhead bulkhead onto right-hand seat. Good thing I have no copilot!" He started to roar with laughter again, then stopped abruptly. "Flight plan Botswana?"

"You tell me," I said.

He nodded and sighed. "Yes, Botswana. They come and pay cash and tell me where to take you." He turned and raised his thick forefinger. "And if I ever talk about it, they will come in the night and drive a stake through my heart." He watched me for a moment with a solemn expression, then erupted into another roar of laughter. Henny liked any joke, but best of all his own.

He flipped a switch on the side of the hangar and a line of blue runway lights sprang into view. I yanked the blocks from the wheels and we clambered in. Stuffing leaked from the seats. The stench of whatever cargo Henny had last carried lingered in the filthy cabin. The Antonov made a short, noisy dash along the runway and lifted into the starry sky.

We headed due north over the Great Karoo. The lights of isolated farms floated on the black expanse of the desert. I sat in the green glow of the cockpit in the copilot's seat, thinking about puff adders while Henny smoked non-stop and bragged about his beloved airplane.

Henny maintained the heading north until we had passed the main air routes into Johannesburg, then turned northeast and crossed the Botswana border.

The sun was coming up when we landed at Sir Seretse Khama Airport and taxied to a distant corner of the airfield. The only other planes in sight carried the military insignia of a dozen countries. One of them was a Gulfstream V with US Air Force markings. The list of people who can pull that kind of ride is a short one, and I could only think of one person on it who might want to talk to me.

16

E veryone has terrorists, old man, *everyone*," a British air commodore was braying into the face of a Canadian brigadier.

The lobby bar of the hotel was packed with men and women in uniform.

"Don't tell *me* about regional conditions," the air commodore trumpeted on. He fixed the Canadian with a bulging eye. "Malaya!" he boomed, settling an argument in which he seemed to be the only participant.

A pair of American marine captains huddled with a small group of Namibian army officers and a South African naval commander. One of the Americans tapped his finger on the table and said, "Software."

A sign behind the reception desk welcomed delegates to SAFSEC, the annual security conference for southern Africa.

Until the middle of the last century the Texas-sized sandlot called Botswana was a sleepy backwater. Its scattered population of herdsmen and nomadic San tribesmen led subsistence lives. That changed abruptly in 1963, when a geologist sampled termite mounds at a place called

Orapa. Among the mineral grains he found were microdiamonds. Termites excavate underground cities to a depth of sixty feet. The geologist decided to see if he could find where the termites got the diamonds. He did, and fifty years later the Orapa diamond pipe still produces 12 million carats a year, and Orapa was just the first pipe they found.

For terrorists, diamonds are even more popular than bitcoin, so Botswana's capital, Gaborone, one of the world's biggest diamond-trading centers, was a natural location for the conference. I'd been to it before, and in spite of the spooks mixed in with the soldiers it always had a comradely air about it. It didn't feel that way now.

"Big security," the desk clerk at the Masa Square Hotel said as she checked us in. "Big VIP."

"Who's that?" I said.

She gave me an elaborate shrug and said she didn't know. That seemed unlikely in a country completely controlled by members of the same ethnic group. The Tswana-speaking majority ran everything from the army to the diamond business. The clerk was Tswana. So was the cop standing at her shoulder glaring at the screen as she entered our names and handed us our key cards.

They put us on the top floor. I could hardly keep my eyes open, but I put my laptop on the desk and found the flash drive the South African agent had given me. I slipped it into the USB port and clicked the play button that appeared on the screen.

The scene was shot at night across a river. The cameraman had used a telephoto lens, but the picture was steady. Whoever shot it had a tripod.

I was pretty sure it was the Chicapa. For one thing, a small diamond barge was sieving gravels on the right-hand side of the frame. But the main clue was the huge industrial dredge working the far side of the river. Arc lamps mounted on steel pylons floodlit the scene, including a landing stage tethered to the shore. A small group stood watching the dredge. The camera started to creep in until the figures filled the screen. By the time I recognized Lime, I'd figured out that the dredge was mining the section of the Camafoza pipe exposed by the river. It was just as João had described it.

Lime was talking to someone sitting at a trestle table, back to the camera. The seated person never turned around, but she didn't have to. The camera shot was very tight at the end of the zoom, and in the abundant light the tips of Lily's ears pushed through her coiling hair and straight into my heart.

I watched the clip a few more times, then shaved and took a shower before falling into bed. I had a feeling there wouldn't be time when I got up.

The African sun was burning a hole in the curtains when loud knocking woke me. I opened the door to a young officer with red shoulder boards. He strode by me into the room, followed by a sergeant, snapped the drapes open, and waved his swagger stick at the overnight bag that sat open on a chair.

The sergeant went through it quickly and expertly, making no comment when he found the Škorpion. He snapped out the magazine and stuck it in his belt, found the backup, and took that too. He dropped the disarmed Škorpion back into my bag.

"Please get dressed, Mr. Turner," the officer said. He waited with his back to the window, his feet planted firmly apart and his hands behind him. Clamped beneath his arm, the swagger stick pointed at me like the barrel of a gun. I could feel it drilling a hole in my back as I left the hotel and climbed into the jeep with the blue, white, and black Botswana flag on the fender. The officer got in beside me and we tore off through the city.

The government guest house sat in the middle of a sprawling fifteen-acre park with lawns and towering fan palms. Jackalberry trees shaded the drive that swept through the grounds in a graceful curve. At the mansion's entrance, two airmen in gray fatigues and sidearms stood beside a white Mercedes limousine. I followed the officer through to a veranda at the side of the house.

Matilda Bolt slouched on a sofa and watched me with her yellow eyes. She wore a white cotton sleeveless shirt and black jeans. Her silver sandals matched the nail polish on her toes. She took a puff on a vape and squinted at me through the smoke.

"You don't look so hot."

My legs had swollen again. The doctor had warned they might.

I sank into a wicker chair.

She fanned the smoke away with a lazy flap of her hand. She was doing her best to preserve an appearance of calm, but every screw that held her together had been tightened with a wrench.

"Just so you know, I had nothing to do with that attack on your numbskull boss. But when I heard about it, I did use it to find you and bring you here."

An air force colonel stepped onto the veranda with a clipboard and some papers. She took another drag on the vape, glared at it with loathing, and tossed it on the table. She glanced through the papers, slashed her pen through some lines, and scribbled her initials in a corner.

"I started this conference," she said when he'd gone. "We used to set the agenda. Now we're the country the others whisper about when our backs are turned. I only get the fancy digs," she flicked a bony finger at the house, "because they're still afraid of us."

"They should be."

"As you, unfortunately, are well placed to understand." Her face radiated menace. I kept telling myself not to take it personally, but I wasn't sure it was the right advice.

She told me how Chuck had been followed, because she had people watching the watchers. He'd thrown off his trackers with the maneuver at Newark, but they'd picked him up again in Miami. They were onto him when he boarded the flight from São Paulo to Johannesburg, with connection to the Cape. That told them where I was. They asked the South Africans to grab me and wait for an arrest team. But in Africa the president had no friends. More to the point, no one feared him. They feared Bolt. That's why I was now in Gaborone instead of in a black site somewhere with the lights on 24/7 and my eyes taped open.

Two Botswanan soldiers stood under the nearby palms, their backs to the house as they surveyed the grounds. The US Secret Service detail stood nearby, sweating in their dark suits. A hundred yards away a secretary bird, its long quill-pen feathers trembling on its head, stalked watchfully across the grass.

Bolt gestured to her detail to stay where they were. "Let's walk."

We went down the steps and followed a terracotta path that wound through the sparse trees to a concrete fountain. A trickle of water dribbled from a rusty spout. Sluggish koi drifted through the turbid water.

"You know the story of the diamond as a Russian treasure," she said. "That worked for us. If the pink came from the imperial treasure in the Kremlin, and Harry got it cheap, then we were outsmarting the Russians." She stirred a finger through the water. "Whether the story was true or not didn't matter. Voters liked it." She pushed aside a patch of algae to peer deeper into the dull green water. "But try to change the story and you have a problem. Because now the original story looks like a lie. The people who believed it feel like suckers, which of course they were. So when Harry changes his story, as he now plans to do, I think we have a problem."

"What's the story now?"

"That the stone might have been a recent discovery. He says he just found out, but I think he probably knew all along."

He did. I could hear Davy's gravelly voice. *The Chinese one with the blue eyes.* Honey Li had seen the rough. She'd been there in Antwerp when the stone blew up. According to Davy, the Russians had called it the Chicapa Pink. So they'd known where it came from. If they did, so did Honey, and that meant Nash too.

Bolt's skin was papery and drawn. She looked dessicated. Her yellow eyes shone with anger. "I loathe that diamond. It's the magic mirror that tells them they're the fairest in the land."

It wasn't the diamond she hated. It was Nash and Honey Li.

"If the diamond wasn't stolen," Bolt continued grimly, "and it was a recent discovery, then Harry's purchase from the hedge fund smells. Because why do they give him a deal if the diamond's not stolen? The other investors are Russian oligarchs. They're not people who grant favors without getting something in return."

The secretary bird paused in its hunt and stood stock-still. Its long head-feathers shivered in the breeze. Bolt surveyed the lawn with a bleak expression.

"I need the company charter for First Partners. That's the only record of who controls it. The company is registered in the Channel Islands. That's where the charter is."

"Remind me why I'm going to get it. I must have missed that part."

She gave me an icy stare.

"Because now you know about it."

A dark shape in the grass had caught the secretary bird's attention. For a moment the shadow remained as still as the bird, then slithered a foot, then stopped again.

"If you're worried about authority to act," she said, "call Tommy Cleary."

I have to admit, that hurt. So she owned Tommy too. She knew I wasn't expecting that. She didn't gloat. It was a card turned over at a poker table.

"You think you've got this worked out, but I doubt it, Senator. OK, I'll get the charter. But I cut both ways. I will not find out what helps you and ignore what doesn't. I keep looking until I find out everything, including who killed Amy Curtain and attacked my kid. And when I do, I won't need Tommy Cleary to tell me what to do."

We walked back to the veranda. The secretary bird was locked in concentration on the grass. I could see the snake clearly now. A bright green boomslang, four feet long. A current of air stirred the bird's long feathers, and it drew back its lethal beak. But the snake struck first.

I spent an hour in my room composing a long message to Patrick Ho, and a shorter one to Tommy and DeLucca. Last, I sent a short query to Tabitha asking if she'd turned up anything on Vanderloo.

Gaborone twinkled in the night. A cool evening breeze was blowing off the desert when I joined Chuck and Lily on the roof.

We took a table at the edge of the terrace. A few waiters gossiped at the bar. On a distant hill the red lights of a communications mast winked against the stars.

"Kgale Hill," said Chuck. "They call it the sleeping giant."

Nobody called it that but the tour-bus drivers. In the Tswana language *kgale* means "the place that dried up," although you had to wonder how effectively that distinguished one location from another in a country mostly covered by the Kalahari Desert.

We made plans to leave in the morning, catching the early hopper to Johannesburg. Lily and I would take the Air France flight to Paris and Chuck would return to New York.

While we waited for our food I filled them in on my conversation with Bolt. Chuck had earlier objected to me sharing information with Lily, but had bowed to what he called the "operational exigencies" when I pointed out that Lily knew more about what was going on than he did. As I'd discovered when I saw that clip from the Chicapa, she knew more than I did too.

A puff of desert air stirred Lily's hair. Just looking at her, a sense of loss came over me. I had made her my instrument. Who would I blame if that instrument was now aimed at me?

Our talk turned to Great Pipe.

"The company that owns the deposit," Chuck said, "what would it be worth on the market right now?"

"Pennies a share," I said.

"But if it's just a penny stock," Chuck said, "how does it play into some dark scheme? Say Nash did buy the Russian Pink with the plan in mind to goose the stock of Great Pipe, because that's where it was discovered. If the stock was chump change to begin with, he could double his money and it's still chump change."

I explained how a mineral exploration worked. The odds were long against any venture succeeding. That's why the stocks traded in pennies. Investors tended to buy large blocks. If Nash were in any way involved, he could easily have a million shares, for which he'd paid pennies a share. If suddenly it were announced that the greatest diamond in the world came from that property, the stock could easily go to $100 a share. Say Nash had a million shares for which he'd paid ten cents a share. That hypothetical holding of a million shares would go from its original value of $100,000 to $100 million.

"In a week," I said.

Chuck thought about it for a moment. "So if Nash did own Great Pipe shares, even if it turned out to be through Lime, you could say he had used his celebrity as a presidential candidate to increase the value of the Russian Pink, and in turn drive up the price of Great Pipe stock when the connection was revealed."

"And you'd be right."

The waiters had cleared the table. Chuck waited until Lily left before he spoke.

"It's a fine line we have to walk, Alex. Bolt is certainly manipulating us, and we can't be sure of her end game. If she's recruited Tommy to her cause, who else?"

If you didn't listen carefully you could miss the duplicity that lurked behind Chuck's bone-headed cautions. I had figured Bolt out long ago. She feared Nash, and was determined to understand what game he was playing. Bolt I understood. It was Chuck who had me buffaloed. I'd never mentioned Tommy.

17

The night drive from Paris took five hours in the rain. We hardly spoke.

"You own stock in Great Pipe," I said when we were near the coast.

"There, was that so hard?" she said coldly. "Really, Alex. You sulk like a child."

"It didn't occur to you to tell me? After the meeting with Fonseca?"

"Yes, it occurred to me," she said in the same cold voice. "But common sense prevailed."

A semi blazing with lights hurtled out of the rain and almost blew us off the road.

"You knew I'd find out about the pipe," I said. "And if I could tie the pink to it, you'd make a windfall."

"God, Alex," she shook her head. "Sergei Lime raped me. He brutalized me and tried to ruin me. Any money I can make from him, I will. I didn't even know where we were going until we got to the Chicapa. He wanted my opinion on the rough. I made him pay in stock."

"It's a scam, Lily. Somebody, somehow, is going to get ripped off."

"Diamonds are diamonds!" she shouted. "Somebody always gets ripped off. We polish that away and make them sparkle. Nash and Lime are going to make a lot of money? Fine! So is Lily!"

The storm was still lashing the port when we arrived. We drove down through the gray stone streets of Saint-Malo and parked behind the hotel. Inside, the light from old-fashioned storm lanterns filled the bar with a silky, orange glow. I got us espresso and a small carafe of marc. We took a table by the window.

I drank the espresso and poured us each a shot of marc, a spirit distilled from the dregs of the wine-making process. It's not for everybody, but on a cold, wet night it goes down like a lit fuse.

Lily stared out unseeingly at the driving rain, occupied with her fury.

"Stop fuming," I said irritably. I was tired too. "Let's just execute the plan. It's a good one."

She turned from the window. "It's a risky, stupid, insane plan. The whole point of that island is bank secrecy. That's what it exists for. A plan that involves stealing those secrets and examining accounts connected to a man on his way to becoming the most powerful man in the world—I don't call that a great idea."

She glared at me, tipped another shot of marc into her glass, and tossed it down.

"Too bad," I said harshly, "because here we are. Somebody's yanking us around. They're yanking you and they're yanking me, and while they were warming up they slapped an innocent kid so far out of her world I doubt she'll ever get all the way back."

Lily poured herself another shot. She filled my glass too and wrapped my hand around it, which is when I realized that I was shaking.

"Is it Bolt pulling the strings," I said, "or Nash? I don't know. But I'm going to find out. So we're going over to that island. We're going to steal secrets and spread alarm and dismay. Because guess what. I fucking feel like it."

Fifteen minutes later a woman in a denim jacket came into the bar and looked around. She caught my eye and nodded. Lily and I got up and put on our coats and headed out into the rain.

The big white ferries that run out to the Channel Islands were tied up in their berths waiting for the morning tourists. We followed a stone quay to an anchorage in the oldest part of the harbor, where an eclectic fleet of *bateaux touristiques* heeled before the driving wind. We stopped at an old trawler with a high bow and a rounded wheelhouse topped with a sign that identified the boat as CHANNEL ISLAND CHARTERS.

In the dim light of the wheelhouse the captain stared at his instruments, ignoring us. He had a cigarette in the corner of his mouth and a bottle of clear liquid on the ledge in front of the wheel. I hoped it wasn't marc.

Lily and I crossed onto the heaving boat. The woman untied the lines from the bollards on the quay and leapt on board. The skipper spun the wheel and we motored out of the harbor.

Past the breakwater, the boat met the full force of the gale. The wind charged out of the English Channel, driving six-foot waves. The boat reared and plunged as it struggled through the wild sea.

The 10,000-ton ferries of the Condor line make the crossing from Saint-Malo to Saint Helier in twenty-five minutes, but it took us a couple of hours to beat our way across. A gray pre-dawn light was seeping into the sky when the lights of Jersey twinkled into view. The seas dropped as the skipper brought us into the lee of the island. The harbor appeared, packed with the kind of yachts that have room on the afterdeck for the owner's helicopter.

In its secret bank accounts, the island of Jersey holds more wealth than some of the first-world countries nearby. Trillions of dollars flow through Jersey's opaque financial structure. A dependency of the British crown, but not part of the United Kingdom, the island is a tax haven.

A winking blue light appeared to port. The captain throttled back and docked at a concrete jetty. I arranged for him to take us off again at eleven. If we weren't through by then, we'd be in jail.

Lily and I climbed into a blue Vauxhall idling on the road.

"Jolly good," the driver said when we got in, an idiotic phrase, even for a recognition code.

"You say the target documents are in Lime's name?" said Lily.

"Yes. The Russians left him as front man. He was the figure known to investors and the banking people."

The Vauxhall whisked us up a hill to a sprawling old inn. The gale was blowing itself out at last, and a shaft of dawn light caught the white gables on the front of the hotel.

"Eight forty-five," I told the driver, and we went inside.

The large parcel from DeLucca was waiting at the desk. We checked in and went upstairs. They'd given us a corner room with big sash windows looking across the strait to the coast of France. Lily disappeared into the bathroom and shut the door. I called down to the desk for an iron and ironing board, unpacked the parcel, and spent half an hour taking every crease out of the charcoal gray suit and the pale blue dress shirt. I used the steamer to take the wrinkles out of a dark silk tie.

I went through the laborious procedures for logging into the darknet mailbox set up by Patrick Ho. There was one message from him, with the alphanumeric formula I'd asked for. He'd hacked into Lime's laptop and logged the keystrokes when Lime accessed accounts. The code changed every day, and Patrick had cracked the date-based formula that changed it.

An hour after Lily went into the bathroom she came out again, this time as an ash-blonde killer in a black Balenciaga dress that stopped just above the knees. I'd been with her when she bought that dress in Paris.

She was wearing contacts that made her eyes look bloodshot. When it came time to depose witnesses to the crime that we were planning to commit, all they'd remember about Lily would be those bloodshot eyes. And maybe the diamond ring—a twenty-carat, top-color white in an emerald cut. When your associates are diamond thieves, you can afford the best.

She sat down at a desk by the windows. I snapped open the tiny plastic case that DeLucca had included, found the tweezers, and spent the next ten minutes carefully applying Lime's prints to Lily's fingers. Even in a strong light it would be impossible to detect the synthetic skin that carried the prints.

The driver dropped us two blocks from our destination. I told him where to wait for us.

Like a lot of other tourist destinations, Saint Helier's small downtown was crammed with the things that day-trippers like to buy—alcohol, T-shirts, and the lethal sweets that conduct a war of attrition on British teeth. But the people who bring the real business to the Channel Islands don't come over on the French ferries or the hydrofoil from Dover. They arrive in private jets that make the flight from London in twenty-five minutes. There are no T-shirts for sale in the buildings that house the bankers, lawyers, and accountants these people come to see.

The Channel Islands Directorate of Companies is located in a four-story glass-and-steel office block. Within fifteen minutes of entering we were sitting in front of a portly man in a navy chalk-stripe suit. He wore a gold signet ring on his right pinkie, the finger he was now running through one document after another. He kept shooting covert glances at Lily's spectacularly bloodshot eyes.

"Most irregular," he would murmur every sixty seconds, in case we'd forgotten he'd just said it. But he was a civil servant, and a civil servant loves a piece of paper. To the rest of the world it is a tiresome document; to him, a pearl to be threaded lovingly onto the necklace of plausibility we needed him to accept. The forger in Paris had done well: company minutes on the letterhead of First Partners. A letter from a Wall Street law firm introducing me as Lily's attorney. Notarized copy of Mrs. Nina Lime's power of attorney to act for her husband. That one carried the bright red wax seal of a notary "in and for the City of London, by Royal Authority duly appointed," as it said in huge gothic capitals across the top. The pinkie with the gold ring caressed the seal with particular affection.

"Most irregular," he murmured again, but you could see that he was in a rapture over the stack of documents.

He nodded and peered at me once more through his rimless spectacles. "And you are Mister . . ."

"Griffon," I said, sliding across the engraved card that identified me as a managing partner in the law firm Ames, Ames, Lowenthal, and Griffon, whose letter he already had.

"Ah, yes," he said, inspecting the card and then clipping it to the impressive pile with a satisfied flourish, as if he had just squeezed a final dab of icing onto the decoration of a splendid cake. He cocked his head at the paperwork, then looked at me.

"Still," he said, "strange that we didn't have your name in the file."

"Most irregular," I said.

The rest went quickly. He buzzed for his secretary. The young man came through the door carrying a small black device with a keypad. The code was the crucial, final step to access the records we wanted to inspect. Lily punched it in. The man took the device back, entered a code of his own, waited for a number to appear, and scribbled it in a log beside the date.

He opened the top drawer of his desk, took out a thin, purple file stamped in gold with the crest of the Channel Islands, and placed it in front of Lily. She opened it. We were sitting side by side, and bent over the contents as if we knew what we would find there and were only verifying it for the legal purposes that our documents stipulated.

At first glance it was a straightforward corporate document. The charter for First Partners gave its incorporation date in Jersey, followed by a dozen paragraphs of legal boilerplate that described the company's business. An addendum showed the redistribution of Lime's original block of shares when he'd been forced to divest. That's the point when Nash bought into the fund. Oligarchs took most of what Lime had owned, Nash a smaller chunk, and Lime retained a sliver.

But then I noticed a second addendum. Dated the same day Nash bought in. It was only a single page, but my amazement deepened as I read. In a few terse paragraphs it established a trading committee of the board with the sole and unrestricted right to buy and sell assets for the fund.

The trading committee's decisions were not reviewable by the board. That was surprising enough. But even more astounding was the degree of independence the committee had. The board could not dismiss or replace committee members without the consent of the committee itself. It was the supreme government of one of the richest asset pools on earth, and it had only two members.

Nash and Lime.

Stunned, I read it again.

Nash would have the real control. That meant he'd sold the diamond to himself, and probably authorized its purchase too. Only Nash had the financial star power to extract that kind of deal from the oligarchs. Only

Nash could deliver the payback they'd have wanted in return. A paycheck presumably to be cashed when he won the presidency.

I scanned the pages with my phone and returned the file.

❖

"That trading committee," I said when we got to the street. "Why would the large shareholders ever agree to such an arrangement?"

"I've heard of such structures in Russia," Lily said. "It lets the oligarchs pack the board with respectable names without the risk that they will actually try to run the company."

"But Lime got the fund listed in London. The British would never allow such an arrangement."

"They wouldn't know about it," Lily said. "They wouldn't have been shown the addendum that makes the trading committee independent. They'd assume the committee was controlled by the board."

"And the large shareholders," I said, because I understood it now, "they'd know Nash wouldn't cheat them."

"Exactly. They're not men that people cheat."

"And Lime is just the signature Nash hides behind."

❖

The second part of our operation would be trickier than the first. Men guard money more carefully then documents.

"The bank is going to find it strange when we show up in person," Lily said.

"They launder money for a living, Lily. Their clients are gangsters and oligarchs and hedge fund billionaires. I doubt there's very much that they find strange. It's a numbered account. Neither Nash nor Lime have ever set foot on the island. Their fingerprints were digitally scanned. The protocol requires only one set of prints for access."

"But I am manifestly *not* Sergei Lime."

"We're not saying you are. You're his wife. The fingerprints and the code are all we need. The bank is required to give access to a person with those fingerprints and the right code."

"And they have never met Lime."

"Lily, it wouldn't matter. We're not saying you're Lime."

Five minutes after leaving the registry we turned onto Bath Street, a pedestrian mall lined with identical nineteenth-century houses. I found a luggage store and bought a small, wheeled suitcase.

"In case we need it for documents," I said, in reply to Lily's questioning look.

Only a small brass plaque with a single word identified the Canning Bank, but that one word said everything the people who worked behind the lacquered black door wanted you to know: PRIVATE.

I pressed the bell.

The door was opened by an ancient, shrunken man with skin like parchment. He wore striped trousers and a black tailcoat and shuffled ahead of us across the worn slate tiles to a door that had been paneled to match the oak wainscoting of the entrance hall. He pressed a plastic card to a panel. The door flew open to reveal a twenty-first century interior humming with the quiet, well-oiled sense of urgency that rich people like to see in those who handle their money. A brisk young woman with black-framed glasses that made her look like an owl took my card and disappeared. She was back in a moment, and ushered us into a small conference room. A tall, fair-haired man in his forties was waiting to show us what a distant smile looked like.

"Mr. Griffon," he said, very smoothly for a man who hadn't known until that second that such a person existed and was struggling to master himself at the sight of Lily's bloodred eyes. He gave us another glimpse of small, even teeth.

"Giles Canning," he put out his slender hand. Lily ignored it and muttered something in Russian. Canning darted his eyes at me. "What can I do for you, Mister, er," he checked my card again, "Griffon."

He had a high forehead as smooth as a pressed white handkerchief. It didn't look as if a wrinkle had ever strayed across it.

He pulled out a chair and held it for Lily. I sat down beside her, and Giles Canning slid in behind his silver MacBook.

"We're here to inspect the accounts held under nominee Sergei Lime. My client, Mrs. Nina Lime, is his proxy and code holder. The fingerprints you have on file are hers," I told him. "We took the opportunity because my client was here anyway on other banking business."

Other banking business had been Tommy's idea. "Make sure that's the first thing you say," he'd insisted on the phone when I'd talked to him from Gaborone. "It's the only thing they really care about—that you might take your dirty cash somewhere else to clean it. Once you say that, he won't be able to think about anything else."

"I see," said Canning, his fingers chattering briefly at the keyboard.

Owl Glasses sprinted in with a tray. On it were three Wedgwood demitasses of espresso. She dealt them out as smartly as a dealer at a blackjack table.

"We also need to make a withdrawal of $5 million," I said.

"I see," said Canning again. His face remained unruffled, as did Lily's, so good for them. They were both hearing about it for the first time.

Canning looked intently at the screen and then at me, confirming that I matched the photo of J. P. Griffon III that Patrick Ho had uploaded onto the law firm's website when he hacked into it at exactly 10:00 A.M. Jersey time.

A good con depends on providing the mark with distractions that make it harder for him to focus on the essential bullshit, which in this case was that someone would walk in off the street and demand to inspect accounts so secret that whoever owned them had set them up at great expense in a jurisdiction whose sole business was providing that secrecy. Part of the distraction we provided was Lily's appearance, her fabulous dress and frightening eyes. And the ring. It was spraying high-priced photons around like machine-gun fire.

"I'm not quite sure I understand," Canning said. "You can review all the accounts online."

"My client needs to have the actual bank ledger entries, not the simplified version you provide online. She needs to see the full details of the sending and receiving entities for every transfer."

"I see," said Canning, leaning back and tapping a pencil against his teeth. He would assume that we suspected malfeasance by some of our associates, a reasonable suspicion for clients of super-secret banks. That by itself would make us more credible.

On Canning's side, he had time. We did not, as I learned when I unscrambled a coded text from Patrick Ho. The civil servant at the registry office must have tipped First Partners that the charters had been viewed. Patrick reported that a Gulfstream registered to First Partners had left London at 9:55 A.M. It was now 10:20. Assuming a flight time of thirty-five minutes from London to Jersey, and another half hour to clear immigration and get from the airport to Saint Helier, we had forty minutes to get what we needed.

No doubt First Partners had been calling the bank too. But the bank's phones, including Canning's own cell phone, had all been routed to a recording that apologized for the temporary technical problems, and asked the caller to try again later.

"We're ready to proceed immediately," I said sharply.

"Of course," said Canning. "I'll have the check drawn up."

"Cash," I said.

"Cash?" said Canning. "You must be joking. Banks don't keep that kind of cash around. I'm sure a man such as yourself, Mr. Griffon," he smiled smoothly, "is well aware of that."

"Look," I said, in the tone of a man just able to restrain himself, "you are not most banks. I happen to know something about your business. Very large sums of cash go in and out of here every day, and $5 million is a long way from a very large sum."

I knew zero about his business, but if people like Nash and Lime were customers he was rinsing cash nonstop.

Lily threw up her hands and erupted in a stream of Russian. I gave Canning a severe look and glanced at my watch. That Gulfstream from London would be landing now.

"We're ready to proceed with the verification protocols," I said.

Canning made the helpless gesture of a man who has tried to do the right thing, and having tried, was ready to let it go. He pressed a button and said, "Miss Frith."

The door opened instantly.

"Please bring in the verification kit," Canning said.

"And the cash and the accounts," I reminded him.

The assistant paused in the doorway. Canning waved her away. He leaned back and tapped his teeth with the pencil. I guess that's what it was there for. "Let's stay with the formalities for a moment, shall we?"

"No problem," I said. "But I'm a lawyer, so it's my job to anticipate problems. We're all grown-ups here, Mr. Canning. We both understand that unusual banking arrangements are part of modern life." I drew a folded page from the inside breast pocket of my jacket and flattened it on the table. I turned it so Canning could read it himself. He stopped tapping his teeth and leaned forward. It was the most recent statement of the Canning family's very private bank account in the Cayman Islands, an account unknown to the tax authorities in London, where the Cannings' holding company was headquartered.

Canning flushed with anger. "You're threatening me."

"You can keep that," I said. "I have copies."

His assistant returned with a black numeric pad identical to the one we'd used earlier. She also brought a glass-topped device with fingertips outlined in phosphorescent green. She plugged it into a USB port and handed it to Canning.

"Please print out three months of statements for First Partners," he snapped at her, "and tell the vault to prepare $5 million in cash. What denominations?" he asked.

"Hundreds," I said. "Put it in a plain canvas bag."

I checked my watch. The plane had landed ten minutes ago. They would be clearing immigration. We had twenty minutes left.

Lily made the most of the diamond ring while she placed her fingertips one after the other against the glass. She made sure she twisted her hand this way and that, as if to find exactly the right angle for the fingertip. Canning was used to rich people, but twenty carats still packed a punch. Owl Glasses gaped. The diamond blazed, and the fingerprint device made little beeps as it accepted each successive print. Lily made the last impression with her right index finger, and as she pulled her finger back, I noticed that the print was hanging to her finger by an edge. I reached forward and grabbed her fingers. Lily yanked her hand back reflexively and stared at me. I gripped her fingers tightly and tried to come up with an expression suitable to a lawyer reassuring his client while I stripped off the hanging print and stuck it in my pocket.

When the print check was complete we went through the same code-number protocol we'd performed at the registry. The passing seconds boomed inside my head like a drum. First Lily entered the series of digits. Then Canning punched in his own checking code and waited for the apparatus to generate the authorization. When it did, he handed the gadget to the girl.

"When the cash is ready, take the slip to Fellowes for counter-signature, then bring it back to me."

"Fellowes?" I said.

"We need two directors to authorize large cash withdrawals."

Lily shot to her feet and stormed around the small room, delivering a storm of Slavic abuse. Bloodred eyes, heart-stopping Balenciaga dress, twenty-carat bling. As a performance it was over the top. But I had stolen another peek at my watch: ten minutes to go. Lily could leap onto the table and do a Cossack leg-kick for all I cared if it would hurry things along.

Canning's assistant appeared in the door with a look I didn't like.

"Mr. Fellowes says he will need to review the account," she said, her voice a whisper.

"Nyet!" Lily slammed her fist on the table. *"Nyet, nyet, nyet!"*

This time Canning looked genuinely rattled. "Let me see to this," he said, closing the door behind him when he left the room. The assistant looked as if the steel gate to the lion cage had just clanged shut with her on the wrong side.

"Those account copies," I told her. "Make sure they are the ledger entries showing all the banking details of wires in and out. We need them now."

She sat at the laptop and typed in a few lines of instructions, and in a moment a printer in the corner began to spit out pages. She handed them to me as they came out. Lily scanned them too. After all, it was supposed to be her husband's money.

I found what I was looking for, monthly transfers to a bank account in Sag Harbor, a town in eastern Long Island.

The assistant handed me the last page just as Canning returned with an elderly man in a black suit and silver tie. He had piercing blue eyes that glittered through his bushy eyebrows.

"Most irregular," he muttered, sitting down and taking out a gold-nibbed fountain pen.

"So I keep hearing," I said in a firm voice, "but sudden unusual trans-actions are an important part of your business, I believe. Those fees you collect must be for something."

"No need to shout," he said. "It's you we are trying to protect."

Canning laid a few sheets of paper on the table in front of the older man. The bony fingers placed the gold nib beside the figure and put a tick beside it. I didn't dare look at my watch. We had less than five minutes to get out of the bank.

I must have made an impatient gesture. The old man raised his head and fixed me with a look of pure malice. He smelled a rat. But the nature of his business gave him no alternative. The very features used to secure his clients' money compelled him to give it to us.

He paused for a moment. I wondered if he might refuse to sign. But finally he drew a breath, shook his head, and scratched his initials on the form beside Canning's. I waited while Canning examined the slip one last time. He pressed a button and a porter came in with the money. We transferred it to the suitcase. The partners stood stiffly by the door as we went out. Lily swept by them without a glance.

The black lacquer door had just thudded shut behind us when I saw them. Three gorillas in good suits headed for the bank with purposeful expressions. Poor Canning.

I steered Lily into the first side street.

It was just starting to rain again. The driver with the Vauxhall was waiting where I'd told him to. Lily and I got into the back.

"Jolly good," he said, and tore away.

"You didn't say anything about stealing $5 million cash in broad daylight," she hissed furiously as soon as we were on our way.

"No."

"And what are we supposed to do with it?" she demanded.

"I guess it'll have to be handled by the one of us who already has a banker in Luxembourg who lets her in the side door after hours to make large cash deposits."

That shut her up. She'd thought that was one I didn't know about.

We were just turning onto the road that led down to the jetty when a Land Rover painted in the yellow-and-green checker pattern of the police went speeding by with its blue light flashing.

The woman in the denim jacket stood on the jetty watching us as we pulled up. She didn't look any more like a deckhand now than she had before. That denim jacket had come out of a Paris boutique. Otherwise it might have done a better job of concealing the shoulder holster. A contact of mine in French intelligence had arranged the charter, and I guess he was not going to let the story write itself without finding out how it ended.

At the jetty I handed the driver a brown envelope. This time he didn't say anything. He was in a hurry too.

As soon as we set foot on deck the boat chugged away from the jetty, swung its bow at France, and began to wallow eastward through the chop. The rain picked up.

A squall came ripping off the Channel. The rain flattened into horizontal sheets and rattled like hail. I couldn't see the port of Saint Helier, but that's where the next siren came from. It started as a low wail and rose to a scream. The sound carried through the wind, piercing the storm. The coast of France lay dead ahead, a gray mass taking shape across the thrashing sea, and still, through the tumult, that tormented sound rose and fell like a soul in anguish.

I checked my email. One from Tabitha. I opened it, and the tiny dust mote of self-congratulation that I was clutching, the fool's prize, blew away on the wind. The awful desolation of the siren filled every crevice of my heart. The department's techs had found a picture from Amy Curtain's phone that she'd sent to a site in the cloud. Shot inside a bar. They'd had to run it through their enhancing software, but there was no mistaking him among the background figures, standing next to Lime, in the same beige turtleneck, his hair parted neatly on the left, his calm face looking straight at Amy Curtain. The new man in Pierrette's life, and inescapably in Annie's too. Tim Vanderloo.

18

I gripped the phone in my hands and stared at the screen as Lily drove. The cell-phone signal struggled to get past a single bar. Twice I started to enter the ponderous security protocols, only to lose the connection. At last I got through to DeLucca.

"Do you know if he's there right now?" he asked when I told him about Vanderloo.

"No. And if I call Pierrette, and he's there, he'll be alert to her behavior."

"I agree. He'd know he was the subject of the call. What about your guy Treacher, the heavy you posted at the house?"

"Augie is supposed to text me if anything happens."

"But Vanderloo would know about him, right? He knows he's there, because your ex knows."

"We have to assume that if Vanderloo's there he's probably taken Augie out. I think I have to show up in person. I'm who Vanderloo's after, and at least I'd have an element of surprise."

"I'll get a special unit ready to go immediately. Call me when you land."

I was losing coverage, so I texted Tommy my flight number and left it at that.

Lily dropped me at the airport. She would drive on to Luxembourg. We made arrangements to contact each other later. When I opened the door she put her hand on my arm.

"Alex."

"I know, Lily."

I got out and shut the door and hurried inside.

As soon as we touched down at Kennedy, I tried DeLucca. The special number wouldn't go through. I tried again three times as we taxied in. I felt as if a balloon were expanding inside my chest, making it hard to breathe. At the gate, I charged up the jetway and ran the length of the terminal. When I inserted my passport in the slot at the automated kiosk, it didn't clear. The screen directed me to report to immigration.

They were waiting for me. A border agent with sergeant's stripes and a face pitted with acne scars pointed to a booth at the end of the row. The officer in the booth swiped my passport and flipped slowly through the pages.

"What was the nature of your business?"

"Holiday."

"Is that so?" It didn't sound like a question so I didn't answer.

"And what's your work?" He held my passport at arm's length so he could compare the picture on the ID page with my face.

"I work for the government," I said.

"Uh-huh. Can you tell me a little more about that?"

"No," I said.

He shot a smug look at the sergeant lolling nearby, and closed my passport.

"Then I'm afraid this is going to have to go to secondary interview," he said.

Keep your temper, I told myself. Do not yell. Do not get crazy. I leaned forward to the glass so I could read his name tag.

"Agent Trottier," I said. "It would be unlawful for me to tell you anything about my work. You already know that. My security grade came up when you swiped the passport. So please understand, because I'm in a hurry: If you delay me in any way, the people who asked you to do it won't be able to protect you from what happens next."

He tried to outstare me. That was never going to happen. He slid his eyes to the sergeant, who decided that whoever was behind this wasn't worth a disciplinary hearing. He shrugged and jerked his head to let me through.

The red tail fins of the Caddy blazed in the middle of the taxi pickup lane. Anybody else, the tow truck has a hook on that car and it's on its way to the pound before you have it in park. Tommy's car was surrounded by cops and nobody was writing a ticket. They were all standing there grinning and nodding their heads while Tommy waved his hands around and banged his fist into his palm and described the intricacies of some past glory involving a running back who had scored a touchdown by getting past Tommy, and then tried it again.

I tossed my bag in the back seat and climbed in, and my terror climbed in with me.

"So this time," Tommy told the cops, "not so lucky."

"Tommy," I said.

He waved a hand at me.

"This time," he said to his eager audience, "this time I deke his blocker and so help me God I nail that kid. Maybe there was some of my helmet in the hit. In those days a helmet hit was OK. Hey, it's what we did. You remember that kid?"

They remembered him.

Tommy heaved a sigh and spread his hands wide—a man surrendering to the judgment of history.

"Tommy," I repeated. He picked up on the tone of my voice and looked at me.

"What can I say?" he said to the cops as he started the car. "Nothing personal. It's how we played the game of football."

"You was never any dirtier than you had to be, killer," an older cop said to a murmur of assent.

Tommy's powder-blue rayon shirt rippled as we roared out into the exit lanes, scattering yellow cabs. We cleared the airport and got onto the Van Wyck. I made a gesture, and Tommy put the roof up.

"DeLucca didn't get hold of you?" I said.

"No. Why?"

"That guy at the meeting in Washington, the one the chair didn't introduce. That FinCEN lawyer told you he was probably MI. Is it this guy?"

I showed him the picture of Vanderloo on my phone.

"That's him." He shot me a sideways glance. "Spell it out. Who is he?

"Tim Vanderloo."

"The guy who's been hanging around Pierrette?"

"And who probably killed Amy Curtain. And who might be inside the ring of security that's supposed to be protecting Annie and Pierrette."

Tommy looked stunned. "But is he there? Have you called?"

"Too risky. Pierrette would give it away. If Vanderloo was there when I called, he'd know what was up just by watching her face. Now I can't reach DeLucca. We can't wait. I have to go there now. Tuxedo Park."

"Call Chuck," Tommy said, putting his flashers on and launching the Caddy up the left-hand lane. "We have to know what's going on. He can

find out. There's an NYPD default contact if we can't reach DeLucca."
We hit heavy traffic.

"In the glove box," Tommy barked. "There's a blue strobe." I handed
it to him and he stuck it on the dash, cutting into the breakdown lane
and shooting by the bottleneck. We were going eighty when he realized
I hadn't called Chuck. He was reaching for his phone when I grabbed it
from the bracket and tossed it into the back seat.

"What are you doing?"

"Let's just say I want to preserve the cone of silence until I understand
who knows what."

His face turned red. "Is that how it is? I'm a bad guy now?"

"Maybe you can throw some light on things," I said, my fear taking the
easy road into anger. "You're the guy who's been having all the secret meet-
ings in DC. Now I hear that you're Bolt's go-to guy. Why is that? Please tell
me what it is you bring to the table. It's not like they don't have lawyers."

We crossed the East River on the Throgs Neck Bridge and blew onto
the Cross Bronx Expressway at ninety. Five minutes later we hit the tailback.

The expressway was barely moving. Tommy fought his way across five
lanes to an exit. He picked his way up to Tremont Avenue and headed
west to the Major Deegan Expressway.

You could measure Tommy's anger by how long it took him to reply.
His basic armament included a full clip of withering repartee. When he
was really mad, he was not so quick on the trigger.

We found a ramp to the Major Deegan and headed north up the
Harlem River.

"This is what you carry with you, Alex. Suspicion and mistrust. You
against the world. You had a rotten hand dealt to you when you were
a kid, so the whole game's phony and you're the only one who knows."

The Major Deegan fed into the I-87. The thruway took a big loop
through Westchester and crossed the Hudson at the Tappan Zee Bridge.

"Are you working for Bolt?" I said.

"It's not that simple."

"You can bet on that, Tommy."

"I'm not sure you understand how bad things are in Washington."

"I would rather eat broken glass than hear that one more time, Tommy. I don't care if the president and Nash are in a bidding war with the Russians for help with their Facebook ads. At the moment, a killer who's already murdered an agent may be holding Pierrette and Annie."

Tommy had been going ninety since we'd left the bridge. We were now at the Sloatsburg exit. We got off and merged into the slow-moving traffic on the state road.

"That was your cue to tell me if there's anything you know that could tell me something about Vanderloo. If you think I can be trusted with how bad things are in Washington."

He'd gotten way past his comfort zone. I could hear it in his voice when he answered.

"I don't know anything for sure. There are these zealots at the White House. Maybe military intelligence, but that's a guess. They believe the president could destroy Nash if only the truth about Nash's dealings with the Russians came out."

"Why would that make anybody come after me?" I said, pressing the speed dial for Chuck. "I'm the one investigating Nash. Isn't that what they want?"

Chuck picked up right away.

"Where are you?" he said, his voice tight.

"Almost at Tuxedo Park. What's going on?"

"There's been some kind of incident there. DeLucca went onto the property and hasn't come back out. The NYPD can't raise him. State police have set up a cordon and are bringing in an armored track vehicle."

"What?" I shouted. "Are they out of their fucking minds? Chuck. Get a grip. Call them and order them to hold off until I get there. Tell them you have two senior Treasury officers with special authority on the way. Tell them whatever you want! Just stop them. We'll be there in . . ." I glanced at Tommy.

"Fifteen minutes," he said.

"You copy that?"

"I'm calling them now," Chuck said.

A mile from the gatehouse we hit the roadblock. Two cruisers blocked the road and four more were pulled up on the shoulder. A squad of troopers in full tac were scrambling out of a bus. A tall man in a gray uniform with a colonel's insignia on the collar strolled up when we stopped.

"You Turner?"

I showed him my ID.

"I got the village cop here," he said, nodding at a kid in uniform.

It didn't take long to get the story. Vanderloo was on the list of permitted visitors. Pierrette had put him there. The Tuxedo Park cops knew him anyway. You wouldn't easily forget that car. They'd waved him through.

When the kid was making his regular evening check of the house, Vanderloo came out on the veranda with Annie and told him everything was OK. The cop asked if he could come in and see Pierrette, because the protocol called for him to visually check. Vanderloo told him no, she wasn't feeling well. Annie just stood there staring. She looked as if she'd been crying. When the young cop got back to the gate he described the incident to the sergeant in charge of the state police detail. They called DeLucca. DeLucca had been assembling a special team, but when he learned Vanderloo was already inside, he decided to drive out immediately, ordering the team leader to follow as soon as he could.

"DeLucca went straight in," the colonel said. "Last message, he was approaching the house. Nothing since then." He checked his watch. "That was ninety minutes ago, and I got here soon after. Now, I've got my perimeter established. I was ready to go in and see what's up. Then the brass called. Said they had to check with the army, on account of this guy who's in there, he's a colonel, and could be on assignment. Then I get another order: wait for you."

"I have to go in," I said. "It's me he's waiting for."

He took a deep breath and let it out slowly. He jerked his head at the roadblock and one of the cruisers eased back out of the way.

"Thirty minutes," he said. "This is above my pay grade, but after thirty minutes, it's not. I'm coming in."

The gatehouse had been abandoned when the state police pulled back to set up their perimeter outside the village boundary. I wanted to check the surveillance system. One of the jobs of the village police is to make sure that once visitors are in, they only go where they're supposed to. I sat at the desk with the monitors, found the camera trained on the house, and toggled in for a closer look.

At the end of the driveway was DeLucca's car with the driver's door open. Vanderloo's E-Type was pulled up in front of the steps. I zoomed into the screen door. I could see right through it to the stairs on the other side of the front hall.

I panned along the front of the house, selected another camera angle, and checked the side. The curtains were drawn on Annie's bedroom window. Those curtains were never closed in the daytime. If Vanderloo was holding Annie and Pierrette, that's where he had them.

But where was DeLucca?

I got up and checked out the office. Clipped to the side of a desk was a twelve-gauge, pump-action Remington. It was the model they call "tactical," because it holds six rounds. I yanked it from the clips, found a box of shells, loaded it, and handed it to Tommy.

"What am I supposed to do with this?" he said.

"See the end with the hole in it?" said a voice behind us. I whirled to see DeLucca leaning in the door. "That's the part you point at the bad guy," he said.

He looked bad. His face was pale. One arm hung uselessly at his side. His hair was full of twigs and his coat stained with mud. He tottered backward. I grabbed him and we pulled him inside.

I stripped off his coat and looked at his bloody arm. I found the medical kit. The property owners of Tuxedo Park hadn't skimped on their cops' supplies. The white tin box with the red cross contained a US Army field-grade medic's kit. I scanned the contents.

"Pop these," I said, tearing open a white paper packet that contained two morphine pills. I shook them out in his hand.

I cleaned the wound with swabs and bandaged it as well as I could while he told me what had happened.

He'd driven to the house as soon as he arrived, put his gold badge on the front of his coat, and was heading for the front steps when a kid in fatigues stepped onto the veranda with a Heckler & Koch MP5 submachine gun and fired a burst. DeLucca threw himself on the ground and got off three quick shots. The kid popped back inside to take cover, but jumped out and fired again when DeLucca scrambled for the side of the house. A round caught him in the arm. He got around the corner and made it to the woods.

"No sign of Augie?"

"I'm sorry, Alex."

We decided that DeLucca would go back through the woods and get in position behind the house to provide a diversion. We opened the arms locker. They had everything in there: flares and riot guns and even bear bangers, a sort of heavy-duty firecracker that's supposed to send bears running for their lives.

"Hey," DeLucca said, lifting out an anti-tank gun. It was already loaded. "This is stuff they get from the military when it's out of date."

"Do you know how to use it?"

"I'm thinking you pull that trigger-shaped thing."

I found an Uzi and shoved it into my belt, added a Walther PPK. I gave DeLucca a ten-minute head start. The sight of him heading unsteadily into the trees dragging that cannon didn't fill me with confidence.

Tommy and I came slowly down the road from the gatehouse. The idea was: Give him lots of time to watch us come. No surprises. We had the roof down. I wanted Vanderloo to think he could see everything there was to see. If you hope to do the trick with the rabbit, keep everybody looking at the hat.

As soon as we arrived, the door to the balcony above the porch opened, and Vanderloo and Annie came out. Except for the pistol in his hand, he looked like he did the last time I'd seen him. Cords, sweater, bland expression, not a hair out of place. Good look for a psychopathic killer.

Annie was wearing her old white cowboy boots with the silver stars, but even with the extra height the heels gave her she seemed shrunken. Her face was white and her eyes bright with terror, and her mouth was quivering. I decided not to say anything to her. If she broke down or became hysterical, Vanderloo would lose some of the control I wanted him to feel he had.

"Unbutton the jacket," he called.

I waited a moment, as if reluctant, then shrugged and did as he asked. I tossed the Uzi on the grass and held my arms out wide.

"Take the jacket off and turn around."

I paused again, then slipped off my coat and turned. The Walther was tucked in the small of my back, muzzle in the belt. I pulled it out and dropped it.

"Pants," he called.

I lifted up the bottoms to show I had no ankle holster.

"You," he called to Tommy. "Drive away. Do it now."

I'd never seen Tommy look so helpless. He stared up at Annie, his face a picture of anguish. There were tears of shame in his eyes as he turned the car around. The red tail fins drifted up the road and disappeared into the trees.

Vanderloo waggled the pistol.

"Take it slowly." At least he sounded calm.

When I entered the house, the young guy with the Heckler & Koch was standing at the top of the stairs. The muzzle tracked me all the way up. He gestured with the gun and I crossed the hall and went into Annie's room.

Vanderloo stood on the far side, by the balcony door, muttering a phrase into his phone. He finished and slipped it in his pocket.

The double doors were open now, showing the view right down to the lake. Vanderloo's pistol was what the military calls an M11. Thirteen rounds in the clip, nine-millimeter parabellum. A stopper. And something else I didn't like. He was wearing latex gloves.

Pierrette sat in a chair, her wrists handcuffed to the arms. I'd expected her to be frightened, but the look on her face was hatred. Her eyes were molten with rage. I'd seen Pierrette angry, but the face that stared at Vanderloo brimmed with murderous fury. He had a mark on his face—a deep scratch that raked across one eye.

Pierrette's wrists bled from her attempts to wrench her hands free. Annie stood behind her, trembling.

"Sit there," Vanderloo said, pointing his gun at the chair beside Pierrette.

"This isn't the way it was supposed to go, was it," I said. "When you planned it, this wasn't the ending."

He tossed a silver key onto the floor near Annie. "Cuff them together."

Annie picked up the key and started to sob. She had no tears left, just big, dry gasps that shook her whole body.

"It's OK, Annie," I said, but Pierrette gritted her teeth.

"Annabel," she said harshly, her eyes fixed on Vanderloo. "Do not cry in front of this person."

Annie unclipped one bracelet from Pierrette and snapped it onto me. The metal clamped the cuff of my shirt tightly to my wrist. I wasn't sure how that would affect the bear banger taped to my forearm.

I studied Vanderloo's face. A killer has a picture of himself. What was it?

"There are better ways to fight this war," I said, betting that's how he'd see himself. "Keep me. I'm a combatant. Let Pierrette and Annie go. I'll give you whatever I know, and that's a lot. Don't dishonor yourself."

His lip curled as he watched me.

"Don't talk to me about honor. That's not a virtue you care about. It's out of fashion. This country's lost that. It needs a leader with spine."

"And you think it's got one."

He frowned. "Got one?" he repeated. "You mean the president?" The idea seemed to stun him. "Are you out of your mind?" His mouth drew down in disgust. "You think that a soldier of the United States, sworn to protect the constitution with his *life*, would support that man?" He glared at me. "I don't understand you, Turner. How could you be so clueless?"

I was wondering the same thing myself. If he hadn't been trying to protect the president, what was he doing? Vanderloo read my confusion.

"The president's a traitor. He's made us weak. We're a laughingstock in the world." Each outrage seemed to cause him pain. "A laughingstock. He made us that."

"So you support Nash?" I must have looked stunned.

"Of course we support Nash!" he spat. "He's fearless. He acts. He doesn't let enemies stand in his way. He wore his country's uniform."

His country's uniform. I heard Tommy's words. *Zealots at the White House. Maybe military intelligence.* So that was true. Except they weren't trying to protect the president. They were protecting Nash. That's why he'd killed Amy Curtain. Now he would protect Nash again. From me. What could I say to gain time?

"Is this the right way to make Nash look good? Nobody's going to shed tears for me, but killing a mother and daughter? For a politician?"

"For a country," he said. "And I'm not killing anybody. He is."

He already had his pistol out, so it was easy to drop the kid with the HK. The bullet hit him in the neck. A nine-millimeter slug at that range: his head was hanging by a tangle of sinews as the body slid to the floor. Annie began to gasp as if she couldn't breathe. Pierrette stared in horror.

Vanderloo stepped across the room and picked up the machine gun.

And finally the penny dropped.

The latex gloves meant the only fingerprints on the Heckler would be the dead man's. Vanderloo would make it look like the kid had shot the three of us, and then he'd shot the kid.

Where was DeLucca? Where were the state troopers?

Then I heard the sound Vanderloo was waiting for. The slap, slap, slap of helicopter blades echoed in the hills. He checked his watch again then looked straight at me. He would wait until he knew for sure it was his pickup. Everyone in the room was concentrated on the sound. That's why we heard the other noise so clearly.

From just behind the paneling. The sound of a floorboard moving against a hundred-year-old nail.

Vanderloo's eyes snapped to the wall. He stared at the paneling. But he wasn't sure what he'd heard and didn't fire immediately into the wall, which he should have, because here's what happened next.

The helicopter popped into view above the hill on the other side of the lake. The clatter of the rotors rose to a roar.

Vanderloo took a step through the door and onto the terrace to signal the fast-approaching chopper. As he did, the piece of panel that concealed the back stairway started to inch open. Vanderloo finished signaling. He turned to step back into the room, where he was sure to spot the opening panel. With my free hand I clutched at the bear banger through my shirt. It was the size of a fountain pen, with a kind of plunger sticking out one end. I guessed that the way to fire it was to push that in.

A tongue of flame shot out through my cuff. The explosive detonated with a terrific bang. At the same time I launched myself out of the chair at Vanderloo, but with one arm fastened to Pierrette, that did not go well.

I collapsed in a heap with Pierrette on top of me, and the barrel of the HK tracking toward my head.

Suddenly a terrific boom reverberated in the woods as DeLucca finally fired the bazooka. For a split second, a quizzical expression formed on Vanderloo's face, and he paused, and Augie Treacher sprang through the hidden door with a tire iron in his fist and swatted away a small but apparently important piece of Vanderloo's head.

He sprawled backward onto the terrace. He lay there with a surprised look on his face, staring at the sky. Augie jumped through the door and snatched the HK. Vanderloo's heels started drumming on the wooden decking.

The sound of the approaching helicopter, amplified by the hills, shook the air.

"Augie," I shouted, "the key!"

He stepped over and unlocked the cuffs. By the time I got free and grabbed the HK, the helicopter was coming in to land on the shore. How many men were in it?

"Annie, Pierrette," I shouted. "Get to the back of the house and into the woods. Augie, there's an Uzi and a Walther on the grass out front. Grab them now."

I was trying to decide how to mount a defense when a large Cadillac-shaped chunk of red came streaking out of the trees and down the road toward the lake. The pilot of the Twin Huey must have had all his attention on the landing, because he took no evasive action as Tommy hurtled off the road, slewed on the grass, and T-boned the chopper into the lake, the car plunging in behind it.

By the time Augie and I made it to the water, Tommy had floundered to the bank and was struggling to climb out. Augie grabbed his hand and yanked him ashore. Behind him, two rotor blades stuck out of the lake in a cloud of steam. The water churned with bubbles and an oil stain began to spread. No sign of the pilot.

"This isn't what I wanted," Tommy said, his shirt clinging to his massive frame. He looked stricken. "I mean," he gestured helplessly at the pieces of the aircraft that projected from the turbulence.

Tommy was used to violence, but not the kind that ended in death. Watching him stand there helplessly, I forgot for a moment how angry I was at him for playing Bolt's game behind my back. And let's face it: The only person standing there who'd screwed up more than he had was me.

That night a vampire moon rose out of the trees and spilled a lurid light onto the black waters of the lake. A military crane arrived and the operators set up arc lights on the shore. They hoisted out the crumpled helicopter.

A black SUV with army plates pulled up in front of the house to collect Vanderloo's body. Two soldiers zipped it into a bag while a young lieutenant stood stiffly by, speaking to no one. Then they drove over to the helicopter and retrieved that body too. The pilot had been alone. The kid Vanderloo had shot turned out to be a Russian contract shooter from Brooklyn.

Pierrette hadn't uttered more than the few monosyllables needed to confirm to the police who she was. Annie's face had frozen into an unreadable mask. She had let me wipe away the specks of Vanderloo's blood that had spattered her when Augie struck him. I might have been dusting furniture for all the emotion she showed. She stared at the night, and each time I managed to catch her eye, she moved another mile away.

Later, when the crane was gone and the moon had slunk from the sky, a pallid dawn oozed into the hills.

My phone pinged. Patrick Ho.

The play on Great Pipe had begun.

19

The first move on Great Pipe came just after 6:00 A.M. Three and a half hours before the New York market opened, a buyer took a single block of a million shares at fifty cents a share. The stock had been trading at forty cents.

Anyone following the stock would immediately wonder: What does the buyer know that made him take such a large position at twenty-five percent above the last price? Who is it? Should I jump in?

Trading programs all over Wall Street would spit out alerts. Now other traders would start to watch to see what would happen. But nothing happened. It went quiet.

Interest faded immediately. Great Pipe was a junior exploration stock. Some insider hocus-pocus. That seemed to be the market's judgment.

Not for long.

Two days later someone took another million shares. At sixty cents. That was at 8 A.M., an hour and a half before the opening bell. Attention snapped back to the little stock, because in two trades it had increased by fifty percent. The feeling now was—what the fuck?

I was waiting for the opening. From my vantage point on the top floor of NYPD headquarters I watched the morning traffic stream across the Brooklyn Bridge into the city. A SeaStreak commuter ferry rounded Governor's Island heading for the Wall Street pier. Trillions of dollars' worth of stocks are listed on the big board in New York City, and tens of thousands of people pour across the bridges, through the tunnels, and into the ferry terminals every morning to trade them.

The market opened. Great Pipe went through one dollar in the first fifteen minutes, heading north. By noon it had brushed past two dollars.

Others began to trail into the conference room. I put my phone away, grabbed a coffee, and sat with DeLucca. Silver Bill Fitzgerald, the police commissioner, was chairing the meeting, but he would not come in until everyone else was in place. Silver Bill knew how to make an entrance, especially when the purpose of the meeting was a dogfight with a two-star general who was coming up from Washington. The general had made it clear he expected answers as to how a full colonel in US Army intelligence came to be returned to them in a body bag with part of his head chipped out.

The general came in scowling. He wasn't more than forty. He had battle ribbons from Iraq and Afghanistan, and a purple heart. His adjutant was a marine half-colonel, and the lawyer he brought along from the office of the judge advocate general was a US Navy captain. They established their beachhead in the center of the gleaming conference table.

As soon as the military were seated Silver Bill appeared. He was a short, thin, sharp-eyed former Boston cop. With only a high-school education and street smarts so sharp you could shave with them, he'd risen through the police hierarchy to run, successively, the three largest police forces in the country.

He wore a pearl-gray summer-weight suit with a dark, silk Ferragamo tie. A starched white linen handkerchief blazed in his breast pocket.

His hair had a part so straight it looked as if it had been put there by a surveyor. The four highest-ranking uniformed officers of the NYPD marched in behind him and arranged themselves across the table from the visitors.

The general asked for straight answers and he got them. DeLucca dealt them out in a series of eight-by-ten glossies of material recovered from Amy Curtain's folder in the cloud, bolstered by printed excerpts from phone intercepts that devastatingly established Vanderloo's complicity in the murder of Amy Curtain, the planned murder of a federal agent and his family, the murder of a foreign national (the kid with the HK), and other acts, "in the commission of which," DeLucca concluded, "he conspired with foreign nationals to subvert the laws of the United States."

When DeLucca was done, Silver Bill's hard blue eyes met those of the officers across the table.

"Are we agreed, then, gentlemen," he said in his Southie accent, "that the late colonel was not a credit to the distinguished service of which our country is so rightly proud, and that he acted wholly without the knowledge or authority of his superiors, and that, therefore, nothing in connection with recent unfortunate events reflects to the discredit either of the United States Army or of the other services represented here today?"

It was a wide door that Silver Bill held open. Clearly he thought the general would step straight through. He didn't. He was a highly decorated officer who had reached two-star rank while still comparatively young. He hadn't come up to New York to have his cheek patted by civilians and sent home again. Also, he seemed to have his own ideas about where things pointed.

"Is that your considered opinion Mister, um . . ." he flipped through his agenda as if looking for Bill's name. He knew Bill's name, and everybody at the table knew he knew. Maybe boardroom tactics is a course they give at West Point. It was not a maneuver that would throw Silver Bill, but it served to make the point that the general wasn't going to sign on anybody's dotted line.

"Your considered opinion, if I may restate it," he continued in a hard voice, "is that Colonel Vanderloo was a renegade who acted solely on his own without the knowledge or support, tacit or otherwise, of superior officers?"

Silver Bill sat back in his chair and gazed at the general. He'd thought of the meeting as a funeral service where the army got to bury an embarrassing situation free of charge. He had wrapped the Vanderloo package as neatly as he could and must have wondered why they weren't just taking it and going away.

"Because if that's your opinion," the general said, when it became clear that Bill was not going to reply, "the opinion that Colonel Vanderloo flew solo, that would be convenient. You could just close your file."

"We *have* closed it," Silver Bill said.

"Minute that," the general said to the JAG officer. "The NYPD has closed the file on murdered colonel possibly implicated in hostile powers' plan to subvert the Constitution of the United States." He looked back at Bill. "So noted."

Bill's smile could have welded steel.

"Let me explain something," he said. "This is New York City. What we do here, in the police, we catch people who commit crimes in the five boroughs, and we bring them to justice. Vanderloo committed a crime when he murdered a girl in Brooklyn. Being dead, he can't be brought to justice, but the crime is solved. See, that's our business right there. Crime," he raised a hand, "solution," he slapped the hand back on the table. "Then we close the file and pick up the next one. We are cops."

"Let's just unpack that statement," the general said. He put out his hand and the marine half-colonel handed him a manila file. He opened it and ran his finger down a column. "The NYPD has almost 36,000 police officers and 19,000 civilian personnel, including highly trained forensic technicians as well as counterterrorism and intelligence analysts." He shut the folder. "You have more people and you pack a bigger punch than the FBI. You are not the town cop pounding a beat. You're the biggest law-enforcement operation in the country, by a very substantial margin."

Keeping his eyes on Bill, he raked in DeLucca's glossies and the records of the intercepts and slid the pile in front of the marine. The officer tamped the loose material together and put it in a briefcase, snapping the case shut and spinning the dial of a built-in combination lock. The general laced his hands together.

"We know you have much more information than you've shown us," he said. "We think it's important for the security of the country that we see it. The point here is: The United States Army doesn't train lone actors. That's not how we work. To my superiors, it's unthinkable that a career officer of Colonel Vanderloo's long service did not believe he was acting with authority. We'd like to see all the intercepts, not just the ones you've produced for this meeting."

He looked directly at DeLucca and me, shoved back his chair, and stood up.

"As soon as you can put them together, if that's convenient. Minute formal request," he said to the JAG officer, and they left without another word.

When the door closed behind them, Silver Bill glanced at his senior officers. "Uniforms excused."

As soon as they were gone, he shook his head. "OK, since we're all security-cleared from the arsehole up, maybe someone can tell me what kind of jackoff bullshit is going on."

"Sir," DeLucca began, but Silver Bill held up his hand.

"I was speaking rhetorically. I don't need anybody to tell me what's been going on because I'm supposed to be able to discover that for myself by reading through the stack of files and debriefs and the meeting minutes that tell this sorry tale. But for the benefit of anybody who's been having trouble following, I'm going to say it out loud as if it was something that fully grown adults had thought up."

He ruffled through some pages.

"Basically" he said, raising the papers and letting them drop, "everything in here is one version or another of some kind of conspiracy to affect the outcome of the upcoming election, starting with the party nominating convention that opens tomorrow. The information about Nash's pink diamond and his secret business arrangements will embarrass him by showing that he's a Russian patsy getting rich with Russian help."

He shook his head at the papers.

"As far as I can see, all suppositional in nature. Have I got that wrong?"

No one spoke.

"About that murder of the young Curtain woman," he said to DeLucca. "Would you call that solved?"

"Yes, sir."

"Fine. Tie a ribbon on this file," he patted the papers, "and send it back to Treasury. If they stumble across a crime anytime soon, tell them to call 9-1-1."

I had just come out of the building and was crossing the plaza when a young army officer stepped to my side.

"Sir, if you could spare a moment? The general would like a word."

The car had a black military license plate with two silver stars. The driver got out and opened the back door, and I slid in.

The general had taken off his green jacket and tossed it over the front seat. The purple heart dangled against the dark green fabric. His tie was loosened and his sleeves rolled up and he was smoking. Up close, he didn't look young. His face was hatched with tiny scars. Plastic surgery had left a smooth strip of scar tissue on his chin.

"You didn't have much to say in there."

"No," I said.

He took a last, deep drag and flicked the cigarette out the open window.

"Yet you're the guy Vanderloo was after. I saw your report. If it weren't for that hood with the tire iron he'd have killed you, and your wife and kid too."

"Ex," I said.

"I beg your pardon?"

"Ex-wife."

"But just as dead." He lit another cigarette. "So I would think you've done some thinking about who exactly was behind it."

One of the cops patrolling the square stopped to run his eye over the car. He wore a helmet and dark goggles and his finger lay alongside the trigger of his Colt M4 rifle. He noted the military plate and the young officer standing outside, and moved on.

"You came up here to find out what we know about Vanderloo," I said, "but I didn't notice anything you had to trade."

He pulled his tunic from the seat and shrugged it back on. With the stars glinting on his shoulders and the ribbons blazing on his chest he looked like a general again.

"Vanderloo should have been sectioned out long ago. Proceedings had already begun for an administrative discharge, which is a way to get rid of crazy people so they keep their pensions. He had friends. Turns out, important friends. The proceedings were terminated. Files disappeared. I'll send you what I have."

His hands were folded in his lap. They weren't a pretty sight. He'd been badly injured, and wherever they'd put him back together, they'd been in a hurry.

"So there's something from me. Now it's your turn. Excerpts from intercepts don't help us. We need to know who Vanderloo was taking orders from, or thought he was."

I watched men and women hurrying across the square, cell phones pressed to their ears as they pursued their lives. A young man pushing a stroller stopped to peer at his child. Suddenly he grinned and stuck out a finger, and a tiny pink hand reached up to seize it.

"OK," I said. "You want the phone intercepts. My guess, some of those have disappeared. I'll get what I can. Have somebody contact me. I'll say where we meet. He comes alone. After that, we never met."

The general rapped a knuckle on the window. The young officer opened my door. When I got out, he closed it and climbed into the front seat, beside the driver. As the car pulled away, the general was lighting another cigarette.

"Sounds like Silver Bill and the rest of you got handed your asses," Tommy shouted. He had the top down on the 1962 Chevrolet Impala he'd got as a loaner. His car guru was ransacking America for another vintage Eldorado. For now, Tommy had to settle for the Chev.

He was irritated I'd found out that the paint was a vintage shade called Twilight Turquoise. That was one thing. Another was, he'd arrived at Police Plaza to pick me up just as I was getting out of the general's car, and my evasions about what we'd talked about were driving him crazy. He was running the unit now.

"That two-star guy, do you even know who he works for?"

"We're all making this up as we go along, Tommy."

"Not everybody. Somebody seems to know exactly where they're going."

He was right about that. An announcement from Great Pipe had detonated on the business wires. An independent diamond lab had established, from an examination of fragments obtained from a "reputable source" in Antwerp, that the origin of the Russian Pink was the Camafoza Diamond Pipe.

We were heading east on Canal Street to Chinatown when Great Pipe's shares went past five dollars. By now the story had swept into the general news. The Pink was the most famous diamond in the world, and Nash and Honey Li the most dazzling couple. Their fame was the gas poured on a bonfire of speculation, and the share price blazed and crackled.

The news feed cut to a live shot at a Nash campaign stop in Iowa. This would be his last appearance before he locked up the nomination in twenty-four hours.

"Guys, guys," he was saying to the sea of reporters, "sounds like a terrific stock. Great Pipe, is that what they call it? Maybe I should buy some."

Doyers Street is a crooked lane that runs off the Bowery. Halfway along, two young Chinese men, bulging out of black T-shirts, stood beside a metal garage door practicing their killer stares. They wore earbuds and had small mikes clipped to their shirts. One of them spoke as we drove up, and a camera mounted above the door panned in our direction. A moment later the door rolled up and we drove down a ramp into a large, white, underground garage.

Ho Wang Wei, Patrick's father, owned most of a block of Chinatown. At street level he had a number of businesses, including a traditional

Chinese pharmacy, the largest kitchen-supply store in Manhattan, and his daughter's fashion shop. Ho's biggest business, a bank, not being strictly legal, hummed along out of sight in the carpeted, sleekly modern rooms that spread through the basements below.

Tabitha's Mini was already parked. Tommy eased into the space beside it indicated by a woman in scarlet overalls.

"Cool," she said, running her eyes along the paintwork.

"Twilight Turquoise," I said. "He picked it for the color."

"Trez cool." She stepped back to snap a picture on her phone. "Minnie Ho," she said, dropping the phone in a voluminous pocket and thrusting out her hand. "Patrick's sister." She led the way through a door that hissed open at the swipe of her card.

Thousands of Chinese immigrate to New York City every year. Some of them, like the billionaire who bought the top two floors of a tower on West Fifty-Seventh Street for $120 million, don't need banking help. Most do. Smuggled into the United States, they arrive without papers. Without proper ID, they can't open accounts at American banks to wire money home, or save, or eventually, as many will, borrow to open a business of their own. So they bank with Ho Wang Wei. He does all those things, and he does them faster and cheaper than American banks. If he'd made himself rich by providing an unlicensed service to people whose kids were going to end up at MIT, sue me, because I'm looking the other way.

Minnie kept shooting sideways glances at Tommy. Suddenly she stopped and put a hand against his chest. Even in the voluminous overalls she was an elfin creature, but her eyes had stopping power. She caught a fold of fabric in her fingers and rubbed it briskly. The shirt was the color of dark moss, with a paler snow-pea piping.

"This heavy rayon," she said, "you can't get it now. It's the quality of the fabric that lets it take on that intensity from the dye." She snatched the phone from her pocket and snapped a picture. She winked at Tommy. "Very cool, big guy. Also, love the hair."

She led the way through another set of secure doors into a dimly lit room. A screen displaying a map of the world took up an entire wall.

Patrick Ho had hacked deep into First Partners. Since we now knew that Nash controlled the fund, the computer had begun to examine all the fund's transactions in terms of how they might benefit Nash. Everything the machine had taught itself about Lime it now applied to Nash. It was unwinding Nash's business secrets by the second, spewing out reams of elaborate transactions. Patrick's software plotted those dealings on the screen, creating a fantastic web of lines that looked like one of those airline route maps in the back of the in-flight magazine.

I slid into a seat beside Tabitha. Tommy scowled at the screen and stomped around in front of Minnie with his chest pushed out. Patrick rattled some keys and the lines vanished from the screen.

"The market's just suspended trading in Great Pipe," he said. "They're demanding the company provide the scientific data that proves the Pink came from the Camafoza pipe. In the meantime I can show you how Nash trades. It's actually kind of beautiful."

He tapped a key, and a light glowed on in London.

"This is not in real time. It's the computer's replication of a pattern. When you gave me the new information from Jersey about how Nash effectively controls the company, we re-ran the analyses of thousands of trading sequences. So we were ready for today. Here's how Nash has been running up the price so far. That light going on in London is a trading order from Nash to First Partners. It's First Partners that actually owned the stock."

Then two pinpoints of light left London and streaked across the map, inscribing bright lines behind them. One line ended in Lichtenstein; the other, Singapore.

"That's the computer showing that as soon as Nash offered some of the Great Pipe stock held by First Partners for sale, two buyers immediately snapped it up."

Four more dots appeared on the map. Instantly, two lines took off from Lichtenstein and two from Singapore. The Singapore lines connected to Hong Kong and Shanghai. From Lichtenstein, the lights went streaking across the Atlantic, one landing in New York and the other in the British Virgin Islands.

"So the original buyers each found two more buyers," Patrick said, as a firework of blazing lines erupted onto the screen. "Now they'll all trade it back and forth among themselves. Sometimes they sell the whole block of shares they've bought, sometimes they split it into smaller lots. The price increases fast."

"Those buyers are all Nash-owned companies," I said. "He sold the stock to himself."

"Correct," said Patrick.

"They're wash trading," Tommy said. "Their only purpose in buying and selling is to run up the price."

"Yes, it's a wash play," Patrick agreed, "but a hard one to prove. Because the price escalates so quickly, all kinds of other trading programs kick in, and soon thousands of investors are trading."

Tommy nodded, then aimed a finger at Minnie.

"This is a highly secret operation," he said to Patrick. "You were supposed to be able to guarantee security. So what about her?" he nodded at Minnie.

"I couldn't have done it without her," Patrick said.

The program kept filling the screen with a tracer fire of trades while silence deepened around this news.

"You're telling me she helped you?"

"She's the fastest coder in New York," Patrick said.

"More than a pretty face, big guy," Minnie said. "All this, plus knockout fashion."

"Sweetheart," Tommy said, "I'm going to need your signature on a very serious non-disclosure document."

She slid a hand under his arm. "Oh, baby," she purred, "please make me sign."

I would have liked to watch Tommy struggle in the quicksand of Minnie Ho, but the market had just posted Great Pipe's scientific data.

News feeds streamed across the bottom of the screen carrying the actual report that Great Pipe filed with the exchange.

From the first phrase, I knew who'd written it. I could hear him in the prose. He laced his sentences together with a crisp, seductive logic. First he established that the impurities contained in diamonds existed in ratios that were unique to the pipes from which the diamonds came. Then he described the technique he'd developed for vaporizing tiny diamond chips and measuring the ratio of the impurities with mass spectrometry.

"L. T. Labs," Tabitha said. She'd been reading it too. "That's the name of the company. Remember you asked me to see if there were any payments from Lime to a company in eastern Long Island? There were. That's the company."

"Yes," I said. I already knew. I'd seen it in the statements from the Jersey bank. Regular payments through a bank in Sag Harbor. L. T. Labs. Lane Turner. The man who invented diamond mineral chemistry. My dad.

"The market is taking the suspension off," Patrick said. "I'll get rid of this old record." His fingers chattered at the board. The lines disappeared. Dots of light remained on the map, marking the places where Nash's trading companies were based.

But now, none of them traded. In the upper right-hand corner of the screen, the price of a Great Pipe share had already passed ten dollars.

The market was feverishly trading the stock. Yet Nash did nothing. His trading apparatus sat there like a giant spider, watching the action with its glowing eyes but not attacking.

"I don't get it," Patrick said. "Why isn't he trading?"

I wondered the same thing. If Nash was running a pure stock play, he would continue to run up the stock by trading among his companies, while at the same time unwinding some of his massive position—selling it off into the rising market in small lots so as not to alert buyers that a large investor was bailing on the stock.

And he *would* bail. Because he knew the pipe's secret. He knew that the conclusions investors were drawing were wrong. The origin of the Russian Pink in the Camafoza Pipe didn't point to a population of other fabulously large and valuable pinks. The only other diamonds explorers had found were the fractured browns.

"Could Nash be hesitant because he knows that you and Lily uncovered his control of First Partners?" Tabitha said.

I smiled at her. She had the decency to blush. Lily's name hadn't been in my report.

"Who are you, masked stranger?" I said quietly.

Then an alert pinged on my phone.

One of Lime's credit cards had been swiped at a gas station in Sag Harbor.

I showed the screen to Tabitha.

She grabbed her keys and I followed her out.

20

We cleared the city. As we headed out Long Island, Great Pipe continued its meteoric climb. The market issued warnings. No one paid attention. At sixty dollars the market suspended trading a second time. The frenzied buying and selling switched to the gray market. Inside an hour, the pressure to clear the swelling backlog of trades forced the market to remove the stop order. Great Pipe blew like a magnum of champagne. It had just passed seventy dollars when Patrick called.

"A European broker is selling 500,000 shares every time the price goes through a five-dollar increment."

"When did they buy?"

"I can't find any record that they bought."

"Maybe it's one of the funds that had an early investment, and they're taking a profit."

"It's not a fund."

"OK." I thought for a minute. "Where's the broker?"

"They're using a New York nominee, but the orders are coming from Helsinki."

Sag Harbor is a pretty, shaded town full of those enormous cedar-shake houses that the original inhabitants would have built if they'd been partners in hedge funds instead of fishermen. The bank was on a side street, leaving the charming, cobbled main drag for the coffee shops and bookstores and sellers of expensive handmade soaps. We parked in a lane behind the bank.

The manager had a roomy, old-fashioned office at the back. A ceiling fan stirred the soupy air. I'd called ahead. The file for L. T. Labs lay open on his desk. He was going through it—what there was. Only a few pages. He was frowning at them. And us.

"Sag Harbor is a long way from Washington, DC," he said, tilting his head back to stare down his nose at my Treasury ID.

The manager was in his thirties. He had a red face, as if he'd just come in from a jog. A hank of black hair fell across his forehead.

"I'm not sure what I can tell you," he said. "This account was closed a month ago. I don't even know if this business exists anymore."

"We just need a few particulars," I said, "such as where they were located."

He pushed the hank of hair from his forehead. It fell back again.

"We only had an address in the city," he said.

"Sure," I said. "And I'll need that too. But what I need today is where the physical premises were and what was the nature of the business."

He nodded and made another futile attempt to brush the hair from his forehead. His face glistened with a sheen of perspiration.

"All I know is what's in the file."

"I know you're familiar with the provisions of the Dodd-Frank legislation," I said in a reasonable tone. "But just so we know what provisions I mean—you're supposed to know the nature of a client's business. By that I mean, you are *required* to know it. That's to prevent the I-didn't-know-what-they-were-up-to defense if we have to prosecute you for abetting a crime."

The sweat was pouring off him now.

"Research," he blurted out. "It was some kind of research company. That's all I know."

"You don't know where they had their building?"

He shuffled through the statements in the file again, then closed it and took a deep breath.

"Look, this account was opened by head office in New York. Deposits came by wire. Mostly it was used to pay bills for L. T. Labs. There was an authorized person for cash withdrawals."

"And he was?"

He glanced at the file. "Lane Turner."

"Where did the wires come from?"

"A bank in Liechtenstein."

"Oh, boy," I said, and after that he shut up like a clam.

"He was more afraid of someone else than he was of you," Tabitha said when we left.

We walked around the corner to the real estate office. The salesman wore a black polo jersey and those faded pink cotton pants that New Yorkers hope will make them look as if they come from an island other than Manhattan. He had the local newspaper spread out in front of him and was deep in a story about local politicians caught up in a corruption probe. There's a surprise. Prime oceanfront properties located in small municipalities with rudimentary oversight, a short helicopter ride from the richest people on the planet. What could go wrong?

"Industrial?" he said when I told him what we were looking for. He had a gleaming bald head with a fringe of wispy hair. "We don't get much industrial interest out here." His shrewd eyes darted back and forth between Tabitha and me. "Mostly what people like yourselves are looking for is a nice summer place."

"Light industrial," I said. "Place for a small plant."

He stepped over to a large wall map of the area.

"The only place I can think of," he said, "is to the south of town, right around here." He drew a circle with his finger that took in a swath of countryside. Black rectangles marked the few buildings that stood along the roads. "There's a place in here somewhere," he said, tapping the map. I stepped closer and saw a long straggle called Old Shinnecock Road. "No idea what they do," he said. "Some kind of lab? Been there about a year. Want to take a look?"

I told him we'd be fine by ourselves, and we'd be in touch. He gave me the sad smile of a man who'd heard it before.

We could have found Old Shinnecock Road by following the news helicopter. It circled at about a thousand feet, the camera operator visible in the open door. A sheriff's car blocked the nearest intersection. A TV truck from the local station was parked beside it. A camera was set up on the roof of the truck, beside the satellite dish. The cameraman was shooting down the road, where two more sheriff's cars were parked by a gate, roof lights churning their message of foreboding into the dry scrub.

The sergeant at the gate just glanced at our IDs. He looked like a man not far from retirement, and Lime's black Ferrari Testarossa parked at the entrance to the building and the sudden appearance of federal agents were telling him that this was not a scene he wanted to be in charge of.

"I'd better call the sheriff," he muttered, reaching for the mike clipped to his shoulder.

"Suit yourself," I said, "but before you do," I pointed to a deputy pulling on blue latex gloves and heading for the Ferrari, "stop that officer right now. We'll get our own forensics." I nodded to Tabitha. "Call Tommy. Tell him what we need."

"One more thing," I said to the sergeant. "What brought you out here?"

"Phone tip," he said.

"Let me guess. Anonymous."

The single-story building was made of concrete blocks and painted a cream color. It looked well maintained. No sign identified the occupant. Orange and black notices that warned RADIATION: DO NOT ENTER were clipped to the chain-link security fence around the property. A police tech with a Geiger counter was coming out the door.

"It's clear," he said.

Inside, daylight poured though skylights and puddled on the polished concrete floor. Against one wall stood a row of benches with flex lamps and diamond scales, and after that, a large, glass-walled office. That's where Lime was sitting.

His chin was resting on his collarbone. His face was paper white. He stared in perplexity at the papers on his desk, as if he were trying to understand exactly what they meant: in the circumstances, a hopeless task. The killer had slashed his throat from ear to ear, severing the jugular vein. Lime's chest and lap were caked in the dark, congealing mess of his own blood. A viscous pool had formed around his shoes.

The sharp, metallic smell of blood filled the room.

I left the office and crossed the empty lab to a door painted in diagonal, black-and-yellow stripes. A red lightbulb was mounted just above the door. A sign warned employees not to enter when the light was flashing. The door was ajar. I stepped into the windowless room.

Thick cables ran from a ceiling duct and connected to the back of the stainless-steel machine in the center of the room. It was the size of a home washing machine, with a thick, steel door that opened into a small space lined with white tiles. I heard Tabitha come in behind me.

"That's Lime in the office?"

"Yes." I swung the door open. In the center of the chamber was a small, clawlike device. Tabitha came in and crouched beside me to peer in.

"What is it?"

"A radiation chamber."

"For what?"

"For irradiating diamonds. They fix the stone in that clasp in there and bombard it with radiation." I stood up. "This whole room is lined with lead."

"And what does that do, when they bombard the diamond?"

"It changes the color of the stone."

"You mean . . ."

"Yes, that's what I mean. They can make a diamond any color. Including pink."

A loud *whoop whoop* sounded just outside, and a flash of blue and red strobes flickered through the door. We came out of the radiation room in time to see Honey Li climb out of a black Suburban. She came wobbling across the gravel parking lot in her heels. Behind her were a couple of secret service agents and the sergeant from the sheriff's department, all looking unhappy.

"You are fucking kidding me," Tabitha said, raising the total number of obscenities I'd ever heard from her to one. She took off for the front door like a shot, hauling out her badge and holding it up and shouting, "Federal crime scene." Honey stepped through the door. "Ms. Li," Tabitha called, "you need to stop right there."

She stormed down the room in a whirlwind of hair. Honey froze. When I got there I could see she was trembling,

"Ms. Li," Tabitha said, "you don't want to come in here."

"But, Sergei," she stammered, "on TV. They said a killing." She grabbed Tabitha's sleeve. "I drove over from Bridgehampton," she said in the same shaking voice.

Honey stared down the room at the open door. Lime's body was just visible, with its awful wound. She staggered, and I grabbed her quickly to prevent her falling. She clasped her head in her hands.

"I'm sorry I've come," she said. "I see how inappropriate this is." She shuddered. "I'm so sorry. I'll go."

"How did you know it was Lime?" I said as she was turning to leave.

It was as if I'd turned a spigot that let ice into her veins. She looked straight at me.

"What are you talking about?"

"You said you saw it on TV. But that wouldn't tell you Lime's name. It hasn't been released."

"Hasn't it," she said. "Well then," she looked around, "I must have recognized the car."

"Wow," Tabitha said as we watched her drive away. "Where do you learn to do that?"

"She has an algorithm for it."

"Suspicious circumstances," I said to the sheriff's sergeant when we left. "That's all you release. Manner of death is a federal secret until the statute of limitations unseals the file in thirty years. Is that clear?"

"Is there even such a category as a federal secret?" Tabitha said as we walked back to the car.

"You have to wonder."

It's only fifteen miles from Sag Harbor to Orient, but you have to take two ferries on the way. So Tabitha had plenty of time to decide how guilty she should feel.

We were the only car on board when we slipped away from the jetty for the first crossing, a fifteen-minute run across the Peconic River. The thrum of the diesels made the interior of the car seem even quieter.

"I wasn't supposed to know that Lily was with you on Jersey," Tabitha said.

"No."

"I'm sorry, Alex."

"You were always too good to be true."

"You suspected?"

"The CIA spent a lot of money training you. For what, to lend you to FinCEN for immediate burial in Special Audits as my assistant?" The ferry slowed as we approached the dock on Shelter Island. "It never made sense."

The boat eased into the slip. The ramp clanked down and the deckhand waved us off. We bumped ashore and took the road to the north side of the island.

"What I can't figure out is who you're working for. Who would be the client?"

"Don't ask me," she said. "My case officer only came up to New York once. Mostly she wanted to know where to buy shoes. You know they don't tell us anything."

"If you say so."

My phone emitted a beep. Bulletins on Great Pipe were coming in fast now. At first, the killing at the lab had been strictly local news. The Suffolk County sheriff hadn't released the victim's name or even said who owned the building. But when Honey Li had rushed from the

Nash estate at Bridgehampton all that changed. The paparazzi staking out the property for a glimpse of Honey caught the black Suburban as it came tearing through the gate, strobes flashing and a state police escort front and back. Boom: Suddenly it was O. J. Simpson in the white Bronco. The news chopper, alerted to Honey Li's cavalcade, had picked it up, and from that moment she towed behind her the rapt attention of the whole country. Suddenly the reporters on the story were from the *New York Times* and CNN.

In less than an hour they'd linked the black Testarossa to Lime. Next they discovered that the building belonged to L. T. Labs. It wouldn't take them long to connect radiation warnings to the science of altering diamond color.

Trading in Great Pipe slowed, then stopped. The price had hit $110. It was as if the market had sucked in its breath and was waiting to see what happened next.

"I'm not getting this," I said. "If this is a stock play, and Nash is running it, what's the murder for?"

"Why does Lime's killing have to be about a stock-market plot? Maybe there are other reasons."

"That's not how we think, though, is it. We don't believe in coincidence. We look at what's happening now."

"OK," Tabitha said. "The share price of Great Pipe increased fast. That's the main event."

"Exactly. Why?"

"The belief that the Camafoza Pipe will hold other sensational pink diamonds?"

"Right again. So the question is: How does cutting Lime's throat help that? And why did Honey Li come over? She had to know she would be followed by the press."

We crossed Shelter Island to the second ferry. Tabitha rolled her window down. The warm breeze stirred her hair. We came to the landing, and the thick smell of seaweed drying on the rocks. If I'd ever had a home, that was the smell it had.

The ferry to the North Fork docks in Greenport. From there it's ten minutes to Orient. We drove through the village and turned into the sandy lane that cuts through a pine grove and comes out on a point.

It wasn't a big house, but it had a kind of perfection. Like everything Dad ever owned. He'd bought the weather-beaten cottage for my mother thirty years ago, when prices on the North Fork were a fraction of what rich New Yorkers were paying in the Hamptons. He'd restored the white trim, and the parking area blazed with a fresh load of sun-bleached shells. Banks of white roses and blue hydrangeas piled up around the entrance.

"Is this where you spent summers?"

"When my mother could swing it. You've read the file, Tab."

The brass lamps beside the door shone and the window panes gleamed. Mrs. Cutler opened the door, so I guess she was still coming every day to make sure not a speck of dust or flake of salt was allowed to settle on my father's world. He inspired that devotion in people. God help them.

He wore his summer uniform—immaculate white shirt, sleeves rolled up to the elbow, khaki pants, and blue canvas boat shoes. His vintage, steel World War II officer's wristwatch fastened with a simple khaki nylon band. Thin, erect, thick white hair.

"Lane Turner," he said in that confident, warm voice, taking Tabitha's hand when we came into the front room. "I hadn't understood I was to have such a pleasure in my dull, old life."

We stood in an awkward silence for a moment until he said to Mrs. Cutler, "So that will be tea for three, then, Hannah."

My father's idea of tea was a meal featuring ham sandwiches on brown bread with English mustard and lettuce, served at exactly 4:00 P.M. Sure, it came with tea—in a beautiful china pot that my mother had used every day. But now the tea was just another part of the ritual. Dad didn't touch it. He hated tea. He ate his ham sandwich and washed it down with three fingers of single-malt Scotch.

"You want to talk about the Pink," he said to me. Then he turned his smile on Tabitha. "That's the only reason he'd come to see me," he said in a confiding tone, as if she might not know.

Turning back to me, he said, "They're saying on the news that the dead man at the lab could be Sergei."

"It's Lime," I said.

"But why? It was a *lab*. And we were closing it. There wasn't anything valuable there. We'd moved the diamonds. I don't understand."

"Why did you have the lab out there in the first place?"

He took a sip of his drink and held the glass up to the light to examine the color. He was particular about everything. But the news about Lime had shaken him.

"It was a good location partly because it's so out of the way. We didn't want anyone to know what we were doing. For me, it was convenient. And for Honey too. They have that place over in Bridgehampton so she could use that as a base when she wanted to keep tabs on progress."

"So she knew where the lab was located and what you were doing?"

"Knew? It was her idea."

"The radiation chamber too?"

"Of course. Once I explained to her how browns could be turned into pinks."

"Dad, for Christ's sake. This is not an academic discussion. People are betting their shirts right now on news about the Russian Pink. If you altered the color and have concealed it, that's going to put you back in jail."

The face he turned to me wore that frigid expression I knew well. And if I thought for a second I'd forgotten it, the boy who had feared its icy splash was there to remind me.

"The Russian Pink? Are you out of your mind?" He clenched his teeth. "I didn't touch the Russian Pink! I analyzed a chip that Davy gave me. It's the strongest, most vivid pink I've ever seen. Alter it?" he spat. "Who on earth would alter such a diamond?"

If Dad had any appetite for truth, that's where you'd find it: inside his fascination with minerals. They were more alive for him than people. The photographs of my mother and me on the walls were like the remnants of a collection he'd once put together before losing interest and moving on.

"If not for the Pink, what was the chamber for?" Tabitha said.

"Browns," he said. "If they have the right properties, they do very well."

"You mean brown diamonds in the Camafoza Pipe?" Tabitha said. "You're planning to change them into pinks?"

"Why not? It's not illegal, as long as the certificates acknowledge that the stone's been treated and enhanced."

But something kept nagging at me.

"If you were closing the lab, what was Lime doing there?"

"How would I know? Maybe he left some papers out there, I don't know."

"There were no papers anywhere. The place was cleaned out. It was completely empty. Except for the radiation chamber. Why was that still there?"

"I guess they were going to move it last. Harry said to leave it."

"Nash? I thought you said it was Honey and Lime who were running this."

"Nash took an interest. He wanted to know how everything worked."

"Why did Nash tell you to leave the radiation chamber?" I said.

"Always probing," he said angrily. "Always suspicious." He glared at me bitterly. Once he'd started, he had to finish. I guess he'd been imagining this conversation as long as I had. "You blamed me for your mother's death."

"Of course I blamed you," I said. "You killed her. You starved her of what she wanted, which was your love."

"I did love her! I loved *you!*"

He looked out at the remains of the dying day. His shoulders registered defeat. The night came on like a fist closing on the sun.

I don't know what attracted him to people like Nash and Honey Li. I suppose no man on earth knew more about diamonds than my father, or less about people.

"This got away on you," I told him. "You thought it was a straight stock play. You would certify the pink as a Camafoza stone. After all, it was. Nash would make a bundle on the stock, and you'd get a cut. Turning those browns into pinks—that would be a nice sideline. As long as no one claimed the stones were natural, you weren't even committing a crime. Except Nash had other plans. There could only be one reason to tell you to leave the radiation chamber at the lab. He wanted it to be discovered."

Blue shadows crept into the room. The ocean lapped at the darkening shore. Fingers of cold night air slid through the open door.

"I think you know where I'm headed, but in case you're too dazzled by your own brilliance let me spell it out:

"You issued a report on the Pink that established its origin in the Camafoza Pipe. The stock in the pipe went stratospheric. Now, at the premises of the lab that certified the Pink, here's the scene: The place looks like it's been hurriedly abandoned. There's a murdered man. And what else? A radiation chamber. How long do you think it's going to take the most aggressive reporters in America to find out that some diamonds can be turned pink by radiation? What's the headline going to be? It's going to be that the lab that certified the Russian Pink had equipment designed to *make* a pink. Conclusion: It's a fake."

He stared at me with a look of real loathing.

"You take innocent facts and weave them into your own sick fantasy," he said. "A twisted, evil fantasy. It doesn't even make sense on the face of it. For it to be true, Nash would have to know that the press would show up. He'd have to know beforehand that something would draw them out there."

"I'm going to let you think about that for a minute."

I checked my phone. The first stories about the radiation chamber had already broken. The market had imposed another cease-trading order. I called Tommy.

"Nash is shorting Great Pipe," I said. "It's a short play."

"Are you sure?"

"He didn't confess it to me personally, Tommy."

"Stop snarling," he said. He was silent for a moment. "Technically, in the strictest legal sense, this is the market's problem."

"Technically, in the strictest sense, this is the problem of all the poor dopes buying that stock right now, Tommy. So call it. Use your newfound power as a big-time fed. Shut down Great Pipe now, or your name will be at the top of my report."

"OK, OK," he muttered. "I'll call the exchange."

As Tabitha and I were leaving, Dad put his hand on my arm. He grabbed the picture of my mother and me in the silver frame and made me take it.

"She loved you," he said. His voice was hoarse. As we drove off, I watched him dwindling in the mirror, an old man getting older, until a bend in the drive swept him from view.

"I don't even know what a short play is," Tabitha said as we left the village and headed west along the North Fork in the gathering night.

I explained that a short play is a bet that a stock is overpriced. The short seller thinks, or in Nash's case knows, that the stock will fall. If he has the right connections, he borrows the shares from a broker and immediately sells them. Then he waits for the market to come to its senses. When it does, and the share price falls, the short player buys the shares back at the lower price, and returns them to the broker he borrowed them from. He pays the broker a fee, and pockets the difference.

"And the Helsinki broker means it was Honey Li," she said, "and Honey Li means Nash." She thought for a minute. "One thing I don't get, though. Lime's murder. It brings the press attention, but the Pink was a huge story. The press would have found the lab anyway, and the radiation signs would have done the rest. Now there's a murder investigation involving a presidential candidate."

"Look at it from the oligarchs' point of view. I doubt they'd have trusted Lime after they robbed him. He was on borrowed time. Also, they don't care what happens to Nash. If he's elected, could he deliver on sanctions relief? Not a chance. The oligarchs were planning on making a killing on the short."

"That assumes they were in on it."

"Trust me—they were in on it. And so was Honey."

"Which means she drove over from Bridgehampton on purpose, to draw attention where they wanted it."

"Yes."

At Southold we stopped at a donut shop and got coffee, then sped out along the black highway.

I felt comfortable with Tab. When you thought about it, what did I have to complain about? They'd given me a spy for an assistant, and sure enough, she'd spied.

The miles unspooled and we settled into companionable silences broken by brief exchanges. Who was running Chuck, and was Tommy fully in the loop? Then, after a long silence she said, "How did your mother die?"

"Cancer."

"Hard on a kid."

A minute later she handed me a handkerchief.

"You keep these just for me?" I said.

"You'd better hope I don't put it in my report."

As we drew closer to the city, the attributes of night dissolved into the stream of headlights, the brightly lit freeway, and, miles away, New York City, blowing its volcano of light into the western sky.

21

A nd what's so great is that it really is cursed," Annie said, gazing at the famous jewel.

"Some of the people who owned it weren't so lucky," I agreed.

"They died horrible deaths," she recited avidly, running her finger down a page of the booklet. "The diamond spread death wherever it went. One man drove off a cliff with his wife. Then Mrs. McLean—she went from being one of the richest women in America to one of the poorest. Her newspaper went broke. Her son died at the age of nine. Her daughter died of an overdose at twenty-five. Her husband ran off with another woman. *He* died in a mental hospital," she added with relish.

Calamity was one of Annie's passions, ranked just below clothes. Her ambition now was to be a designer. Tommy had introduced her to Minnie Ho. Minnie had taken a step back and cocked her head.

"I totally get the boots," she'd said. "Let's make something to go with them."

Today it was a pink buckskin jacket spattered with sequins, black jeans, and the trademark cowboy boots. Her hair spilled over her shoulders in a tawny coil. We turned our backs on the Hope Diamond and made our way out of the Smithsonian Institution into a bright February, Washington day. I hailed a cab.

The dome of the Capitol blazed against the blue sky. We crossed the Anacostia River and headed southwest out of the city. Twenty-five minutes later we arrived at the gate of Joint Base Andrews. The MPs checked my ID and Annie's carefully against a list, and summoned an Air Force car. It took us out across the runways to the corner of the field where Air Force One sat running up its engines. We climbed a gangway at the rear section of the plane.

A young airman blushed at Annie and led us forward through the empty press section to a small cabin. It was furnished with a pair of sofas and a writing desk. The airman went away, and returned with a tray. I helped myself to coffee and Annie poured a glass of orange juice. Five minutes later, we watched through the windows as a party of high-ranking officers assembled near the forward gangway. Soon the dark green shape of Marine One came clattering into view.

Ten minutes after takeoff the airman poked his head in the door. "The president will see you now, sir."

I followed him forward, through a large cabin where staff were working at computers or busy on the phone. Flat-screen monitors carried newsfeeds from around the globe. The next compartment was the forward communications room, where air force personnel in headsets sat at a row of monitors, keeping the president in touch with American military commanders at bases around the world.

We climbed the staircase to the upper deck. Two Secret Service agents stood at the door to the executive suite. A marine lieutenant wearing the gold aiguillette of a presidential aide-de-camp rapped sharply on the door and opened it.

Matilda Bolt was sitting at her desk, the presidential seal mounted behind her on the wall. Her chief of staff, looking harried, was tidying a stack of papers.

"Have that done by the time we land, Bill," she said. "I want to go over it before we get to the school."

He shot me a glance as he hurried from the cabin. Bolt leaned back and gestured to the empty seat facing her.

Even in the plush cocoon of the president's cabin, with its thick carpet and oversized chairs and acoustic paneling, the insistent din of the machinery of government never stopped. It clamored just beyond the walls. It hummed in the fabric of the plane. The urgency and might of the greatest office in the world.

"You've taken a leave of absence," she said, pinning me with her yellow eyes. It was only two weeks after her inauguration, and already the burden of office had printed itself on her face. She had gray half-moons beneath her eyes and the lines around her mouth were etched more deeply. Her lips adopted the sardonic smile that was her natural expression. "I could use someone with your talents."

When I didn't reply, a ripple of malice twitched across her face. It faded quickly, erased by the relentless pressures of the presidency. In New York that morning, a deranged gunman with an assault rifle had shot his way into a school. She was on her way to the scene to console the parents and the nation for what was inconsolable.

Our own business was simpler: She needed to know that I wasn't going to be a problem. She was the most powerful person on the planet, and I knew how she'd gotten there.

Others who knew pieces of the story had been swept up into the administration. Tabitha had an office in the West Wing where she prepared the intelligence report called the President's Daily Brief. The PDB is the most sensitive intelligence digest in America, so Tab's future was assured.

In addition to running the department, Tommy had the rank of assistant deputy secretary of the Treasury. That gave him some extra weight to throw around. You couldn't really buy Tommy's loyalty, but like all lawyers you could rent it.

Chuck left the department and moved to DC, where he joined a high-powered K Street lobbying firm whose partners expected a stream of contracts to follow in his wake. Chuck had promised as much, hinting that it would be his reward for keeping his mouth shut about certain things he knew. But spreading it all over town that you are going to be keeping your mouth shut is sort of the opposite of actually keeping your mouth shut, and the line of Chuck Chandlers came to an abrupt end one afternoon when Chuck walked in the front door of his new house in swanky Chevy Chase and met a bullet coming the other way.

The two-star general got a third star.

As for Patrick, his father's banking operation got a license. Any quibbles about how they'd amassed their capital had been brushed aside. For now.

That left me. I'd been expecting the summons. The problem, as Bolt would see it, was that she had nothing I wanted. This made me the *i* that didn't have a dot. When she'd sent for me I'd already planned the trip to DC with Annie, so a pass arrived for her too.

It was a no-press flight to New York City. Air Force One takes off when the president boards and lands when it reaches its destination. The pale-blue 747 doesn't circle waiting for a landing slot. It's cleared before it gets there. A commercial flight from Washington to New York takes fifty-five minutes. On Air Force One you're there in half an hour.

"We won't waste time," she said. "Harry Nash very nearly became president." Her face tightened with distaste. "Fortunately he was destroyed by his own greed."

We both knew that wasn't true. Nash didn't suddenly become greedy. Greed was his profession. In a world foundering in lies, the stark simplicity of Nash's greed had seemed like a kind of truth. *Guys, who doesn't like to make a buck?* Greed was the founding motive of Bolt's deal with Nash. He provided the glitter of his name, the throat of Honey Li, and the diamond to hang against it. Bolt supplied political credibility; Nash was the glowing bubble of magnificence that would float them to the nomination.

"Nash was the package you picked yourself," I said.

"Elections aren't about ideas. I'd never even have got through the primaries," she said. "Just look at me."

It was as if her weariness had peeled off the armor and revealed the girl she'd been: a bony kid with serpent's eyes and a cleaver for a nose. A life of playground jeers and, later, eviscerating editorial cartoons. She glanced out the window. A few hundred yards away, a pair of F-16s kept station on the plane.

"I didn't know what Harry was planning. That's why I reached out to you. My sources told me you were the only one who could figure out what he had in mind."

"No," I said, "that wasn't why you contacted me. You didn't care what the scam was. You only needed me because you suspected Nash was going to double-cross you."

"I'm not sure what you mean."

"Nash was never supposed to be president. That was always going to be you. Nash's job was to get you as far as the nomination. He would pull out on a pretext at the last minute. Your party would have no choice but to hand you the nomination. Nash's reward was whatever he made from the Pink. Yours was the presidency. You thought Nash had decided to take both. That's the reason you wanted me to penetrate the bank in Jersey. It wasn't to protect Nash. It was to give you the proof you needed to threaten him."

I think in a way she was relieved to hear the truth plainly stated. For just that moment, she was not alone with it.

"It was my turn," she said, looking out again at the F-16s. Her fingers curled into fists. "*My* turn. Time for the power to come to me. No one lets you have that power. You take it."

Matilda Bolt would spend the rest of her life wrapped in a capsule of deference—protected, courted, privy to the world's secrets. She'd paid a heavy price for it, but she'd made the first down payment long ago.

"So you threatened Nash with exposure and he came to heel."

The plane shuddered slightly as the undercarriage went down.

"Where you're going to have a problem," I said, "is the murder of Lime. You've seen the stories. They can't leave it alone. The reporters on the story—they'll find out eventually how he died—his throat slashed so your running mate could cheat investors."

We sat for a minute with our own thoughts. Nash had come out in front of the mansion to face the press, Honey beside him. He'd said how sorry he was investors had lost money. He blamed himself, didn't think it was right to continue his campaign. *And guys, I lost my best friend and partner, so I think I'll leave it there for now.* And he disappeared inside the house.

"Harry's a cold-blooded man," Bolt said, "but not a monster. He told me his plan had been for the police to be called to an illegal entry. The local TV channel would be tipped. Once they got onto the story, they'd discover the radiation chamber, and the stock price would fall. But the murder? That wasn't Harry."

She glanced at her watch.

"Let's finish our business. You seized the Russian Pink as part of your investigation. I understand you've finished whatever tests you wanted, so please, give the man his bauble."

"That's part of the deal? He gets the diamond and the pardon?"

"The pardon is for the people. It clears away investigations that would have consumed the country. Now the nation can move on."

"I'm glad there's a happy ending."

There was a knock on the door, and the chief of staff put his head into the cabin. "Madam President, we land in fifteen minutes."

"Bill," she said, "Mr. Turner's daughter might like to come up for a look."

"Yes, ma'am," he said, closing the door behind him.

"I'm told you have a report but have refused to file it. I'm going to guess it's one of those if-anything-should-happen-to-me-or-my-family situations?"

"Yes," I said.

"You understand there's a flip side to that."

"I do."

They must have brought Annie up earlier, because when the door opened this time she was right there, her eyes popping out of her head.

"Wow," Bolt said, "that's what I call color." She came around the desk and fingered the western-style fringe of Annie's jacket. "What do you call it?"

"Prairie Blush," Annie whispered.

"Got a phone?" Bolt said, and she put out a skinny arm and hauled Annie in for a selfie.

"I hear you're a designer," she said, reminding me, in case it might slip my mind, even for a second, how easily she could find out whatever she wanted to find out. "Can you make me one?"

"Totally," said Annie.

"Then I guess we're cool," she said. But it was me she was looking at.

The girl with the blonde crew cut had the front door open about one nanosecond before my hand touched the bell.

"Is that something they teach at butler school?" I said as I stepped into the marble vestibule.

"Yes, sir," she said. "It's right after the part where we learn how to deal with serious household emergencies, such as how to use the new remote."

"You're worth every penny right there."

"You might not think so when I tell you they found the bug I put in it."

We were passing through the long corridor that led to the back of the mansion. The pictures had all been packed away. The Nashes were moving to Singapore and selling the house.

"Do they suspect you?"

"Probably. They're not stupid. They have the place swept for devices every month or so. It was only a matter of time."

The butler agency had been Tab's idea. She'd recruited the woman in charge of assignments and we'd put in our own agent.

"Any discussion of what happened to Lime?"

"Not in front of me. She was pretty upset when she got back to Bridgehampton after the drive to the lab."

"She knew she'd be followed."

"But not what she'd find when she got there."

Nash and Honey Li were waiting on the patio. It was a clear day, and the enclosure made a suntrap so that even in February they could sit outside in coats and have their coffee in the sunshine.

Honey was draped in an ankle-length mink. Nash wore jeans and a camel hair coat. His Converse sneakers were parked on the wrought-iron table.

I put the brown parcel beside them.

Nicky floated in with a silver tray and placed a pair of scissors in front of Honey. She snipped through the Treasury seals, folded back the paper, and took out the box. She opened it, and the diamond splashed her face with rosy light.

She gazed at it with a desperate expression. "We think it's worth even more now."

"Even more than what?" I said.

"Oh, come on," Nash said in his upper-class Boston drawl. "More than what it was worth before that nonsense that it was a fake."

"And how much is that? You paid First Partners $40 million for it, which is what they paid Barry Stern. That's supposed to be you getting the fabulous deal on a priceless diamond. But half the world thinks you got suckered by a fake and the other half thinks it's you who faked it."

"Don't be an ass," Nash said. "We have a certificate."

He didn't really look like Kennedy. His eyes never stopped darting. He was like a pickpocket with good teeth and hair who'd stumbled on Kennedy's barber.

"The certificate is from one of the most respected diamond labs in the country," he said. "It certifies that the Pink is a genuine pink, not artificially enhanced."

"Let me tell you how this works," I said. "Let's say you decide to sell the diamond. You take it to one of the big auction houses. They don't laugh in your face, because you're Harry Nash."

Nash tried on a lazy grin, but it wouldn't stick, so he screwed around with his phone as if he wasn't really paying attention. Honey, though—she was watching me fearfully.

"The auction house will stall for time. They'll say that for a stone like this they need at least three independent labs to certify it. You waste another couple of months getting the extra certificates, but guess what? When you come back the auction guys say the market's not good at the moment. They don't advise selling. Demand is soft. So you wait a year and try again. But you'll get the same answer. They'll never try to sell your diamond. They're afraid of it."

He wasn't looking at his phone now, and Honey was clutching the diamond to her breast as if to give it life.

"Bullshit," Nash said. "The certificates prove the value of the stone."

"They don't. A certificate is a piece of paper. It describes a physical object. Nothing more. Only a dealer can say what the diamond is worth. Anyone likely to think of buying a jewel like the Pink would never do so without the guidance of one of the two or three dealers in the world competent to judge it. Ask yourself what they're likely to say to their clients. They'll say don't touch it. It's tainted. You took what could have been the most valuable jewel in history and slimed it. You made it part of a stock play. An essential part of the scheme was raising doubts about whether the diamond was even what it was supposed to be. You'll never get back from that."

In the diamond game a buyer's fear of being taken for a fool is the single biggest hurdle a dealer has to clear before he makes a sale. That's the same whether it's an inexpensive engagement ring or a ninety-carat, top-color white. Diamonds have a secret language, and the buyer knows he will never learn to speak it. The dealer has to get the client to trust him. Who would trust Nash?

Honey's knuckles were white as she clutched the diamond. God help her, I think she loved it.

Nash stood up and looked at her. There can't have been many times in his life when something he'd planned had come apart. He looked bewildered, and for just a second, fearful for his wife. But when he turned his eyes to me, he'd got back to a place where he was comfortable. Scorn.

"You've got everything figured out, is that it?" he said. "You nailed the short, and Bolt used that information to force me out?"

Contempt radiated from him. Honey reached out a warning hand.

"Harry. No."

"Play it out," he said. "How does Bolt shame me off the ticket? By revealing I was behind the short? She can't do that without blowing herself up too."

He shoved his hands deep into the pockets of his coat and looked around at the mansion, as if annoyed to find himself still there.

"If she carried out such a threat, it would wreck her. I'd say it had been her idea, and let's face it, it was."

"Harry," Honey pleaded again. "It's enough."

But he kept his eyes fixed on me.

"So she doesn't reveal it to the public, does she? Who does she talk to?"

You think nothing can surprise you. But I hadn't seen this.

"Your partners," I said. "The Russians." I thought it through. "She told them you were permanently crippled. That if the details of your deal with them came out, the deal that let you control the fund, you'd never be able to help them. She convinced the Russians, and they convinced you."

He forced a smile onto his face. An expression hacked out by a blade.

"Next time you're in the office," he said, "see if there are any orders to unfreeze Russian bank accounts."

"Maybe she set you up from the beginning," I said, getting up to leave. "You were always her Trojan horse to get to the nomination. She must have suspected you'd try to take the presidency for yourself. If she had a deal with your Russian partners, who knows when she made it?"

He made a gun out of his hand, pointed it at me, and pulled the trigger.

"Now you're getting somewhere."

Tommy was waiting outside to drive me to LaGuardia. He still had the Impala. Minnie liked it.

I reviewed my conversation with Nash. He waved his hand.

"The bad guy speech at the end of the movie."

"Cut the bullshit, Tommy. Bolt screwed everybody. You helped her. You got your reward."

He shrugged. "You can't play the game if you're not on the field."

"Come on, Tommy. I'd be surprised if you even know who the teams are."

Tommy wasn't taking me to the airport as a favor. That's not where things stood with us. Our friendship had been punched too many times to be getting off the canvas anytime soon. But Tommy was my boss now, and extended leave or not he needed to make sure I understood what the consequences would be if I revealed what I knew. I'd thought Bolt and I understood each other, but I guess she thought I needed the message driven home by a hammer like Tommy.

I listened to his heavy-handed message as we went up the FDR. Traffic was snarled at the toll gates on the Triborough Bridge and slow through the tangle of construction around the airport. I waited until we got to the departures drop-off. We sat there for a few minutes, both of us staring straight ahead.

"I thought you knew me better," I said. "Nobody has anything to fear from me. But that's a two-way street. So make it clear when you report this conversation that if somebody gets nervous about me, and so much as a shadow of a threat falls across my family, I'll come back. You will never see me coming. And so help me God, I will pull the house down."

We still hadn't looked at each other, and he didn't look at me when he replied.

"Everybody knows you're a serious guy, Alex."

"I sure hope so, Tommy."

The flight to Montreal arrived late in the afternoon, the sky already shading to purple. My car had been sitting in long-term parking at the airport since I'd left it there on my way to Brussels. A truck came out from a garage to boost the battery, and I followed him back for an oil change. Another $250 got it detailed at a carwash. A 1978 BMW 530i. Metallic blue. Four-speed manual, like pushing a knife through butter.

I drove onto the expressway that led into the city. The first flakes of an early snowstorm slanted through the headlights.

Half an hour later I tossed the keys to the valet at a downtown hotel and checked into a room on the top floor. I changed into a bathing suit, grabbed the bathrobe, and walked the short distance to the pool. I dropped the robe and slipped into the heated water and swam through the narrow tunnel that led outside into the gathering snow. Wisps of vapor rose from the bright-blue water. The lights climbing up the side of Mount Royal glimmered through the gauze curtain of the snow. The pool was empty except for a lone swimmer slowly doing lengths.

I stood with the water to my waist. The snow fell more thickly now, and the lights of the city filled the sky with a soft glow. The traffic streaming across the St. Lawrence River bridges melted into a magical tableau of drifting lights and rising steam and the white cascading sky.

The swimmer turned at the end of the pool and came crawling back: strong, thin arms pulling through the turquoise water and the falling snow. As she passed, I sank to my chest and swam beside her.

The snow danced around her elvish ears. The wind shifted into the north and came rushing down the mountain with a howl, erasing the city. We sank to our chins in the water and watched the blizzard stream through the sky.

Later, in the room, as she watched me with her speculative Russian eyes, I reached under a pillow and pulled out the little package I'd hidden there. Lily sat up and unwrapped it eagerly, flinging the paper aside until she got to the dark-green velvet of the innermost layer. Her eyes shone as she ran her fingers over the rectangular shape. She folded back the fabric reverently. The Virgin and child emerged in a blaze of gold leaf. He didn't look so irritable this time. Lily sighed and pressed the icon against her naked breast.

"Alex, that is so adorable." She held the icon out at arm's length and tilted her head. "Did you steal it from poor, dead Sergei?"

"At the time, he wasn't dead."

"That makes it so much better," Lily beamed.

We'd left the curtains open to watch the snow fill up the city. I was wondering what we would do in the morning. Drive further into the snow.

She lay back in the pillows and cradled the icon in her arms.

I told her about Nash and Honey Li.

"Yes," she said dreamily, holding the icon out again to ravish it with her eyes, "they destroyed the reputation of the jewel. Call it moral closure."

"Well, the bad guy's still a billionaire and his Russian partners got away with murder, so maybe not."

"You worry too much. There were rules Sergei lived by. He should have told them about the pipe from the beginning. They were Russians, darling," she said, running her finger down the edge of the gold frame. "There were worse ways he could have died."

The snow brushed by the window like tufts of cotton wool. A soft blue light fell on Lily's face and on her breasts.

She'd never looked more beautiful. Maybe that's why I searched so desperately for an explanation other than the one right there in front of me. How would Lily know there were worse ways to die if she didn't know how Lime had died? It was the detail we'd never released.

I reached up and pushed a lock of hair away from the tip of her ear.

I went through the short list of people who knew the manner of Lime's death, and discarded each one as a possible source for Lily. I pulled each name aside, one by one, like veils, until I could see Lily clearly, as I suppose, at the end, so had Lime, his last sight on earth her calm gray eyes.

I had no illusions about Lily. Nor Lily about me. The five million we stole from Nash had become $62 million, thanks to Great Pipe. Lily had got in early and bailed when the price hit eighty dollars. She'd seen the short coming a mile away. Naturally she'd tried to get the money out of her Luxembourg account before I twigged.

We left in the morning and drove north into the mountains, into the snow.

ACKNOWLEDGMENTS

T hanks to the many friends who read drafts: Ellen Vanstone, Cathrin Bradbury, Jefferson Lewis, Stephanie Wood, Douh Knight, Carlos Pitella Leite, Clair Lamb, Alex Beam, and my longtime agent, Michael Carlisle. Special thanks to Susan Walker and Paul Maloney for their meticulous reading of the galleys. I'm grateful to my friend, the editor and agent Trena Keating, for early advice and for pointing me to Leslie Wells, a veteran editor with an unerring eye for pace; and to my editor at Pegasus, Jessica Case, for her enthusiasm. My greatest thanks as always are to my wife, Heather Abbott, a merciless reader of drafts.

Those who've shared their diamond expertise over the years are too numerous to list, but I must thank my friend Richard Wake-Walker, the distinguished diamond valuator; Donald Palmieri, whose Gem Certification & Assurance Lab in New York has certified such staggering diamonds as the 1,111-carat Lesedi la Rona; and Chris Jennings, one of the great diamond explorers, with whom I've spent many happy hours discussing our mutual obsession and the outlandish characters who populate it. Any errors are mine, never theirs.

ACKNOWLEDGMENTS

My account of the market in junior exploration stocks comes from knowledge gained writing books about two colossal contests: the 1983 Hemlo gold rush on the north shore of Lake Superior, and the 1991 Arctic diamond rush, which began when explorers drilled through the ice of a frozen lake and hit a diamond pipe—a discovery that made Canada the world's third largest diamond producer. The market that makes such discoveries possible is a hair-raising casino—if anything, even crazier than the version depicted here, as the author, sadly, can attest.

ABOUT THE AUTHOR

Matthew Hart has reported on gold and diamonds for *Vanity Fair*, the *Atlantic Monthly*, the *Wall Street Journal*, the *London Times*, and many other newspapers and magazines. He was a contributing editor of the New York trade journal *Rapaport Diamond Report*. His award-winning book *Diamond: The History of a Cold Blooded Love Affair*, was translated into six languages and made into a four-hour dramatic miniseries starring Sir Derek Jacobi and Judy Davis. His book *Gold: The Race for the World's Most Seductive Metal* was adapted into a National Geographic television special. He has travelled from the Arctic to Angola in pursuit of diamond stories, and *The Russian Pink* is his first thriller. He lives in New York City.